# divas of dutchess

## erica-faye nicole williams

# dedication

To all of the girlies working hard and making it happen no matter what—this story is for you. Keep going. ✨

# prologue

My name is Jaliyah Camille Whitfield and I just turned 25-years-old a few months ago. I was born and raised in Mount Vernon, New York, but my family and I moved to Poughkeepsie, New York about seven years ago. My family consists of my mother, my father, my two sisters, and me. My immediate family is not too big, but my extended family is a whole 'notha story. Damn near all of my aunts and uncles made the same move up to Poughkeepsie about a year or two after my parents did. Now, it's just like old times.

I'm five-feet-six inches tall, with almond-shaped, honey-brown eyes that shimmer in the sunlight. I have thick eyelashes that curl at the ends on their own, and I *used* to have thick eyebrows as well, but they are currently in the early stages of growing back after surviving my over-tweezing era of the late 90s. I have a smooth, buttery-brown complexion with a small mole beside my lips, straight Janet Jackson style.

My hair is dark-brown and super curly like Tia and Tamera's in *Sister, Sister before* the silk presses, so I usually rock it up in a loose bun or I keep it braided. I have a flat stomach, slender hips and thick thighs. I'm a size 7/8, and my booty is not crazy-big, *but* I *do* have a *little* fatty, so finding jeans that don't expose my *coin-slot* when I bend over can sometimes be a challenge.

I remember when I used to look at my mom and say to myself that I wanted the shape that she has after I have my children. I wanted a big booty with hips and a flat stomach just like hers. Well, I have all of that right now. The only difference is that my mom has had *three* kids and she's forty-plus. My mother was teeny-tiny before having kids. You could see the bones in her chest she was so small. I got a long way to go if I plan to follow in her footsteps. I would actually have to *lose* weight before getting pregnant. Figure that one out.

I graduated with my Associate in Arts degree in Communications about four years ago and since then, I have been in and out of school on and off. My current job has nothing to do with my major, but that's not uncommon in this day and age. Sometimes, you just have to get in where you fit in. Every so often, I enroll in college to earn credits towards a Bachelor's Degree in *whatever* they will give me one in after I turn in my transcripts from *all over* New York State. I'm always changing my major. I know that I'll get it one day. Not one day soon, but one day.

I have no idea of what I want to do. I've been at my current job for three years. Sometimes I can hardly believe that. I *do* enjoy making mixed-media art and writing. I get my passion for writing from my mother. When I was younger, she would always help me with my essays and book reports. She always knew just what to add to give them that special *razzle, dazzle.*

Speaking of my mother, let me tell you a little bit about her. My mother, Deena Whitfield, has always been such a prissy missy. She collects and keeps *anything* and *everything*. She has every single one of me and my sisters' drawings that we have *ever* made for her. She loves flowers and little things. She thinks everything is *darling* and *ornate.*

She loves glass figurines, vases, and candles. She loves to

shop in stores like Home Goods and Bed, Bath and Beyond. She and my Auntie Tiffany recently opened a card and gift shop named *Heart and Soul*. Opening that store was a dream come true for her. She still works as a financial analyst at a busy real estate firm in Manhattan, but the store is where her whole heart lies. I am so proud of her. My mother is so soft spoken and polite. She flashes her billion-dollar smile and she wins your heart. You would never guess that she grew up on one of the roughest blocks in the South Bronx and she got into fights at least once a week between middle school and the twelfth grade.

Yeah, my mom was born in Buckhead, Georgia, but she grew up in the Bronx, New York around the time when the whole hip-hop era was just beginning. She still has the original flyers in a scrapbook for Kool Herc, Grandmaster Flash and a bunch of others. She kept the flyers as a reminder of all of the things that she *could not* do while she was growing up.

My mother is absolutely beautiful. She has one of *the* most banging bodies out of any 47-year-old that I have ever seen. She has a warm-brown skin tone, large, honey-brown eyes like mine that turn down on the ends like Nicole Richie's, a huge smile and gleaming white teeth.

She is all of five-feet-two inches tall, with a voluptuous figure. She's quite curvy, but she carries it confidently. Still, she refuses to go outside without a shirt that hangs lower than her jeans pockets or a long jacket. I try to tell her to take it off and show off her shape, but she always declines.

Another thing about Mrs. Deena is that she hates and I mean absolutely *hates* to exercise! She will do anything and everything short of dietary supplements to lose weight. My mom has been on every diet from here to China. It's quite comical. I remember when she was on her vinegar and honey kick. Then it was the cabbage soup diet. She was drinking something called "Noni Juice" for a while.

Then, oh yeah, how can I forget the, "I'm just gonna eat saltine crackers and drink water until I feel light-headed" diet. Oh and her brilliant idea that comes up about every two to three years, *"Y'all, maybe I should start smoking crack for a little while and then get off of it. Shee-yit, I'll be skinny than a mug! Hot dog!"*

So yes, in conclusion, my mother is a fabulous, fly and amazing Black woman. Growing up, my mother always reminded me of Claire Huxtable from the Cosby Show. She's drop-dead gorgeous—like, jaw-on-the-floor pretty. But those elbows? Baby, they have seen some thangs! If she misses a day of lotion, they are rougher than a cat's tongue! Thankfully, she keeps the Jergens on deck.

She says that her elbows look so bad because she never got to go *anywhere*—her *or* my aunts. They were always leaning out of the window of their third-floor apartment in the six-story walk-up where they lived, watching everything.

Now that I think about it, all of my aunts have elbows like that. My grandmother kept them on a tight leash, as did my parents when my sisters and I were coming up.

Now—there are times when I can be a *little* rude and overly sarcastic, and I get that from my pops, Lonnie Whitfield. Since I have already given you the low-down on my mother, let me give you the low-down on my pops.

Lonnie was born in Mobile, Alabama to Ruthie Lee Gaines and Charles Whitfield on June 5, 1957. He was born in Alabama because my great-grandmother had passed away a few days before my grandmother's due date. My grandmother chose to attend the funeral although her doctor had warned her of possibly going into the labor in the middle of the funeral service. Well, my dad had a *little* more class than that. He at least waited until they lowered her casket into the ground. Then just like that, my grandmother's water broke and it was off to the hospital. Little Lonnie was here. Once my pops was born, they hauled it back to the Bedford-Stuyvesant section of Brooklyn, New York where they lived before finally settling in the Bronx.

My father is a retired Lieutenant from the New York Police Department. He wanted to become a police officer since he was a little kid. It's so funny because, once he became a cop, a lot of my aunts and uncles followed in his footsteps. He should have worked for the recruitment office.

From what my grandmother and others have told me about my father, he was a talented little kid and he is an even more talented man. My father can build anything. He can play any instrument. He can sing any song. He is extremely creative. He can make anyone and everyone laugh. He's the best.

Although we do not always agree, I know that his main concern is making sure that my mom, me and my sisters are taken care of. He is such a worrywart when it comes to *his girls*. He is the Tom Hagen of our family. You know, the consigliere in *The Godfather*. He is always there to help everybody. This one has to move. This one has an operation on Thursday that they need to get to. This one needs a ride from the airport. This one needs quick entry into a rehab program. Well, that wasn't anyone in my family, but, you get my drift.

Oh, and ladies—let me tell you. He is very, very good-looking. Think Billy Dee Williams in *Mahogany* after he tells her, *"Success is nothing without someone you love to share it with."* That is how cute my daddy is. The way he and my mother met is even cuter.

### April 1977 - Bronx, New York

*"Deena," a 14 year-old Sharisse Whitfield screamed. "How many times are you gonna play that doggone Deneice Williams song. I mean it is nice and all but, that is the twelfth time you've*

*played it in an hour. Come on, play something else already. I wanna be "Free" to dance!"*

This was an everyday ritual for the Whitfields, but this was my mother's first time visiting their house. Every day, the Whitfield kids would go home to dance and play records after-school while they did their homework. My Aunt Sharisse or "Reesee" was a freshman and my mother and my Aunt Sydney were seniors and very good friends.

*"Okay, so put on "Get on the Good Foot" then!"*

*James Brown rang out loud and clear and Sharisse tore it up. She began dancing coolly, then wildly all around the living room. She put the "foot" in good foot! Deena did her usual cool but controlled dance that would become signature for her.*

*"I'm gonna be so sad when y'all graduate and leave me all by myself," Reesee said as she got up to get a glass of juice. "I hope that nobody bothers me."*

*Deena and Sydney looked at each other and rolled their eyes.*

*"Hahaha...," Deena screamed as she laughed hysterically. "Yeah Reesee, someone is really gonna bother you. You fight, cuss people out and act a damn fool all year long and you think that someone is gonna bother you. You and your little crew who act just as bad if not worse than you do? I heard your big mouth all the way down the hall today fourth period. And that's a damn shame."*

*Then Deena looked at her sternly and said, "Girl, I didn't know that you could cuss like that neither."*

*Sydney shook her head laughing and singing along to the record. "Oh, you ain't know? Her mouth is just as trashy as she wants it to be. Chile, I would be so shamed to let folks hear me talking like that. And what were you so mad about anyway Reesee that your lil' ass was cussin' like a man in the halls?"*

*Sharisse exhaled deeply and rolled her eyes up in the air. She took a long pause and then finally said, "Bobby Reed told me he thought I was cute and he wanted to take me out on a date some-time. So I cursed him out, and I told him to take his damn mama!"*

*Just then, Claude Whitfield, the oldest of the Whitfield siblings entered the apartment. "You done told who take his mama where," Claude asked as he juggled a large art canvas and some art supplies. The girls all went over to help him with his things and then Sharisse answered him.*

*"Bobby Reed. He asked me out on a date and I got embarrassed, so I cursed at him and told him to take his mama on a date," Sharisse finished.*

*Claude laughed uncontrollably. "That's my girl! Keep your mind on the books, not the boys!"*

*"Nuh, uh!" Sydney said. "That was just plain mean of Reesee. She should not have told that boy all of that! He is just as nerdy and corny to begin with. She probably gave him a complex now."*

*"I don't care what he got now!" Sharisse laughed. "He was just trying to be cool in front of his friends and I put an end to that mess!"*

*Claude put the rest of his things down, introduced himself to Deena and then went off to shower and get ready for a date with one of his many women.*

*About fifteen minutes went by, and the front door opened again. A young Lonnie Whitfield walked in to find everyone partying and having a good time. He immediately noticed Deena. He had seen her around here and there and they'd always say, "Hello" to one another and keep it moving. He had always thought she was really cute.*

*She looked up and caught him staring at her. "Hi," she said shyly as she went to sit down.*

*"Hi," Lonnie said as he walked over and sat down next to her. "Um, I've noticed you around sometimes. I, um…I know that you hang out with my sisters. I mean, I've seen you when I walk them to school sometimes on my way to the train station."*

"*Yeah, I know. I've seen you too Lonnie.*" *Deena smiled at him.*

*Surprised that she knew his name and even more surprised that she was there, sitting in his living room with him he said,* "*You know my name?*"

"*Of course I do. You're the brother of my best friends. Plus, you're cute.*"

"*I think you're cute too,*" *he said to her smiling.* "*I always…*"

"*Deena and Lonnie! I don't mean to interrupt, but how are y'all just gonna sit down and talk in the middle of all **my** fun!*" *Sharisse yelled as she cut off the record player.*

"*Come on now y'all! Mommy will be home in a little while and y'all know good and hell well that I'm gon' get in trouble for cussin' in the hall today! This may be the last bit of fun I have for a while! So can we please save the chit-chatter for later?*"

"*Whatever, Reesee!*" *Lonnie yelled pissed that she had cut his rap short.* "*Will you just shut up!*"

"*You gon' dance?*" *she asked grinning.*

"*Yeah, I'm gon' dance; but only if your friend here will dance with me.*"

"*Your friend here?! Boy, her name is Deena! Why you so rude for?!*" *Reesee yelled with a voice full of attitude.*

"*Well, I didn't get a chance to ask her what her name was because you interrupted our conversation!*" *Lonnie yelled back.*

*Realizing that she **had** interrupted their conversation she said,* "*Oh. Okay then. I'm sorry, Lonnie.*"

*She lowered her voice back to normal and smiled at him.* "*You still gon' dance for a little while though, right?*"

"*I'll dance with you,*" *Deena said as she got up off the sofa.*

*Flattered beyond belief, Lonnie said to his sister,* "*Hell yeah I'm gon' dance!*"

"*Now, that's what I'm talking about!*" *Reesee ran back over to the record player and put on Marvin Gaye's "Got to Give it Up".*

*Sydney, Deena, Reesee and Lonnie all threw their arms up in the air and clapped to the beat. Claude even re-emerged to get his dance on before he went out for the evening.*

*"May I have this dance?" Lonnie asked Deena as he extended his hand to her.*

*"Yes, you may," she obliged grinning from ear to ear.*

*She took his hand, and they shared their very first dance—and they've been dancing together ever since.*

So, that's how they met. At the time, my father was 22-years-old and my mother was 18-years-old. Let me had tried that when I was 17, 18-years-old. That would have been my natural ass. I mean my dad had a mustache and sideburns and everything!

To make a long story *somewhat* short, they began to speak on the phone regularly and they saw each other around here and there. Finally, my father asked my mother out on a date. They went out to the movies and to the disco almost every single week-end. They fell in love and they made love.

Eventually, after a few years of hot lovemaking sessions, my sister Angela slipped through the cracks. If you let my grandmother tell it, the reason why this occurred was because they had sex *"too strong"*. My parents' response to this was, *"Well, what other way is there to have it?"*

They had already been dating for four years and had broken up for a record of ten minutes during that whole time. My father told me that he always knew he wanted to marry my mother; Angie just sped up the process.

So, my mother got pregnant at age twenty-two and my father proposed to her. They got married and had a small wedding in my

Uncle Claude's apartment in Queens. After their nuptials, they moved into a cozy little two-bedroom apartment in Westchester County, New York. They proceeded to have more children, me and my little sister Nicole; and we lived happily ever after.

———

When I first moved to upstate New York, *Did I hate it?* In the words of *Sex and the City's* Mr. Big, "Absofucking-lutely!" I could never go anywhere because you needed a car to get everywhere. Do not get me wrong, there are corner stores and Chinese food restaurants around, but you have to drive to get to them. Everything is at least a five-minute drive, which equals about a three-hour walk for me. It was complete bullshit! I didn't have a license; only a permit.

Almost all city girls get their permits once they hit sixteen and then don't get their licenses until they get into a situation where they absolutely *must* drive. In Mount Vernon, everything is at your fingertips. Cabs, buses, trains. You don't need to drive. I have even known a couple of people who just rocked with their non-driver IDs like it was *all-to-the-good* for a minute. In Mount Vernon, all you needed was one friend or a boyfriend or girlfriend with a car to get to the Galleria Mall in White Plains or the Cross County Shopping Center, and you were straight. They had trains and buses to get to those places as well though.

Eventually, me and my sister Angie got with the program and we started taking driving lessons. We got our licenses around the same time and my parents told us that there was no way that they were going to buy us both cars. They bought one used car and we had to share it. At first, it was fine, but I do not even have to tell you how that turned out in the end. Let me just say that although my older sister Angela is the quietest and most passive and reserved out of the three of us, my black ass somehow ended up *upside down* inside of the non-lit fireplace in our family room with a face full of soot at the end of a fight for the car keys one night.

Pissed at the fact that we were even fighting, my dad took the car away from both of us for about a month. At the end of the month, he told me that Angie could have the car and that he and my mother would give me some cash towards a small, reliable car. I took the money and went out to look at some used cars. Unfortunately, I could never find one that seemed to suit me. When I finally *did* find one that I loved, the Car Fax report on it showed that it had been submerged in the Hudson River for a few days a couple of years back.

Now, while I was going through all of this nonsense looking for a whip, I was mad at the fact that Angie had a practically new, *used* Honda Accord, and my parents had bought it off one of our neighbors. My parents must have paid about three-thousand dollars for that car, and it was only about a year or two old.

After several failed attempts at a used car purchase, I banked the money my parents had given me and I decided that I was going to buy a new car and just make car payments. I got a job, saved up some more money to come up with a bigger down payment so my monthly payments wouldn't be so high, and I bought my first brand-new car. *That* was the easy part. The hard part was that my parents would not put me on their insurance. My cousin Cory had crashed his car about a week or so before I bought mine. And of course, my auntie and uncle had to bring their asses over to my house complaining about how their insurance had shot through the roof because of *his* dumb ass! So that stuck me with a car payment, a car insurance payment *and* jobs that would not give me any kind of hours whatsoever!

Now, I'm gonna let y'all in on something that you may not know, because I had to find out the hard way—*listen up. You* *cannot pay for a muthafuckin' thing on $6.50 an hour at fifteen hours a week!*

I cannot believe that the government even takes taxes when people are making that little bit of money. That's some shameful shit! And the little bit of money that I had left over after I bought and customized my car went to the first few months of my car *and* car insurance payments. Ain't that about a bitch! And, don't even get me started on the cost of gas, oil changes and running over nails in the street!

I couldn't even buy a pair of damn panties! Now, how that look?! Driving around in a *fire-ass* whip and my coochie is uncovered—just flappin' in the breeze!

I know! It don't make a bit of sense! Well, that's exactly what *my* black ass was doing. Here is where my story begins.

# part one
## friday

# chapter one

I t was the summer of 2004. I had just turned 21-years-old, and my family and I had been living in the Town of Pough-keepsie for about three years already. I was working at a sneaker store in the mall and it was not working out *at all*. It seemed like my bills were coming in faster than my money. 20 hours per week at $6.50 an hour was just *not* cutting it. I had just bought my car, and my payments were a little over $150.00 a month. The car insurance payments were almost $200.00 a month. That was more than the damn car note! I had to find a job paying more hours ASAP.

I saw that the clothing store in the mall—DIVAS—was hiring for a full-time sales associate, so I went in bright and early one Friday morning with my résumé and cover letter in hand and applied. To my surprise, I got an on-the-spot interview.

DIVAS was your typical store for girls in their tweens to mid-twenties and those women who are thirty-plus going through their second, third and fourth childhoods. They carried everything from lingerie to lollipops. It was a nice store, but I wouldn't be spending too many of my paychecks there.

I wasn't dressed at all for an interview. I had on a pair of jeans and a Clemson University hoodie. Luckily, my hair was done because me and my sisters had gone to a concert the night before.

I asked Janet, the assistant manager, what time the manager was expected in. She said, "thirty minutes or so." I ran around that store and threw me together a little outfit. I found a brown and black short plaid skirt, a white baby-tee, a black cardigan, and some flesh-colored stockings. Classy, but sassy. I was sure to style my outfit around my black and brown Diesel shoes that I was wearing that day. While shopping for my interview outfit, I also bought two pairs of lounge around sweat pants and a cute black and silver sparkly dress.

I should *not* have been spending money. But, there are times when you need to spend money to make money and scared money don't make no money—*honey*! I purchased my clothes, and changed in one of the *many* fitting rooms in the back. Just when I was about to go over and take a look in the lingerie section for some Hello Kitty boy shorts, Janet called me into the backroom. When I got back there, I was greeted by a short Latina, with wide hips, thick thighs, big boobs and a flat, flabby heart-shaped, cellulite-laden ass. You could see it through her pants.

She was wearing a pair of tight, gray spandex leggings and a black and rhinestone studded JLo shirt with some gray Timbs. Her stomach hung a little from under her shirt and I could see that she had her navel pierced. I also noticed that she had a pencil eraser holding her belly-ring in. It looked terrible. It was hard as hell not to do it, but I didn't stare. I needed a job and she was the one who was going to give it to me.

She wasn't small, but she wasn't plus-sized either. Maybe a size 13/14—and she had to be about five-feet-four inches tall. She was dripping from head to toe in 10 carat, yellow-gold— you know, the Fordham Road/Diamond District 2000 type jewelry that you see in the store windows. She wore everything from what looked to me like an engagement ring, to a huge nameplate, to a crucifix and a Mickey Mouse with her name on it. She had about five or six earrings in each of her ears, and wore bright-green, artificial-looking contacts. She had a pale-olive skin complexion, and her lips were dark in color like those of a smoker. Her hair was long, extremely curly and dyed blonde. I knew that it was dyed because her black roots were showing.

She introduced herself as Carmen Soto. When I went to shake her hand I noticed how long and decorated her nails were. I guess she saw me looking at them because she said, "I get my nails done every week and I try to change the color like every day to match my outfits."

After she said that, she offered me a seat by her crowded desk and this is how the meeting went down.

The first thing that she asked me was, "Are those your real eyes?"

"Yes they are," I responded.

"Cool," she said. "They're real beautiful. God bless your eyes mami."

She took a sip from her water bottle. "Janet must have seen something in you because I been told that bitch about setting up interviews for me when I walk through the goddamn door."

I laughed at that. "You remind me of my Aunt Reesee," I told her.

"Well, is your aunt chill?" she asked me.

"Yeah, madd chill."

"Word?" she smiled.

"Yup."

"Damn, well that sounds just like me," looking over my application she continued, "Jaliyah is it?"

"Yeah, it's Jaliyah, but everybody calls me Jah-dee," I told her feeling comfortable already.

"Get outta here! There's a girl who works here that we call

Jah-dee. Her name is Jacqueline. The Jah-Dee comes from her first name combined with her middle name which is Deanna.”

“Oh, okay,” I said not knowing what to make of that. I had thought that my nickname was one of a kind. I guess not.

“Ooooooh,” Carmen said shaking her right hand as if she had just burned herself, “she gon’ be pissed when she hears your nickname. That bitch gon’ be like, *‘What the fuck!’*”

I laughed. “I ain’t tryna cause no trouble now! That has been my name for a while. All my life to be exact.”

“I know sweetie.” She placed both her ballpoint pen and my application on her desk.

“Well, it’s obvious that we ain’t gonna get a real interview goin’ on here so let me just let you know that you’re hired. I like you. You came here with your resume and everything—and the little Power Puff Girls in the corner of the page is so cute! No one who’s *ever* applied here lately has done that. You will bring some flavor to the store. I have only been the manager here for about eight months now. When I got here, the staff was all white. I had to go recruiting like the Reserves and shit.

So far my staff is three white girls, Janet (the Assistant Manager), Janine (who was known to always be vacationing and a minor or under 18), and Taylor (a Head Cashier who always seemed to call out). Two Boricuas including Jacqueline, and myself and now four Morenas including you, Nadia (a minor), Cordelia (a minor) and Michelle. But I don't know how long Michelle is gonna be here for.”

She paused briefly and smiled, “Jaliyah, I don’t want the type of store where minorities feel that they are gonna be discriminated against as soon as they set foot through the door. Feel me?”

From that moment, I could tell that DIVAS was the kind of store that I needed to be working in. I hadn’t made that many girl friends in Dutchess County since I had moved up there a few years before. This place was full of them. Maybe I could *finally* meet some nice people.

Before I knew it, Carmen had me taking some kind of a personality test that I was required by law to pass to be officially hired into the company. It was basically just a whole bunch of common sense questions with *yes, no, maybe so* answers. After I finished, she called in my answers. Once I was cleared, she asked me to fill out my tax information and she called up the District Manager to get my starting salary based on my prior experience.

"A-ight, look ma-ma, we're starting you at $8.00 an hour. But, I'ma hurry up and train you so I can push for you to be on management so you can at least go up to like $10.00 an hour. I know how bills can be and trust I had enough of them when I was your age. Struggling and what not. Yo, I've been there and back. Let me tell you how—"

Just then Janet, the assistant manager walked in and told Carmen that she needed her on the sales floor ASAP.

"Hold on a minute okay," Carmen said as she got up to go assist Janet, "I'll be right back."

After Carmen left, I sat there looking around the backroom that was full of holds, layaways and new clothing shipments for that week. Carmen's desk was kind of in the middle of it all. Like I said, her desk was crowded as hell. Part of the reason was that she had a twenty-inch television and a PlayStation 2 on top of it. Before I could even form the question of *why* in my brain, a pretty Spanish girl a little shorter than me walked in.

"That's Chino and Robert's shit." She came and sat down in the chair where Carmen had been sitting. "What up, I'm Jacqueline but you can call me Jah-dee."

"What up, I'm Jaliyah and you can call me Jah-dee too."

*"Why would I do that?"* she asked in an annoyed tone; clearly confused.

I stared at her, my eyes focused, "Because that's what they call me. That's why."

She could hear the annoyance in my voice. "That's what's up," she said.

She looked at me kind of funny, and said sarcastically, "So you're our newest *Diva*, huh?" She threw up air quotes with her fingers for emphasis on the word diva.

"Are those your real eyes?" she asked not taking hers off me for a second.

"Yeah, they are. Are those your real eyes," I shot right back at her.

"Yeah," she said. "Nah, I'm lyin'. I bought em' last week."

She smiled. Jacqueline was really beautiful. She was Puerto Rican with a pale-white skin complexion. Her hair was a deep-auburn with blonde highlights. She wore gray contacts, a baggy, gray Rocawear velour hooded sweatsuit, and some gray Nike Uptowns with the white check and white bottoms.

"We can wear sweats here?" I asked her.

"Nah, we can't, but I'm here picking up my check." She rolled her eyes with exasperation and smiled. "All we can wear in here is dresses, dress pants, shoes and boots. No jeans and no sneakers. Not even jean skirts or shirts. No bellies showing, except for *Carmen's* of course," she let out a light chuckle, "and no tattoos showing. We wear jeans on holidays sometimes though. It's wack."

She paused. "Yo, you wanna come out with me and my girl Stacey tonight?"

Shocked that she had just given me the fucking third degree and then flipped the script I said, "I'm actually busy tonight, but thank you for the invitation."

"Oh, no problem. Trust me. Not all of the girls in this store are as cool as Carmen and me. I'm from the Bronx and she's from Brooklyn."

"BK all Mutha Fuckin' Day! Holla!" Carmen yelled as she re-entered the backroom.

"Yo, Carmen," Jacqueline asked, "when are Chino and Robert gonna take this shit out of here! It's hardly no room for shit!" Those fools need to go find jobs and stop fuckin' chillin' back here all day! It's too fuckin' crowded in this bitch!"

"I know, I know! Robert is my man and I love him, but he really needs to find his no-good ass a job because this bitch here is about to leave his sorry, tired, triflin' ass! For real, for real!" Carmen commented agitatedly as she opened the emergency-exit door to smoke a cigarette.

"You smoke?" she asked me lighting up a Newport.

"No," I said. "I don't really drink too much either."

"Yo, Jah-dee, you heard that? She's so cute. Real innocent like. Like a baby. How old are you anyway?" she asked taking a few pulls off her cigarette.

"I just turned 21."

"You know what," she said. "I'ma call you Baby Girl. From now on, when you walk up in here, your name is Baby Girl.

"Yeah," Jacqueline interjected. "Either we can call you Jaliyah or we can call you Baby Girl because I'm the only Jah-dee around here," she said jokingly with a hint of seriousness.

She caught my side-eye and switched up her steeze, "Nah, let me stop fuckin' around. This way they won't mix us up."

"Mix y'all up," Carmen said inquiringly. "You're a slut and she's not. How could anyone mix that up?"

"Shut up," Jacqueline said.

Just then, two dudes approached the backroom.

"Hi baby!" Carmen yelled and ran to kiss the taller of the two guys. He was crazy cute. He looked just like that guy who used to model for Sean John, Will Lemay.

As soon as they walked in, Jacqueline's whole mood soured.

"That's my fuckin' cue. What up Robert? Later Carmen. Later Baby Girl."

Then she left.

No sooner than Jacqueline left, Carmen closed the door behind her and said, "Baby, you just missed it. Me and Jacqueline almost got into it. Yo, she was talkin' so much shit about you. I told that bitch that I know she's my girl and all but, I will bust her shit if she ever comes out her mouth about you like that again. Shee-yit, don't fuckin' try to play my man!"

Robert just licked his lips, straight LL Cool J style, pulled her up close and kissed Carmen on her lips. I couldn't believe how homegirl had just lied on Jacqueline like that and *she* was the one who was talking most of the shit. Well, I couldn't call it because I had only known these people for two hours.

"Fuck that bitch Jacqueline yo! She is such a hoe! A fuckin' slawed out bitch! We call her Teen Wolf because she's so hairy. The first time I hit it, she didn't even have her pussy shaved. It was so hairy that it was coming out the sides of her panties ma!"

"Chino!" Carmen yelled, embarrassed for Jacqueline. "I spoke to her about that."

She looked over in my direction. "It's true. I had to let her know that it carries odor down there when you don't shave."

"What! Oh excuse me," Chino said looking at me. "I just don't fuckin' like that bitch. Me and her used to go out."

"A bad break up I'm guessing?" I said frowning.

He gave Carmen a pound. "Let's just say that my peoples Carmen handled that shit! But uh, fuck her. What's your name ma?"

"My name is Jaliyah but my friends call me Jah—" before I could finish he said, "Jah-dee. And even if they don't, that's what I'ma call you to piss that bitch Jacqueline's ass off!"

He laughed like a little devil. "I'm a wild boy mami!"

"That you are Chino! That you definitely are papi," Carmen commented.

Now, let me tell you. Chino looked good too. He had a tanned brown complexion and deep, blue eyes. He too, had the signature dark lips that were proof that he smoked way too much weed and a low haircut. His body looked to be pretty toned from what I could see of it through his shirt. The only thing was that he was short. Crazy short. He had to be about five-feet-three or five-feet-four. Like I said, I'm like five-feet six inches myself. How's that gonna look? *Come on now.* Anyway, before I knew it, a whole two and a half hours had passed. It was then when I realized that Carmen didn't do much for her to be the store manager.

I got my things together and I went to use the bathroom before I left. The bathroom was extremely clean and pretty inside. It had orange and fuchsia flower painted walls and all the perfume, EPT tests, condoms, and feminine hygiene products that any girl would ever need. I heard Carmen's muffled voice outside the door saying, "Our bathroom is the bomb right! Robert and Chino just finished it last week!"

"We still waiting on the check though!" I heard Chino yell.

"Papi, you got paid!" Carmen said.

"Yeah, but weed ain't dough ma. That shit don't pay the bills. Besides, you and ya man here smoked like the whole bag. I must have took like two, maybe three hits off that shit. I went to the bathroom to take a shit and y'all straight dunned that shit."

He knocked on the door. "Yo, Jah-dee, you taking a minute in there. What up?"

Right at that moment, I opened up the bathroom door and walked out smiling. I looked right at Chino and said, "See, now you know you ain't even right! How you gon' try and play me and I ain't even been working here a whole day? Shit, I ain't even started working yet."

"I'm sorry ma," he said motioning me over to him with his

hands. When I walked over to him, he hugged me and kissed me on the cheek.

"*Ill*, don't let him kiss you!" I heard the assistant manager Janet say as she walked into the backroom. "You don't know where his lips have been!"

"Yeah, but I bet a couple of people up in here know where yours have been, right?" he snapped back at her snidely.

With Chino's last comment, Carmen shot him a look that I will never forget. Robert wasn't paying much attention to anything that was going on because he was steady focused on rolling his blunt. He didn't see the looks that were being exchanged amongst the trio. I decided to leave. I had had enough DIVAS for one day. I confirmed my start time for the following day, and then I was out.

# chapter two

On my way out of the mall, I stopped in Best Buy to buy another copy of *Prince's Greatest Hits* because my younger sister had just discovered that he is one of the most talented and sexiest men on the planet and had stolen mine.

When I left the store, I saw this *fine* guy standing in the lobby eating a slice of pizza. Now normally, I didn't approach dudes. I let them come to me. But yo, this guy looked sooo good. You had to see him. He was about six-feet-four inches tall with a toasted-chestnut complexion. Just a fine-ass, dark-chocolate brother with a goatee, a low hair cut, and waves that spun 360 style. He had low eyes and a diamond stud in each ear.

He wore a crisp, white wife-beater with a pair of dark-blue DKNY jeans, a leather belt and some tan nubuck Timbs barely laced. He had two tattoos on his neck. I could see one peeking out from the neckline of his beater. Let me see, who can I compare the brother to so y'all can really feel me? Oh okay, my man Idris Elba, you know—Stringer Bell from *The Wire*. I know! Off the hook!

I made eye contact with him instantly.

"Looks real good," I smiled.

"You look real good," he answered back looking up at me.

"Thank you. So do you." I paused. "Hi, I'm Jaliyah."

"Nice to meet you Jaliyah. My name is Quincy."

"Oh, Okay—like my man "GQ" from Juice, huh?" I said smiling.

"Yeah, just like GQ. I see you got jokes. That's cool cause you cute. I'll let it slide."

"Oh, you think I'm cute?" I asked tryna front as if I ain't know the answer to that already.

"Nah, I seen it a thousand times," he said smiling, "you want me to be like, yeah ma. Ell yeah! You know how dudes be leavin' the "H" out of hell when they really be feelin' something."

He took a big-ass bite out of his pizza. "You are bangin' though," he said in between chews as he gave me a once over and nodded his head. "Yeah, you bangin'.'"

Now I was stuck because I have never had anyone say some shit like that to me. I don't know. I was a little tight with his comment, but him saying that I was bangin' kind of pacified me a little.

"So you work up in here?" he asked me.

"Yeah, as of like maybe three hours ago. Give or take a few minutes. I start tomorrow at that store DIVAS."

"That clothing store that *stay* blasting that techno music all the time," he said. "Aww naw! My mans used to do security in the mall and he use to say that everyone stayed stealin' from that store."

I laughed as I thought back on my sordid criminal past. "I used to do that shit too and I had the money. I was just trying to fit in with the wrong crowd at the time. It was not even worth it. I got banned from so many stores in high school. Got my ass whooped by my moms."

I shifted my weight to my right foot. "I had to hold the stolen merchandise while they took a Polaroid of me and then taped it up inside the store. I still used to go in though after a few days. They had so many pictures of muthafuckas that there was no way that they were remembering me!"

I smiled. "Stealing is bullshit. It is the best feeling when you can walk up into any spot with money and just spend it on whatever you want. To me, that is like one of the most ultimate highs you can ever experience," I said proudly knowing that I was one of the brokest bitches in the mall that day.

"Oh, so what are some other ultimate highs?" he asked.

"Well," I said. "Music is one of em'. Spirituality is another. Happiness is definitely one. And uh, making love and being in love. But not fucking. Like actually making love when you are in love with the person that you're being intimate with. I think that would be a great high."

He just looked at me and licked his lips. I noticed that he did that a lot before he spoke. He looked into my eyes when he spoke to me too. I don't think he blinked once. Well, maybe that's an exaggeration. If he did, I didn't see it.

"You're a smart girl. I know that just by looking at you. You got yourself together. In school or about to finish. You probably have your own car and all that right?" he asked.

I hesitated. I didn't want to say yay or nay to that question because with most guys, when you say *Yay* to the fact that you have a car, they say "Yay" and then they try to hop they asses right on in.

I guess he sensed my hesitation and smiled at me. "Don't worry, I got my own whip too so I ain't gon' be tryna scheme and what not."

"Yeah, I have a car." I said.

"See, I knew it.

He finished the last bite of his pizza and said, "May I give you my number so you can call me if you're not too busy with DIVAS and everything else? I mean, that is if you don't have a boyfriend or anything."

"No, I don't have a boyfriend. You think that I would've said anything to you if I did?" I asked him somewhat offended.

He laughed. "The way that you women are nowadays. You can't put anything past y'all." He took another bite of his pizza.

"You could be engaged with a seed at home and get in my whip with me and take a ride like it's all good. I once had a girl sit down and have lunch with me while her husband was school shopping with their kids!"

I rolled my eyes and said, "Anyways! That ain't me, and yes I would like to have your number," I told him with a bright, but not overly thirsty smile.

He wrote it down on a piece of his pizza plate that did not have any oil on it and told me that I could call morning, noon or night. I'm sure y'all ladies have heard that line before. Yeah, it's call morning, noon or night until we do. Then it's a problem. *You know.*

I took his number and said that I would call him, but before I turned to walk to the parking lot, I asked him, "Why didn't you ask for my number?"

"Well, I know how you girls get when you give a guy your number and he calls you either too soon, or too late. We can never seem to get that right. Then y'all be on some, "Girl, this nigga keep callin' me! I think he crazy girl! I just don't know what the problem is. I mean, what *is* the problem!" he said in the stankest girl impersonation I have ever heard; complete with teeth sucking and neck rolling.

I laughed. "Well, let me throw this one at you then. Here, keep your cell number, and take mine."

I quickly scribbled my number down on the plate. "And you use that shit nyucca! I'm giving you a chance to get it right this time."

"Thank you. I'll try real hard to get it right, Jaliyah."

"You better" I said smirking. "You better get it so right that I ain't even write down my name with my number. If I'm worth remembering, you won't forget."

"I know that's right ma," he said.

"Yeah, it is. So you best not call me on some, "What up Shiquinetta!" or some "How you doin' Liquidacia?" type bullshit either."

He laughed. "Nah, I ain't gon' forget you."

I pushed the lobby door open. "Okay. I'll be expecting your call."

"Later Jaliyah."

"Bye Quincy."

Then I walked out into the beautiful summer weather.

# chapter three

**I**t took me a minute to find my car because I don't ever freakin' pay attention to where I park. I'm just happy that I can do it. I failed my driving test like four times before I passed. All four times were because of that parking bullshit. Let me tell you how… nah, that don't even matter because I'm going to end up getting emotional, and I'm gon' start talking about something that has nothing to do with the story.

I used to be *so* scared to drive. I used to go so slow. People would be honkin' and shit. I ain't give a goddamn. I would try to tell them to kiss my ass and give them the finger, but they would speed past me too quick. But trust, if they asses were going just a little bit slower, I would have told *them* a thing or two about *their* stuff and what *they* had going on that day. See there I go— Anyway, the day was beautiful and summer was all up and through the air.

I went from aisle A to C until I *finally* found my baby parked in aisle C-6. I named my car Pearl because it is the color of a pearl. Sorry, I don't have a story behind that. It's pretty self-explanatory really. Pearl is a fully-loaded, 2004 Honda Civic. I hooked my car up like the boys do. I wasn't really into cars that much until I got one. It has the hottest rims, sound system, all lat. I have lights under the car that light up hot-pink at night and everything. It is really nice.

I put my bags into my trunk and got into my whip. I opened up my Prince CD and put it in to play. "I Wanna Be Your Lover" blasted from my speakers. I was going to take the quick way home, but the weather was so nice and *The Artist Formerly Known As* was sounding so right that I decided to ride down to my hometown of Mount Vernon. I wanted to visit a couple of my peoples, and I had not been down there in a good two to three months. Yeah, it was an hour plus drive, but I didn't mind.

I felt the energy as soon as I crossed the Tapanzee Bridge into Westchester County. It was like, even though I didn't live there anymore, I knew that I was home. I called up my man Mos (pronounced like Most) to let him know that I was coming through.

Mos is a guy that I have been friends with since I was about eight or nine-years-old. He is one of my closest friends. He is one of the coolest and most down to earth dudes that I know. He's about six-feet-two inches tall, with a chiseled, toned body. I always describe him by saying, "Imagine if Allen Payne and Shemar Moore got together and had a baby." That's Mos.

I call him Mos because when we were younger, whenever you asked him a question, his answer was always, "Most likely" or "Most probably" or "Most" something. His real name was Shawn. He said that he would be home at around seven or seven-thirty that night, so I told him that I would be through there later on.

I asked him if he would have eaten something by then or if he wanted me to bring him some grub from my girl Alicia's house because she stay in the kitchen. Of course his greedy ass said that he, *most probably would have eaten something by then, but to bring him a plate anyway*. You know how that goes though. A greedy Negro ain't gon' never change. I got off the phone with him and I continued towards my exit.

# chapter four

The first stop on my agenda was my girl Cheyenne's house. I remembered that my mom had put some clothes in the cleaners after her last doctor's visit a few blocks from there, so I decided to pick them up for her. Can you believe that woman had *$87.34* worth of clothes in the cleaners? If I had not taken them out, I don't know when she would have gotten them. My mom tried that *leaving her clothes in the cleaners forever* bit at the other cleaners around the corner from where we used to live once.

She came back like a month or two later than when she was supposed to and the man said that he had given her clothes to the Salvation Army. Now you *know* that my mother flipped out, right? She hopped her tiny five-foot-two inch frame over that counter and started pressing all types of buttons looking for her clothes. The clothes behind that counter started spinning super-duper fast! The man called the police on her.

She wasn't arrested. They let her off with a warning. About a week later, my mom saw the cleaner's wife on the train wearing her five-hundred dollar Donna Karan pants suit that my father told her she ain't had no business buying in the first place. To this day, she can still talk about that incident for an hour straight without stopping whenever we bring it up.

I pulled up in front of my girl Cheyenne's crib.

Shy and me have been kickin' it heavy since pre-k. There was a time when we were clashing a lot because she just wanted to wild out once she got into high school. She was always smokin' weed, drinkin' and fuckin'. For a minute, her name was all over the place. She had been with so many dudes that it was crazy. Old ones, young ones; it ain't matter. If there was a girl at a party walkin' around yellin' out, "Where the weed at!" it was her. If you met her now though, you would never know.

As soon as Cheyenne let me in, I took off the skirt and cardigan that I had bought from DIVAS and threw on one of the two pairs of sweats that I had bought earlier. I liked dressing up, but not when I was just tryna kick it with my peoples.

"Thanks for doing my hair Jah. Girl, you know I miss you livin' down the hall right? Your moms and pops just up and moved you to West Bubblefuck and what not!" Cheyenne took a pull from her cigarette.

"I don't have no time to do my hair let alone anything else between working and going to school for this CPA bullshit. I don't know why the fuck I chose to major in accounting!"

She tapped a little ash into her New York Knicks ashtray. "Ooh girl, have you heard the new Mystique Soulchild CD?!" she asked turning on her stereo excitedly.

"Nah, I have not had a chance to hear the new *Musiq* Soulchild CD. Sweetie, there ain't no "T" in his name," I told her.

"Oh, there ain't? Fuck it. I been callin' that nigga Mystique since his ass came out. He know who I mean. Shit."

I poured myself a glass of apple juice and stole some sugar cookies from the cookie jar. "So, you like my ride out there?"

"Yeah Jah, that's fire right there. It's real cute." Cheyenne rolled her big, brown eyes that complemented her rich, cinnamon-brown tone perfectly. She scrunched her face up.

"Dalvin wrapped my whip. He hit a fuckin'—I don't even know *what* he hit that nigga lie so much. Now Chris, Chris has her moments, but she don't lie."

Now y'all, Christina—Chris for short, was this chick who had just moved to New Rochelle from Florida not too long ago. The first time I saw her I actually felt my bottom lip drop. She was gorgeous. Now, I ain't into girls, but the thought has entered and exited my mind a few times—and lately with this *L Word* show on Showtime?! They *always* have so much fun on that damn show! They make it look like being a lesbian is a non-stop party! Now, I know that is not true, because no one's life is a non-stop party, but they do a hell of a job of convincing you. And the sex scenes—off the meter!

Back to Christina though. The girl is beautiful. She has a deep, butter-scotch complexion, green-amber speckled eyes that almost close completely when she laughs, long, pretty eyelashes and loose, curly, sandy-brown hair with natural blonde highlights that get even brighter in the sun.

All of that aside, Chris is mean as shit—and completely insane. So naturally, I didn't say much when Shy told me that she was talking to her again. You see, Chris brings nothing but drama whenever she appears. She has a psycho-ass ex-girlfriend who is always up in her business. When Chris is told to handle the situation, she always ends up right back with her ex-girl. I told Cheyenne that she should just leave Chris and Chris's whole situation alone. Shy has fought over that damn girl too many times to count.

I sipped my juice. "Oh, word. Chris? I thought that she had a girl and what not."

"Nah, they broke up. I'm tired of these fools. Black, White, Puerto Rican, Dominican, Italian, Russian, Japanese, Thai, shit...

African. Fuck em'. They ain't shit. They ain't shit individually and if they all blended into one, they *still* would not be shit. I'm tired. I don't have no more patience." She took my glass and drank the rest of my apple juice.

I looked at my empty glass and sucked my teeth.

She rolled her eyes. "What? You could get some more."

That was *definitely* true, so I got up and poured me another glass.

"Anyway," I said to her, "I guess you gotta do what you gotta do. If being with a chick is what's gon' make you happy, then go for it."

"I know that's right." She took another pull from her cigarette. "So *Jah*, what brings you down here today?"

"Oh, I came from a job interview a few hours ago and I got the job. I wasn't doing anything so I hopped on the highway and came through." I grabbed a few more cookies.

"You done went and got you *another* job ma? What you doin' now?"

"I'm working in this clothing store called DIVAS. Me and you went in there the last time that you came to visit me."

"Oh, you mean that store with all of them white girls up in it that think that you tryna steal shit. How you gon' work up in there and respect yourself Jah-dee?"

"First off, Shy, you *were* stealing. Second, they are starting me at $8.00 an hour. Third, the manager is just as Puerto Rican as you are."

She rolled her eyes. "Oh, then she's cool people," she said sarcastically. Then she yelled, "Jah-dee, stupida, that don't mean shit. Where is she from?"

I looked at her and smiled, "Brooklyn."

She rolled her eyes. "I can't stand Brooklyn bitches!"

I waved my hand at her. "I know you can't. Honestly, I don't think you can stand too many people; whether they are from

Brooklyn or anywhere else, but Carmen is cool. She got this fine-ass boyfriend too. Yo, that muthafucka is bangin'. He got this friend. Yo, he looks good too. The only thing is that he's so freakin' little."

Cheyenne interrupted with her usual, "Hook a bitch up!"

I sucked my teeth at her. "Bitch, I thought you swore off dick! I ain't hookin' you up with shit."

"Oh, yeah. I be forgettin'. Good thing Chris wasn't here. That bitch is jealous as shit. She don't hardly like *your* ass."

"For real girl?" I asked her faking disappointment. "Cause I don't give a *fuck*. I don't like her smug-ass either. Crazy bitch! Me and you been knowin' each other *too* damn long. She better fall back with that bullshit."

I turned off her CD and put on WBLS. Wendy Williams was on the radio.

"I know, I told her. She don't hear me though," Cheyenne said as she got up to get the wide-tooth comb and a scarf to tie her hair down with.

"Yo Shy," I called into the bedroom to her, "for some reason I think that there is a lot of drama up in that store. It's just a feeling that I get from it. I met this chick named—"

Before I could finish, she interrupted with, *"What's her name! Where she at!"*

"Yo Shy, can I finish?" I asked her.

"I-ight," she said.

"Cool. Like I was saying, her name is Jacqueline and instead of everyone calling her Jackie, like normal people would, they call her Jah-dee."

"Bitch, that's your name," Shy said as she handed me the comb.

"Bitch, I know." I responded in agreement. "Anyway, she seems like the jealous type. I mean, she got a little bit tight when she heard that everyone calls me that too. Carmen said that she was going to get upset before I even met her. They're all calling me "Baby Girl" though because I seem "innocent" to them. Chino, the short guy, he said that he's gon' call me Jah-dee just to piss Jacqueline off. That's fucked up right?"

"Well, yeah just let them think that you're innocent or whatever because I don't want to have to come up there and whoop everybody ass." Cheyenne looked in the mirror and applied some MAC lip-gloss.

"I'm getting too old for that mami. Word. And, that Chino instigatin'-ass nigga is gon' have Jacqueline hatin' on you and then you or me or Nicole or Angie is gon' have to fuck that bitch up. You know how we used to do. I know you ain't forgot. It ain't been that long."

Cheyenne has a way of hypin' situations up. Everything always comes down to fighting with her. She's *extremely* aggressive. However, I really can't blame her. She used to see her pops beatin' up on her moms when she was small. That is until her mother moved into the building where I was raised. Let me see, I am 25-years-old and I have fought about twenty times in my whole life beginning at age ten. All because of Cheyenne's ass. Maybe once or twice it was because of me, but all the other times were because of her. She fought too damn good one-on-one, so bitches would always try to jump her. I was not letting that go down. We were always getting suspended from school, but we both managed to graduate in the top percent of our high school class.

"Yo Jah, are you going to see Shawn tonight?"

"Yeah, I told him that I would come through at about 7:30, 8:00 o'clock the latest."

"I heard that he been seen a few places with that chick Lela. You know the one who I fought back in the day and beat her ass? Yeah, her."

She took one last pull from her cigarette and put it out in the ashtray.

"I don't know what the fuck he sees in that bitch. Trey told me that Shawn said that she look madd good and this and that. In my opinion, Shawn ain't never had no good taste except for when he was going out with Dominique. *She* was pretty. The rest of them chicks were fuckin' ugly as *fuck*. He be gassin' them up to be like that. Trey told me that whenever Shawn stops to talk to his peoples outside or wherever, she sucks her teeth and shit. Just showin' her whole ass."

She laughed. "And you know that Trey don't lie about other niggas. He may lie about his own shit to certain people, but he don't lie about anybody else to no one. He runs his mouth like a straight up girl. That's where I be gettin' all of my info from. Alicia gets her info from that nigga too. All she tells him is that she gon' cook for him. Once he eats, he runs his mouth all night til he goes to sleep. That's my word. Til' his big ass head hits the fuckin' pillow."

Now, Trey best friend of Mos, is one of the realest dudes I know. His way of describing himself is, *"Yo man, I'm cooler than the other side of the pillow B!"*

He's much realer than a lot of people, but the majority of the time, I think that he gets the definition of the word *real* confused with the definition of the word *rude*. He told me that I looked like a turtle in a toupee once back in 9th grade.

"Ooh, girl," I said excitedly, "I met this fine-ass cutie in the mall today! Delicious. Freakin' dark-skinned, tall, muscular, Stringer Bell looking muthafucka. I think that he's gon' call me tonight."

"You gave *him* your number?" She took my glass of juice and drank it again. "You must have been really feelin' him because you don't be givin' anybody your number. But I'd give my number to Stringer Bell too though."

I took my empty glass back from her and just stared at it.

"Damn Jah, don't be lookin' at your glass like that! You can *get* some more!"

Again, that *was* true, so I finished braiding her hair, kicked it with her for a little while longer, then I left to go and check my girl Alicia.

The first thing I did once I left Cheyenne's apartment before anything else though, was head to the corner store to buy a dollar bottle of apple juice that I could enjoy in peace.

# chapter five

I drove by the park to see who was out there. I kicked it with some people, and then I drove to Alicia's apartment. Alicia's place is always so nice and neat. Everything has its own, special place. She has had her own crib since she was 19-years-old. She met this dude and he was the head of A&R at some record company. He was ten or eleven-years-older than she was. *Gross, I know*—nevertheless, they fell in "love", and she bounced from her mom's crib. The relationship didn't work out—but, there wasn't really anything for her at her mom's crib anyway. Her mom was always hanging out. And her pops—*"Yo, what pops?"* is what she always says.

When we were growing up, Alicia practically lived at my house. Cheyenne used to get jealous of that sometimes. They are both my friends, but sometimes I think that they tolerate each other for my sake. They disagree just to do it. God forbid if something ever happens to me because them two are gonna have it out straight Fat Joe/Cuban Link style.

Alicia is shaped like a supermodel. Straight up and down. She is five-feet-ten-inches tall, and a size 2 in clothes. Her posture is immaculate. She used to take ballet when she was younger and traveled to the city a lot. That's how she met that A&R guy. She is very fair-complexioned with deep-brown, almost black eyes. She has long, straight, dark-brown hair that usually grows to reach the arch in her back when she doesn't cut it. Her pops is Italian and her mom is Japanese and Jamaican.

Alicia is so lady-like. You will rarely hear her curse anyone out. But when she does, oh honey, she curses muthafuckas for filth, I tell you!

When I entered Alicia's apartment, I was met with the nicest aroma. Oh, it smelled so good! I went into the kitchen, opened up a pot and sniffed the cloud of steam that rose from it. "Yo ma, what are you cookin' up in here?"

"Oh, I'm making some pepper steak, some corn and some mashed potatoes with cheese on top. Trey is coming over. I need some information." She began cutting the tops off strawberries.

I snuck one and ate it. "What kind of information?"

She smiled. "Girl, information about me and him. We've been kickin' it with each other these past couple of months and I just want to know where our relationship is going. "Tonight," she took a deep breath, "I'm gonna ask him."

"Oh snap, you feelin' Trey? I definitely been outta the loop too damn long. Why you ain't tell me?"

"I ain't want you to judge. You know how you can be." She took out another pint of strawberries and rinsed them in the sink.

I didn't blame her because I do know how I can be. I shook my head.

"Girl, Trey is good peoples. But, he's just such a whore. You remember all of those conversations that we used to have back in high school?"

She laughed. "Yeah, it'd be like five, six of us just sitting around talking about any and everything."

## Mount Vernon High School, 1998

"Yo T, you is a nasty muthafucka! Runnin' around here with all these nasty, groupie-ass bitches! What the fuck is wrong wit' yo' ass? You gon' stop when you be done caught some-thin'!" Alicia yelled at Trey shaking her head in disgust.

Trey stopped drinking his soda and yelled "Yo, who you yellin' at like that nigga! Yo, you have madd hostility towards me like. You better ease up. You gon' make me catch a case in this bitch!" He went back to drinking his soda.

She rolled her eyes hard. "Nigga, who the fuck you callin' a bitch nigga?! Your stank-ass girl's a bitch! That's what nigga!"

Trey stopped drinking his soda again. "Nigga, ain't nobody call you no bitch! I said that you gon' make me catch a case in this bitch! I called the cafeteria a bitch! Calm down!" He went to drink his soda again, but then he said, "And you callin' my girl a bitch, I bet she whip ya' ass!"

"T, your girl ain't gon' do shit. I will stomp her lil' 4 foot noth-in', bitch-ass........"

---

Alicia laughed again. "Yeah, we were crazy back then. We were always arguing."

She paused. "It's not like that so much now though. Me and him are here with ours." She said gesturing with her hands. She smiled again. "I could actually see myself spending the rest of my life with him."

Now, I could not believe that I was actually hearing this. Alicia falling in love with Trey was like Pam falling in love with Martin. You just can't picture the shit.

I asked her, "So what's up with old girl? She ain't claiming him no more? Last I heard she was fighting every bitch that went near him."

"She's been away at school and they broke up for good a while ago. They still keep in touch though. She knows that he's seeing someone, but she just doesn't know who."

"*Well*," I said, "if she comes back home tryna start some shit with her street-ass cousins, call me up. I'm here!"

"I know. I don't think that it's gon' come to that though. Can you believe that he is still messing with that chick all the way from high school? We hated her ass back in the day. She wasn't flyy at all. She used to hang on to his ass though. She ain't hardly ever let him outta her sight."

"Girl, you ain't never lied." I stole a few more strawberries and sprinkled some sugar on them.

"The food will be ready soon. You can take some for you and Shawn if you want to. I have more than enough."

"Thank you!" I cheesed as I took two more strawberries.

"So, what is going on with you?" she asked.

"Girl, I met this fine-ass guy today! His name is Quincy and he seems very cool. So cool, that I gave him *my* number and gave him back his. That's what's going on." I winked at her.

"Well, go ahead and do the damn thing girl! Shee-yit, we ain't gettin' no younger!" She took a swig of her glass of water.

"I know that's the truth." I licked the sugar off my fingers.

Alicia could always make me feel confident about any situation. She reminded me of my mom so much. There were times when I would get jealous of Alicia and my mom's relationship. Then I saw the relationship that she had with her mother, and I practically moved her into my house.

"*Jah-dee*, will you stop eating all of my strawberries girl! They are for the cake!" She snatched the strawberry from me.

"Nah see, that ain't right because you know that strawberry shortcake is my favorite. I have it every year for my birthday. The only time that I ain't have strawberry shortcake is when I was like one-year-old because I did not know what a strawberry was! But once I turned two, it was on. I could spell strawberry and everything!"

She laughed. "Bitch, you can't spell strawberry now!"

"Yes, SCRAWBERRRR! That's how you spell it! Yup, that's how you spell it! What you know about the scrawberrrr! Holla!"

Right then, my cell phone rang. It was Mos.

"Where you at black-ass?" he asked as soon as I answered, his voice full of attitude.

"I'm at Alicia's house. Where are *you* at?" I asked him back.

"I'm in my crib waiting for you to come by nigga. I'm hungry. I've been sitting here," he said in a way that made me just want to slap his damn face. "Leave and come and see me!"

I rolled my eyes. "Fine brat. I'll be there in a little while!"

"Okay, I'll be here," he said sounding cheerful now.

I kicked it with Alicia for like another half an hour, and then I headed across town to see Mos.

On the drive over I thought about our friendship. We really *had* been kickin' it since forever. Sharing dreams and aspirations. I remember the day I told him that I was going to be a doctor. I remember the day he told me that he was going to be a *fire department*.

Nope. Not very smart back then—just *smart-mouthed*.

# chapter six

I pulled up in front of Mos's house at 8:05 pm. I stopped to get gas on the way, because I knew that I was going to be at his crib for a few hours and I never stopped for gas late at night by myself. I called him from my cell to let him know that I was outside. When he opened the door, he looked like he had been sleeping. He was wearing some blue jeans and a white tee. He had on a black du-rag and some socks with rainbow colored happy faces all over them. Before I could even comment on the socks he said, "Don't hate ma, you know you want me to hook you up wit' the foot-ees!"

"Yeah, maybe a month ago when I needed something to wear to Pride with Shy!" Once I realized that I was still outside I said, "Damn, can I get inside or what? I mean, what up?" I pushed my way inside of the door, knocking him off to the side.

"It look like you already in to me *nigga*!" He closed the door behind me and yelled out, *"Ma, Jah-dee here! She tryna knock your brand-new door from the Home Depot off the hinge!"*

"Shut up!" I said pushing him.

His mother came out of her bedroom just a smiling away.

"Hi baby, I haven't seen you in ages. You look so pretty! You look like you done gained some weight too. It looks good on you though. You look real nice!" She gave me a hug.

"She look i-ight!" Mos said as he searched my bag with all the food in it.

"She look a little ashy to me though around her knuckles and her lips." He took my bag with the food in it and went into the kitchen.

"Mama Thomas, I been eating the same as I always have. The only thing is that now, it's catching up with me. I eat, and it all stays right here." I rubbed my stomach.

"You gettin older. Don't worry about it though. It goes with your height. You look beautiful."

Me and Mos's mom were so close. We talked about everything. Her and my mom are good friends too. They are always getting into something together. His mom was right there co-signing when the whole dry cleaners incident went down.

Mos came back out from the kitchen with a full plate, stuffing his face. I just looked at him.

"What?" He took in another mouthful of food. "Yours is still in there!"

"*Ill*, don't yell! You sound like a bitch any damn way when you yell. Your kids ain't gon' never take you seriously. They gon' be like, *whatever Daddy*."

"Oh yeah, and I'm gon' be like well whatever my foot outta ya little asses!" He took another bite of his food.

"Boy, you ain't gon' say shit." I walked into the kitchen. "Wow! You couldn't even fix me a plate?"

I got a plate out of the cabinet and heated up my food. He didn't know about the slices of shortcake that I had stashed in my car. Nah, he wasn't gettin' that. He was too greedy anyway. He never gains an ounce of weight. I hate how guys can do that. Eat madd food and still be skinny.

"Did you leave some food in there for me?" he asked.

I almost caught a case with that line. "Nah, pain in my butt, I ain't leave nothing. You hardly left me anything. You better lick my asshole, that's what."

"I won't lick it, but I'll *definitely* put some pain in it!" he laughed.

"Oooh, now I know you ain't getting fresh and talking to me like I'm one of them bitches you be running round with! Boy, I bet you wouldn't even know where to start if you got a chance to get some of dis' pussy nigga!" I shot back at him.

He wrinkled up his face, "Yo, why is your mouth always so grimy Jaliyah? Why you always gotta get so ignant about shit. You need to sit down and focus!"

He laughed. "Remember when Tyrese said that shit in *Baby Boy*?"

I laughed. "Yeah, that nigga was wildin'. *'See that's why we so divided now as a people because we don't have focus'.*"

I laughed some more. "Yo, that movie was real though."

He rolled his eyes and shook his head. "Yeah, *real* dumb!"

"Didn't me and you go see that shit in the movies?" I asked.

He turned on the TV. "No ma, we watched the bootleg right here in this living room."

"Oh, I forgot." I sat down on the couch. "Yo, what you think about me trying out to be on The Real World on MTV?"

"Do you ma! I just can't wait to come and visit and shit when you do get on that shit. I'ma just wild out for no reason. I'ma be fightin' with niggas. I'ma stay looking directly into the camera. All lat!"

I rolled my eyes. "You would be the one to go on there and just super O.D. You'd be trying to start off your acting career from that show and what not."

"Please believe me!" He took the remote and turned to BET. "So, what's going on with you P-Puff? You look like you tryin' to get a little thick on a brotha!" he said slapping me on the thigh.

"Not purposely. And why do you always call me that dumb shit? You've been calling me that for like two years now." I rolled my eyes.

He laughed. "Because, you look like a Power Puff Girl when you get happy, sad or mad."

"So basically, I look like a Power Puff Girl all the damn time?" I poked him in the side.

"Pretty much. Yeah." He poked me back.

"Fuck you Mos! That's why I got some cake and you don't nyucca! I ain't giving you none neither."

"You better take that bass out your voice chick! Remember who you talkin' to now. I will kick your ass like I did back in the fifth grade. Ain't no thing to do it again. Anyway, it don't matter if you give me any cake or not because once you go get it to eat it, I'll just thug you for it punk girl! You know your greedy ass ain't gon' hardly wait til you get all the way home to eat some damn cake!"

He took a spoonful of my mashed potatoes and smiled. "Ain't it crazy how other people's food always tastes better than your own?"

He got up, ran into the bathroom, and locked the door.

"Ain't nobody even chasing after your stupid ass so you can stay in there all night!" I yelled from the living room.

Well, he stayed in the bathroom for like twenty minutes. When he finally came out he said, *"Coming out, feeling about, ten pounds lighter*!"

He put his hands on his stomach. "That food fuckin' killed my stomach Jah-dee! Tell Alicia that I'ma kick her ass. As a matter of fact, let's call up Kimora Lee Simmons right now."

Remembering that Trey was gon' be over there, I said, "Yo, B, ya man's over there and I don't know what you would be interrupting if you called there."

"What chu mean you don't know what I would be interrupting? Nothing. Them niggas ain't doing shit!" he yelled laughing. "All they do is argue about bullshit!"

"You don't know what they doing!" I yelled. "Mind yours nigga!"

"A-ight, fine," he said upset that he did not get his way. "Damn, I wanted to fuck with them niggas." He thought for a minute.

"A-ight then," he said, "I got the Spit cards my nigga! You ready for me to wax that ass?"

"Oh, I should be asking you that *son*!" I cracked my knuckles. "You don't want none of this here!"

For those of you who don't know, Spit is a card game that is somewhat similar to Solitaire, but instead of one player, there are two players playing against each other at a ridiculously fast speed. I have heard about, been a part of and witnessed countless fights surrounding Spit games.

I had beaten Mos in about ten games of Spit before he decided to gracefully bow out for the night. His moms even got in on it and beat him about three times. What a loser. Before I left outta there though, I let him *thug* a piece of strawberry shortcake from me. I felt it was only right.

On that long ride home, I thought about what I was going to wear tomorrow at work and then Quincy popped into my mind. Quincy, with his well-sculpted body and pretty smile. I thought about how he licked his lips before he spoke and how smooth and sexy his voice was. Most of all, I thought about how he had better call me soon.

My cell phone rang. It was my mom.

"Girl, you better get your butt in this house. You know that me and your father don't like you driving up and down the highway all hours of the night!"

"Mom, I'll be there in about twenty minutes," I told her.

She calmed down. "Okay, well just be careful and call when you're on the block so I can see you in, alright."

"I'll be downstairs!" I heard my father yell out in the background.

"Forget it, your father will be downstairs," she said.

"Okay," I answered. "See you in a little bit. Love you."

"Love you too," she said.

We hung up, and I threw on my Lenny Kravitz, *Baptism* CD. My favorite track ended just as I pulled up into my driveway. *Perfect timing.* My cell phone rang again.

"Hello, is this Jaliyah?" a deep voice that I didn't immediately recognize said on the other end of the phone.

"*Maybe*, who's this?" I responded coolly just knowing that it was Quincy.

The voice paused for a bit and then said, "This is Robert."

I thought for a minute. "*Robert who?*"

The male voice on the other end of the line chuckled a bit. "You know Robert who. You met me earlier ma."

I thought for a minute, and then it came to me. This was my boss's man Robert. Right then, I knew that there was about to be some shit.

# chapter seven

I froze. I could not understand for the life of me why *Robert* would be calling me at almost midnight and how *he* had gotten my phone number in the first place. The last thing that I wanted to do was to get caught up in some bullshit at work. That was one of the worst things anyone could do. I regained my composure and spoke again finally.

"How did you get my number? What do you want? I ain't tryna get mixed up in no bullshit, you hear!" I said sternly, anger quickly taking over.

He laughed lightly. "Damn ma, calm down. Nah, it's just that me and Chino are chillin' at Carmen's crib smokin', you know drinking a little bit, and we wanted to know if you wanted to come through and chill. You know, chill, talk, whatever."

"Are you outta ya mind! You still ain't answer me neither! How did you get my number?" I yelled again.

"Oh, I got it out of Carmen's phone. The managers keep all of y'all numbers in their cell phones. Don't worry, she ain't here. She went out to the club with Jacqueline and some other chick. She told me that she would stay over Jah-dee's house since it was closer to the club or whatever." He paused to take a pull off his blunt and said, "So ma, you comin' through or what?"

I sucked my teeth. "*Hell* no you crazy fuck!"

He laughed hysterically. "I'm just playing with you!" Then I heard a whole bunch of laughter in the background.

"Carmen is sitting right here beside me. You have just been initiated. We wanted to see if you were worthy of the name "Baby Girl" mami."

Just then, Carmen got on the phone. "You passed the test! Yo, we had you on speakerphone! You sounded too funny! Yo, at least I know that I can trust you around my man!"

"I'm sorry ma!" Robert yelled in the background.

"Y'all are buggin' out!" I said attempting to regain my composure. "I was like, this nigga is crazy and he is on some straight bullshit right now!"

"Yeah, I know." Carmen laughed uncontrollably. "Yo, I fired a girl the day after I hired her once because she said that she was going to come over and ride his dick the way I never could!"

"What?" I said. "That's— *special*!"

"Yeah, I know. Anyway, let me let you get back to what you were doing. I have to go. Robert already got my jeans unbuckled and now he's tryna pull em' down. He's tryna fuck me from the back and shit."

In the background, I could hear Robert whispering something and then I heard Carmen moan directly into the phone.

"Ma, I'll, mmm, see you tomorrow. Mmm." Carmen struggled to say through her moans.

"Oh, okay. Do the damn thing. One."

I could *not* believe what had just occurred. I got my mom's clothes out of the back of my car and went to key in the code to open up the garage door. My father must have seen me in one of the ten cameras that he has surrounding the perimeter of our house and let me in.

"Hey Daddy," I said as I walked into the basement and gave him a kiss.

"Hey," he responded. "You had better be careful riding up that highway so late."

I rolled my eyes and sucked my teeth in my mind, but kept quiet. "Okay."

"So, how are Cheyenne, Alicia and Shawn?"

I yawned a little. "They are all good."

"Shy is still nuts!" I laughed.

My dad laughed. "She was nuts when she was 4-years-old."

He looked at the clothes I was carrying. "Oh, I see that you got your mother's clothes out of the cleaners for her?"

"Yeah,"I said. "Almost a hundred dollars worth."

He took the clothes from me and we walked upstairs. "I'll give it back to you in the morning."

"Thanks Daddy," I said and gave him a kiss goodnight.

"Okay, goodnight," he said and he went into his room. I got a quick peek of my mother nodding off before he shut the door.

I set the house alarm, and went into my room to shed my dirty clothes and put them into the hamper. I showered, lotioned up, plugged my cell into the charger, and hopped into my bed.

I cut out the light, and I laid in bed a minute thinking about all of the day's occurrences. From getting the job at DIVAS to meeting Quincy. I knew that my life was going to be interesting for the next few months. Every few months or so, my life will be calm. Nothing much going on, and then all of a sudden, I'll have a million things going on at once. The only question was, *was I prepared?*

Just as I was about to knock out, my cell phone rang again.

"Hello!" I yawned.

"Oh, I'm sorry Jaliyah. Did I wake you?" an unfamiliar voice asked on the other end of the phone.

"It depends on who this is," I responded.

"It's Quincy," he paused.

"Oh, okay then. In that case, I'm cool. I just need someone to talk to who isn't completely out of their mind." I laughed.

"Well, that's me. I'm good for tonight anyway. "So what's going on? Has it been that bad since you left me earlier?" Quincy asked me.

"Um, lemme see. My boss's man called playing on my phone talking about how he wanted to get with me. He said that him and his man were smoking a blunt and he wanted to know if I wanted to come through. He said that Carmen wasn't home and this and that."

"Word? Is Carmen your boss?" he asked me.

"Yeah, that's my boss. So I started getting a little shook because the last thing that I want to get into is problems at work, you know. So I'm thinking in my mind like, *What is going on?* So then, when I start to like spazz out, I hear a whole bunch of laughing in the background. Then, Carmen got on the phone on some; "I passed the test" bullshit. She wanted to make sure that I wasn't after her man because she don't trust nobody."

"I don't even want to talk about it. It's so stupid. But uh, what's going on with you?" I asked him yawning silently.

"Ain't nothing. I just got off work a little while ago." He yawned.

"Damn, you work some late ass hours," I told him looking over at my digital alarm clock.

"Nah, I was just trying to get some overtime in. I got the call after I saw you in the mall so I went in," he explained to me.

"So what do you do?" I asked him.

"I'm a cop in the city. I've been with the NYPD for about a good eleven years now.

Now, this shocked the hell outta me. "For real?" I asked. "Wow, my dad is a retired Lieutenant from the NYPD. He's been off the job for about six years now though. I got a bunch of aunts and uncles on the job too."

"Oh, wow. No kidding," he said. "My family is kind of the same way. All law enforcement," he laughed. "Okay, well that's one thing we have in common."

"Well, you look mighty young to have been on the job for eleven years. Shit, you got what, nine years and then you'll be retiring, huh?"

"Well, I'm studying for the sergeant's test this December so; I plan on making Sergeant and then continuing to climb the ladder. You know."

He sounded like he took a sip of water. "I don't have any kids or anything like that so I'm cool for now."

He laughed lightly. "I'm not *that* young though."

"Well, now I kinda figured that. You gotta be 21 to even be hired into the NYPD. So if you got on the job at 21, which you must have done, you gotta be like what, 32, 33?" I asked feeling a lot more awake than I had when he had first called.

He laughed. "I'm 35-years-old."

I was stuck for a minute. He was a 35-year-old fine piece of ass. "*Get* the fuck outta here!"

He laughed again. "Yeah, I'll be 36 in two months."

Now, I had never dealt with no one fifteen-years-older than me before. Maybe three or four-years-older, but not fifteen. Now, I knew that if me and him did start dating officially, I would have to tell my pops his age.

My pops always fronts like that if I ever fell in love with a man that was 50-years-old, he wouldn't care. Yeah, right. It didn't take me too long to figure out that when it comes to my father, everything is all-good as long as it isn't happening. Let it happen, and watch him flip mode like Sybil.

He must have sensed that I was having a conversation with myself in my mind because he said, "Jaliyah, I hope that my age is not going to cause problems." He chuckled, "I promise you I am young at heart."

"Nah, you just had me stuck. You look younger." I cleared my throat. "But, 35 is not old. My parents were 35 once."

He laughed. "You're a funny girl." He paused. "Maybe you want to get together for dinner and you can tell me some more of your funny jokes?"

I thought about it. I definitely wanted to go. Not to just tell some damn jokes though. That was for sure.

I paused. "When's your birthday?"

"What?" he asked confused.

"When's your birthday?" I asked him again. "You said it's in two months which is September. So that could mean that you're either a Virgo or a…"

"I'm a Virgo. My birthday is September 4$^{th}$," he answered before I could finish.

"Oh, you have the same birthday as Beyonce!" I told him.

He laughed, "So is that a good thing?"

"It's a great thing," I told him. "And do you know what's even greater, my dear GQ?"

I sat up in my bed and smiled in the darkness. "I love Beyonce!"

"Ohhhhh…shit!" he laughed acting extra hyped up. "You believe in astrology and all of that stuff though?"

"Not really," I answered. "I just know that I don't like any Gemini men, except for the ones who are related to me. You know, "Like my father, and my cousins and my friends. In my opinion, Gemini men suck. They lie too much about random shit. I dealt with this one Gemini cat and oh— that boy could lie! Just a ball full of lies!"

I yawned. "But that's old news. Just as long as you're not a Gemini, we're cool. Oh, or an Aquarius. I *hate* them!" I took another look at my digital alarm clock. "So, yes, I would love to have dinner with you. What do you have in mind?"

He paused to think. "How about either the Red Lobster or the Olive Garden?"

"Hmmm…let me see. Red Lobster is cool," I said laughingly.

I thought about the black and silver dress that I had bought at DIVAS. Nah, what the hell was I thinking. That sparkly shit was too much for Red Lobster. People would think that I ain't never been nowhere. I continued to think about it.

I must have been pretty quiet during all my thinking because Quincy interrupted my thoughts again and said, *"You there?"*

I caught myself. "Oh yeah, I'm here. I was just putting together my outfit in my mind."

He sighed and said, "Ahhh man. You're one of those that take a year and a day to get ready, huh?"

I laughed loudly. "Yeah and so!"

"Jaliyah, shut up!" my sister Nicky yelled and banged loudly once on my door. "I'm tryna sleep!"

"Shut up Nicky!" I yelled back loudly.

"Oh, I have a brother named Nicholas too," he told me.

"No, I don't have a brother. Nicky's my sister." I rolled my eyes. "I have two of them to be exact. *They're both pains in my ass sometimes!*" I yelled loud enough so she could hear me if she was still standing by the door. "My big sister Angie is getting married soon and she'll be outta here in a few weeks. I'll miss her though."

We both yawned simultaneously.

"I'll give you the directions to my house tomorrow sometime. Or I can just text you the address and you can MapQuest it if that would be easier," I said. "You gotta come in and meet the parents, though. My father and my mother don't like me going out all willy-nilly like. They take down your license plate number, social security number." I paused for a second. "Oh, by the way, what *is* your last name?"

"I understand that. I have seen so many crazy incidents on the job. I totally understand that." He took a second to answer me. "It's Chase".

"Oh okay. Sergeant Chase!" I laughed. "It's got a nice ring to it."

"Don't it though!" he laughed.

"Yeah, it does," I told him. "My last name is Whitfield. Jaliyah Camille Whitfield." *Jaliyah Camille Chase has an even nicer ring to it,* I thought to myself. Again interrupting my thoughts he said, "Well then, you best be getting to sleep Miss Jaliyah Camille Whitfield."

He let out a yawn. "I'm good. I don't have to work for the next two days."

"Yeah, I know. Your swing shifts." I yawned. "Tomorrow is my first day. I just plan on this job being temporary. I cannot be twenty-one-years-old making under ten cash an hour. That's crazy."

"You should join the police department. You could retire in 20 years. You get a pension, benefits."

"Recruit much?" I said laughing. "Yeah, I looked into that. My dad convinced me to take the test. I did, but I haven't heard anything back from them yet." I told him.

"They'll get back to you," he said. "A lot of old timers are retiring. You'll get in." He paused.

"Oh, but a bit of advice for tomorrow morning; don't wear heels. I know for a fact that standing all day is no joke. This is coming from a man who's had to stand on patrol in the rain, in the snow and in the hot ass sun with about fifteen pounds of equipment on, eight hours a day."

"Okay. Will do." I said.

"Okay J," he said. "I'ma see if I can catch an episode or two of *The Wire* before I go to sleep."

I smiled to myself. "You know, it's crazy that you said that because you look just like—"

He cut me off. "Please don't go there. I hear it all the time!"

"Oh, okay," I laughed. "I'll talk to you tomorrow."

"Goodnight," he said in a low sexy voice.

"Goodnight Quincy."

Then at 12:45 am, I turned my cell *off*, and knocked out.

# part two
# saturday

# chapter eight

"*My Goodies! My Goodies! My Goodies! Not My Goodies!*" Ciara blared from the stereo in my bedroom at 5:40A.M.

I had forgotten to take the alarm off from the morning before. I had planned to sleep until at least ten, seeing as how I had to be at work at eleven. It did not happen that way. I knocked on my mother's bedroom door.

"Mom! I picked up your clothes from Mount Vernon yesterday! Did you see them? I don't know where Daddy put them in there?"

She opened her door in her bathrobe. "Thank you sweetie. You went down there to do Cheyenne's hair?"

"I really went to see everyone," I told her.

I wanted to talk to my mom since I had been out all day yesterday.

"Tell Daddy to sleep in. I know that he usually drives you to the train station, but I'll take you today."

"Whatever you wanna do. Don't you start work today though?" she asked.

"Mommy, how do you know that I got the job? I didn't tell anyone yet."

"Don't you get every job that you apply for?" she smiled.

"I'll go and throw on some sweats and I'll be in the kitchen waiting for you okay." I ran into my room to get dressed.

I decided that I would talk to my mother about Quincy on our ride to the train station. My mother and I always talk. We do not always see eye to eye, but I would rather get advice from her before anyone else. I agree with Russell Simmons. He once said, "No matter what your stupid friends tell you, you learn something greater at home."

My mother was finally dressed and ready, coffee cup in hand. We hopped into Pearl, and were on our way.

My mother looked around and did a quick spot-by-spot inspection. "Hmmm, I'm surprised that this car is still clean. It still smells like new on the inside."

She took a piece of paper towel out of her purse and began to wipe at the windshield.

"Ma," I said, "what are you doing? Sit back, I can't see."

"Oh, this window is nasty Lee-Lee! You got to clean that. It looks like lil cats been dancing all across the window. Just a two-steppin' to and fro' with their little paw prints." Her southern accent rang out loud and clear.

You would *never* know my mother had an accent if you were one of her coworkers. She keeps it on lock at her job. The only time you can get my mother's southern accent to come out is if you call her up on the phone at work and say something extremely rude and ridiculous to piss her off.

Like sometimes, my father will say laughingly, "Let's make your mother get mad at her job."

Then he will call her up say something about how poor and trash acting *her* family was back in the day. Of course, this always riles her up because *his* family was just as poor and trash acting as hers if not more so!

It's so damn funny. She falls for it every single time!

But yes, my mother was in the car just a wipin' at the window. I remained calm knowing that she would be off on her merry way in about ten minutes. I exhaled quietly.

"Ma, I think that this job is going to be an experience, *for real*." I said, laughing as I merged.

"Why you say that Jah-dee?" she asked me taking sip of her coffee.

"I can just sense the drama up in there. My boss is a freak. Last night she had her man call me up and—it's just crazy."

"She had her man call you up for what?" she asked, ready to fight.

"To see if I was gonna try and talk to him." I laughed.

"Jah-dee, don't get involved in those things. Just go there and do what you have to do. Tell em' to cut the check!" she laughed.

"Mommy, I met this really cute dude at the mall after my interview yesterday." I said glimpsing out of the side of my eye to see her reaction.

"What he look like?" she asked.

"Oh, he's real tall like Mos, he's has a smooth, dark-brown complexion like daddy, pretty hair, and—"

Before I could finish, my mother interrupted me with her usual, "Oh, well, you don't like him then! You only like the ones who look like the bottom of my boots." She laughed.

"You know what, I ain't even telling you no more. You always got something to say. You just as bad as grandma," I rolled my eyes playfully.

"What does he do?" she asked.

"He's a cop in the city."

"Oh, Lord Jaliyah. Following in your mother's footsteps."

"You see your daddy." She nudged me. "You sure you wanna go there?" she asked jokingly.

"We're going out tonight," I told her.

"Oh, you don't waste any time. Where are y'all going? Who is this boy? You know I want the info before you set foot out that door and I want to meet him!" she started to raise her voice.

"I know, I know, I know ma," I laughed. "You will have all of the info on him."

I smiled devilishly. "Oh, and he's not a boy."

I glanced over in her direction. "He's 35-years-old."

"What!" she yelled almost spitting out her coffee.

We pulled up to the train station. "Look, we're here!" I announced, "Get on out!"

"Get on out my black ass!" she said as she removed her Gucci shades so she could look into my eyes.

"Ma, you are just too much for your own self this morning!" I laughed.

She smiled. "Yeah, keep laughing. I'ma beat your behind!"

"Mom, I'm 21-years-old. You're buggin' out right now!" I laughed uncontrollably.

She opened the car door. "You ain't gone make me late talking about this foolishness. I'll see you when I get home. What time is this *man* coming over?" she asked me.

"We didn't talk about the time, but I'm thinking like 6:30, 7:00 the latest," I told her.

She looked at me under-eyed. "Yeah, well I'll be there sho nuff"! Believe that!"

I laughed. "I bet you will!"

She closed the car door and spoke through the open window. "You keep right on laughing!"

"You looking really nice this morning mommy!" I told her.

"Mmm hmm," she said. Then she turned to walk away.

"Mommmmy!" I yelled. "Wait, come here!"

She turned around and began to walk back to the car.

I got out and ran to her. "You didn't give me a kiss."

She gave me a kiss and a hug. "Oh girl, you called me back for that?"

"Yup," I said as I kissed her again.

"Crazy girl!" she said.

She went off on her way. Once I saw her up on the train platform, and I saw the train pull into the station, I drove off.

It was almost 7:00AM, so I decided to drive back home and get at least three more hours of sleep. That did *not* happen though. I drove back to my house and just as soon as I was about to run upstairs and hop back into bed, the phone rang.

"Hello, may I speak to Jaliyah?" a girl asked.

"Yes, this is Jaliyah."

"Hey, it's Janet, the assistant manager at DIVAS. Um, I wanted to know if you could come in at 9:30 instead of 11:00 because I could really use the extra help. I want to hurry up and train you on register because I have a feeling that someone is getting fired today."

I hesitated. "Um, yeah, whatever. It's cool." I responded although I was a little pissed that I was not going to be getting any more sleep.

"Okay, so I'll see you in a couple of hours. And thanks for doing this." Janet said.

"No problem Janet," I told her.

Then I hung up the phone.

<h1 style="text-align:right">chapter nine</h1>

I slept for about another hour, then I got back up out of my bed, threw on my Babyface CD, and I went to my closet to pick out something to wear to work. I did not really want to wear a skirt on my first day, so I picked out something simple that I could wear with my pink and gray Timbs.

I chose a pair of gray, form-fitting slacks, a pink, short-sleeved, slim fitting top that said, *Girlicious* on it in rhinestones, and a gray zip-front hoodie just in case the AC was up full blast like it was in most stores during the summer months.

I found my gray DKNY bag under my bed and loaded it with gum, candy, lip-gloss, tissues, my wallet and my JLo *Glow* perfume. I did a once over in my full-length mirror behind my door, kissed my dad, and I was off.

I got to the mall at 9:30AM sharp. It didn't open up until 10:00, but everyone else was inside of their stores going through all of their opening procedures; counting the registers, straightening, cleaning up. When I got to DIVAS, no one was there. The gate was pulled down, it was dark inside, and there was not a manager in sight. I waited for ten minutes, still no one showed up.

Fifteen minutes, twenty minutes and so on. Before I knew it, the mall had opened, and DIVAS was still closed.

"They always open late," I heard a girl's voice say.

I looked around to see who had said it.

It was the girl at the jewelry stand in the middle of the mall.

"They always have to pay fines because they are always late," she repeated.

"Really," I said. "I just started today. My name is—"

"Jaliyah," she said.

"*Do I know you?*" I asked.

"No, you don't, but Chino was telling me that a new chick named Jaliyah was starting tomorrow and that you looked good and this and that." She smiled and licked her lips. "*He wasn't lying.*"

She took out some Windex and began to clean the top of her glass counter. "My name is Sabrina. I am the manager here at Gold and Go."

Sabrina was a white girl who was about six-feet tall. She had an uneven tan, short, spiky black hair with fire engine red high-lights and her makeup was atrocious. She had on about five chains that were badly tangled into one another, numerous ear piercings and a hand full of rings; courtesy of her store discount, I assumed.

She motioned me close to her and looked around suspiciously, "Look, don't get too close with anyone up in there. They are all a bunch of—"

Before she could finish, Janet who seemed to have appeared out of thin air said, "I am so… so… sorry Baby Girl!" There was *so* much traffic from Middletown to here. I-84 was backed up for days."

"You come here all the way from Middletown?" I asked her shocked that she would travel so far to work for probably not even fifteen bucks an hour. Middletown was a good forty-five minutes to an hour away from Poughkeepsie depending on traffic.

"Yeah. I applied to the DIVAS over there, but they needed me here. So here I am. She stopped and stared at Sabrina for a minute with an evil-ass look, then she said, "We better get started before we get hit with yet *another* fine."

She unlocked the gate and bolted into the back to flick on the lights and turn on the music.

JLo's "All I Have" with LL Cool J blasted out of the speakers.

"I'll see you later," Sabrina said as a customer approached her jewelry counter.

"Okay. Nice meeting you."

Janet exited the backroom just as I was entering the store and said, "Don't start dealin' with the chicks in this mall. Bitches here are real silly sometimes, you know."

I noticed that Janet was just about my height with blue eyes and wavy blonde hair. I also noticed that she looked a whole lot nicer yesterday than she did today. Today, she looked quite run down and tired.

"Yo, I am so tired. I went to Club Compaq last night and it was crazy up in there. I got so many numbers. Look at my face. I still have my club makeup on from last night." She grabbed my wrist and took me over to the register.

"Okay, I'm going to be setting up the tills in the drawers and I want you to just stay on the floor until Jacqueline gets here. She should be in at 10:30. Just um, watch the fitting-rooms, and help whoever needs help, and blah, blah, blah. If you need anything, ask me okay."

"Okay," I answered taking mental notes on every task she assigned.

She handed me a rainbow-colored, coiled wristlet with a key hanging from the bottom. "Here is the key to the fitting-rooms. Oh, and Baby Girl, don't fuck with Sabrina out there at the

Gold and Go. She's a jealous hoe. She wants to work up in here, that's why she's always startin' shit." She sucked her teeth.

"Oh, I just met her this morning while I was waiting for you. She seemed nice enough." I folded a sweater that was on the counter. "I didn't know that y'all had beef though."

Janet began to count the first drawer, "She's a cunt bitch!"

I laughed. "Damn, Janet. You a mean somethin' ain't you!" I said smiling.

She laughed. "No, I just don't like dealing with bullshit. Especially all of the bullshit that comes with working at this store. I'm 27 -years-old, and I've been here for almost *three* years now."

People began to enter the store.

"We got customers," Janet said. "If you need me, just holla okay."

"Yeah, I will," I said as I headed over to the fitting-rooms and waited for anyone who needed to be let in.

I took a few glances in the mirror at myself. I was looking very cute that day. My outfit flowed together nicely.

As I walked away, I heard a voice say, "Yeah, that mirror will get you every time. You can't help but look at it whenever you pass it."

I turned around to see Carmen walking towards the backroom.

"Hey Baby Girl!" she shouted.

"Hey Carmen! You look nice."

"Thank you. You look cute yourself." She smiled.

"*Yes, she does*," Chino said and smiled at me as he headed towards the backroom. Robert just smiled and went into the back.

Just then, Janet ran into the backroom and began asking Carmen a bunch of questions.

"So, you firing Michelle today?" I heard her say.

"Yeah, that bitch got a lot of fucking nerve. Trying to get me fired. You know that I am way too slick with my shit. She lucky that I ain't flip on her. She don't know that *I* know that she's the one who said that shit."

Carmen opened up the emergency exit door and lit a cigarette.

"What time is she supposed to work today?" Janet asked.

"She comes in at two o'clock," she answered taking a pull of her Newport. "Did you give Baby Girl her fitting-room keys and her DIVAS bag?"

"I gave her the key, but I didn't give her the bag yet."

"Well, make sure you do."

"Okay."

Realizing that I was on the floor by myself, Carmen said to Janet, "Get back on the floor mami before it gets too busy out there alright. Do not worry, you won't miss a thing. I'll let you know when everything is about to go down. I promise."

Janet left out of the backroom and Carmen yelled to her, "Close the door J!"

Just then, Jacqueline walked into the store.

"Yo, I had some night last night!" She yelled. "I got the worst fucking hangover right now though."

She looked at me. "What up Baby Girl?"

"What up Jacqueline?" I asked.

"Nothing much," she responded taking a sip of her Sprite. She looked in Janet's direction. "Yo, J, Michelle get fired yet?"

"No, Carmen is in the back. She said that Michelle don't come in until 2:00."

"Damn, I can't wait for that shit. Michelle got a temper too. I don't think that Carmen has ever dealt with anyone like her. That's why she ain't all rah-rah with her shit."

"Whatever. Carmen will whip that bitch's ass." Janet said rolling her eyes.

"Don't mind us." Jacqueline said smiling at me. "Damn, I gotta pee. Yo, J, what are they doing back there? Is it a safe zone or no?"

"Shit, I don't know." Janet yelled. "Go and see."

Jacqueline shook her head in disagreement, "Nah, I don't feel like having Carmen scream on me this early in the morning. You know how she be on that shit."

"Yeah, I know." Janet began ringing somebody up.

"She be all like, "*I know you knew that I was in here sucking my man's dick and you just wanted to see how big his shit was!*," she shook her head imitating Carmen to a T. "Yo, I get so tired of that shit."

"I'll just go and use the mall bathroom. I'll be back." Jacqueline headed out the front entrance.

Walking over towards Janet I asked, "What is wrong with the bathroom in the back?"

"Oh, you'll find out soon enough I'm sure," she smiled. "You ready to learn register?"

"Yeah, okay." I said. "Just let me run these fitting-room returns back on the floor real quick."

"No problem. I'll be at the counter when you're ready. Oh, and before I forget again, this is the bag you have to carry from now on. We all do. It's to prevent theft."

She handed me a clear shoulder bag that said DIVAS on it in rainbow letters.

"I know, what do you do when you're on your period?" she said. "Lucky for me, I don't get my period."

She smiled and tapped her upper arm, "Depo Shot".

However, for you monthly crampy campers, "We keep pads and tampons in the bathroom which I'm sure you've seen already."

"Yes I did," I responded.

"Okay, cool."

I switched everything from my purse to my new DIVAS bag and then began putting the fitting-room rejects back onto the floor.

Just as I went to hang up the last two pairs of jeans, Jacqueline came up to me and said, "It's this gay guy who comes up in here. He loves to talk shit and he loves to steal. He usually hangs out by the jeans so just watch him if he comes in."

"What's all the whispering about? I mean, can I know?" Carmen asked coming out of the backroom with her two men.

"That guy is in the mall shopping so you know that he's coming in here." Jacqueline answered.

"Oh, Baby Girl, you are gonna laugh your ass off when you see this guy. He tries stuff on in the fitting-rooms and everything. He's a fucking thief." She laughed.

"He pops so much shit to Janet because she's white. He only talks shit to the white girls in here." Chino said.

Carmen turned up the stereo. "You can argue back if you feel like it when he does say something smart to you though. He *will* say some smart shit to you every now and then."

"Oh, her song must be about to come on." Jacqueline laughed.

N.E.R.D.'s "Lapdance" came on and Carmen climbed up onto the sales counter and began dancing around and singing, *"Ooh baby you want me! Oh, ooh baby you want me! Now, you can get this lap dance here for free!"*

"Come on pa! Get up here and dance with me," she yelled to Robert as he walked away blushing.

"Fuck that, I'll dance with you ma!" Chino said as he hoisted his tiny frame up onto the counter and began doing the normal bend the girl over and hold onto her hips type dance with Carmen.

"You don't mind that Robert?" I asked as I watched Janet ring up a customer.

"Please, that shit don't faze me no more. I ain't a jealous nigga, you know. I know that I got a crazy girl. I just deal with that shit. I blow a lot of trees." He pulled two-nickel bags out of his pocket and showed them to me.

"Don't be talkin' shit papi! You ain't wanna dance!" Carmen yelled mid grind.

"Baby Girl, you ready to ring some customers up?" Janet asked me.

"I don't know. I don't think so." I said.

"Well, I have a feeling that Carmen wants you to be a key-holder so come here, and I'll walk you through it." She motioned me over.

"Can y'all get up off of the counter so I can have some room? Damn." Janet said as she began removing hangers from a young female customer's t-shirts and skirts.

"Okay, first, you take all of the hangers off of the clothes. Then you take all of the skew numbers off the price tags where the perforation is. Sometimes it will already be ripped off, but that's okay.

We don't have a high tech system yet, so we have to type in each number manually. Then you fold each item up and you can either put it in the bag as you enter each one or, if you want, you can do it after. It doesn't matter."

After Janet walked me through a couple of more customers, I got the hang of it. Before I knew it, it was 1:30 and Carmen told me that I could take my lunch. I grabbed my purse and just as I was about to leave, a tall, very slim, light-skinned black guy walked into the store.

He had on a pair of rhinestone-studded Baby Phat jeans, a tank top with his belly-button showing and a pink du-rag with a clear ponytail bo-bo on the end of it. Upon closer observation, I saw that he had the nerve to have on a ruby and emerald jeweled belly-ring with cherries hanging from it.

So... *this* was the infamous gay guy who stole. I decided to hang out for a while and watch the show. He walked past me and said to one of the three girls in his entourage, "What is *that* bitch looking at? She must be new. She had better not start any shit. That's all I know. I hope that heifer heard me too!"

He juggled his many *air-filled* shopping bags as he headed towards the jeans.

"Girl, I am gonna wear Richard's ass out right tonight! Shee-yit! The more I think on it, he should really be getting all up in my stuff tonight. After all the bullshit that he put me through! Had me crying night after night into my pillows. Forgettin' my routines for my dance solos at the club and what not!"

He held up a purple, paisley sundress to his small, frail frame.

"I was so distraught and disorientated one night that I got up on stage and started doing the "heel and toe" like it was going out of style to "Greatest Love of All!" I was trippin'!"

"Yeah, you were trippin' that night girl! I saw that show and it was terrible," one of his crew agreed while adding another pair of jeans to her already massive pile.

He shot her a nasty look, before stopping to admire himself in one of the mirrors along the sidewall. He began to apply some pink, shimmery lip-gloss.

He continued, "Oh, but he's so fine! He's my king! He's my rock! He's my—"

Before he could finish his one-man act, Jacqueline, who had not taken her eyes off of him the entire time said loudly, "Hello, welcome to DIVAS. Can I help you with anything?"

He rolled his eyes, sucked his teeth and snaked his body around to face her. "*Yes*, as a matter of fact, you can help me by taking your piña-pineapple ass *back* on across to the other side of the store!"

He laughed and looked at one of his girls and imitated Jacqueline in a terrible, heavy, high-pitched Spanish accent.

"*Can I help ju weeth anything*? She must have lost her ever-loving mind. *Did I ask for her help? Hoe!* Funky bitch!"

They all laughed and travelled a little deeper into the store until one of them spotted Carmen chillin' in the cut watching their every move.

"Oh, Jameka," one of the girls whispered to him as she put down her many pairs of jeans that she had been carrying around with her the whole time they had been in the store, "the manager is up in here today!"

He locked eyes with Carmen. "I can't stand that bitch. We might as well roll out." Jameka swiftly placed the paisley sundress back where he had found it and headed towards the door.

But not before he turned around and yelled out, "*Fish*!"

With that last outburst, Jameka and his entourage were gone.

Carmen walked over to me.

"I was getting ready to come over there if he didn't leave."

She took a sip of her water. "Baby Girl, you better go on your break. It gets real hectic around here in about an hour or so."

"Okay, I'm going." I answered.

"She's so cute," Carmen said as she smiled and pushed Robert.

I left to go on my break. I had no idea of what I wanted to eat.

I liked the job so far. All of the girls seemed so helpful and nice. I got a thirty-five percent discount off all merchandise. I was feelin' it.

I looked down at my bag and smiled. I was officially a DIVAS girl.

# chapter ten

"Bitch, you just firing me because I fucked Janet's so-called man. You need to stop frontin'!" screamed an angry, gorgeous, deep-mahogany complexioned black girl who looked like she had just stepped off a Paris Runway.

"No, Michelle we just think that it's in our best interest to let you go. You haven't been getting the work done. You just haven't been pulling your weight around here." Carmen calmly added, "I don't know shit about you fuckin' Silk."

"Oh, yeah, but you know which man I was talkin' about. That bitch done had so many niggas up in her twat that she don't even remember no more; so how can you?" Michelle walked over to me.

"Oh, you must be the girl replacing me. Shee-yit, have fun! These bitches up in here are full of shit. After everything that I put up with in this fuckin' store!"

She hurled her keys over the counter. "Lyin' and shit! Yo, on some real, fuck all y'all! I'm out!"

"Look, Michelle, I'm not finished talkin' to you. I don't appreciate you throwing your keys either," Carmen said irritated as fuck.

"I don't give a fuck; you ain't my boss no more bitch! You lucky that I don't beat your fat, funky ass!"

"Look, watch your fuckin' walk and your talk bitch. I'm the store manager, but I am a BK bitch first and I will fuck—"

Out of nowhere, Carmen jabbed Michelle in the mouth on the sneak and they began tusslin'. I could not believe it! These bitches were banging it out right in the doorframe of the backroom.

It ain't take but a second for a crowd to gather around. While we were all watching the fight, we didn't pay attention to all of our merchandise *walking* out of the door. We got robbed crazy during that minute and a half.

Carmen jabbed Michelle first, but Michelle came back and snuffed Carmen's face three times. Then, Michelle somehow managed to get Carmen underneath her and it was a wrap. Michelle started to finish her off.

When Janet saw that Carmen was losing, she ran to the phone and called security. They came in no time and broke shit up.

"Not again ladies," an old, white, male security guard said. "Now, this is the *fourth* time in two months. You young ladies need to find a more uh…lady-like way to settle your differences. You are all so pretty. Why must you continue to act like this? Every day it is something else."

He looked at Carmen, "*Please*, try for me." He escorted Michelle out of the store still ranting and raving.

"Yo, I know that this shit ain't over yet," Jacqueline whispered. Then she walked away.

I went and got a box of clothes to hang. As I dragged the heavy box full of clothes to the front of the store, I could hear, *"That's fucked up!"* and *"They some scandalous bitches!"* being murmured throughout the store.

I assembled a hanging rack, and I went to work hanging up junior and plus size shirts and dresses.

"Oh, let's see if you can beat Michelle's old record. That bitch used to be able to hang up like five boxes of clothes in two hours. Carmen gives out gift certificates and different little bonuses when you are a fast hanger."

I looked up to see Chino standing next to me.

He smiled and began talking about what had just happened between Carmen and Michelle.

"That shit was crazy right?" He held up two hands full of empty hangers. "We got hit bad during that shit. I found at least twenty-five empty hangers on the racks. Mostly jeans."

"Damn, they had a field day!" I said.

Chino looked me up and down. "Ma, you look real good."

"I've been told before." I smiled as I glanced at him. "You ain't bad yourself."

"Yeah, so I'm a good looking nigga, you a fine-ass chick, we need to get it poppin'. What's really good ma?" he said in a low, sexy voice.

"You serious? You playin' right?" I raised an eyebrow at him and leaned in close.

"You used to mess with Jacqueline right?"

"True story," he responded in a deep, smooth voice.

"So, now, I can't get with you. Even if I wanted to, I couldn't. I ain't like that Chino. And anyway, mixing business with pleasure ain't my thing homeboy."

"Okay, okay. I respect that." He began to walk away. "But, I ain't through yet. I'm a firm believer in getting what I want."

"Yeah, well I'm a firm believer in sticking by my word pa. Now, lemme get back to work before they do me like they did Michelle."

"Oh, never that, baby. Never that." He licked his lips. "But just know—that bitch brought all of that shit on herself." He looked me up and down, and rubbed his hands together.

"Lemme let you finish up, 'cause I know for *damn* sure that I don't wanna see you go anywhere! Except maybe to the telly wit' me."

He laughed and yelled out, *"I got room keys!"*

I laughed, "Later Chino," and then I went back to hanging up clothes.

Before I knew it, three hours had passed. It was almost time to leave, but I still had one fifteen-minute break left to take. I got to thinking about Quincy and how fine he looked yesterday. I wondered if he was lying about not having kids. I had forgotten to ask him if he had ever been married or had any psycho ex-girlfriends hanging on for dear life. I mean, the nigga *was* 36-years-old. Well, he was about to be anyway. Hmm, I figured if Jay-Z and Beyonce could make it work, then why couldn't we if it came down to it.

*Damn, what would I do if we went back to his crib?* I thought.

Nah, no, no—I couldn't go there just yet. He looked *so* good though.

I mean, I could handle my business on my own if it came down to it later on that night *after* the date. All it took was two *C* batteries and a little Maxwell to set the mood. I started thinking about how it would be if it did eventually get to that point where Quincy and I were going to go all the way. I mean, in my mind, I was a pro when it came to young guys, but I didn't know anything about grown men.

You see, young guys have all the stamina, but they are easy as hell to please once you know what to do and how to do it. Nine times out of ten, their favorite position is doggy style. They like when you can take that shit kinda rough, and they like when you can throw that shit back at them. It doesn't really take that much to get them open. Shit, you can be in the crib wrestling over the television remote and before you know it, *boing*—their shit is standing at attention.

Now, I didn't know how it would be with Quincy. He was a

cop so he probably had been with a whole bunch of bitches down to do freaky shit. He had probably handcuffed them and everything. The girls probably pretended like they were prostitutes and he was the John and then he flipped it on them and said, *"You're under arrest! Spread em'!"* and then they got it poppin'.

I began to think that I was thinking too much. I decided to go find Carmen to ask her if I could take my last break.

I headed towards the back of the store to her "office". I remembered what Jacqueline had said about knocking if the door was closed, but this time, the door was cracked a little bit. I pushed it open slowly, and no one was back there. Or so I thought. I took another look and I was greeted by a bunch of moaning and slapping noises coming from the bathroom. I turned around and bounced. Carmen was probably getting a quickie in with Robert.

Quietly and slowly, I closed the door back slightly, just as I had found it. When I turned to walk away, I heard the toilet flush in the bathroom. I hurried to the nearest clothing rack to pretend like I was straightening up. The back door opened up, and Carmen came walking out.

"Baby Girl, you wanna go out to the club with us tonight? It's gonna be off the hook!" she smiled.

"Nah," I said, "I made plans already. But, who's going?"

"Just a bunch of us, Robert, Chino, Jacqueline, Janet. It's gonna be *fun*! Mami, you should come!" she whined.

"Janet, come and help me get this line down!" Jacqueline yelled from the register. "Jaliyah, is Janet still on her break?" Jacqueline asked punching away at the register keypad.

"I didn't even know that she had left for her break. I'm still waiting to take my break myself," I told her.

"Fuck! I'm coming Jacqueline!" I heard Janet's voice respond.

"Then come on!" Jacqueline yelled.

Immediately, Janet stormed out of the backroom.

"If that bitch keeps fucking with me I'm gonna kick her ass one of these days real soon." Janet said underneath her breath.

"Baby, don't even worry about it." Carmen told her.

Janet opened up on the second register and yelled to Jacqueline, "Damn, I was eating! You couldn't wait?"

"Yeah, I *bet* you *were* eating," Jacqueline said with an attitude. "Just not food though right?"

"Fuck you bitch!" Janet said.

"Alright." Carmen interjected, "Enough of the bullshit. Let's just get these two lines down."

Carmen stared at Jacqueline as if she were trying to see through her. "Watch your mouth around my customers, please."

Jacqueline rolled her eyes. "Fine."

Carmen rolled her eyes. "I'm going to go and get some ice cream. Baby Girl is coming with me."

"What?" Janet asked.

"Why," Jacqueline said.

"Because she is the *only* one up in here who I don't want to knock the fuck out right now. We'll be back."

Carmen got both our bags from under the counter. "You ready?"

Surprised that she was going to get ice cream in the middle of all the chaos at the store, and even more surprised that she asked me to go with her, I obliged.

I didn't want to get into the middle of whatever was going on, but hanging clothes was driving me out of my mind. I took off my fitting-room keychain, put it in a drawer behind the register and I bounced with Carmen.

# chapter eleven

We walked out into the crowded mall, past the Baskin Robbins, and out of the front door.

"I thought that we were going to get ice cream," I asked as we walked out into the parking lot.

"Yeah, but I want ice cream from my crib," she snickered. "This is my car right here."

Her car was a black, Acura Legend coupe. It had tinted windows and the hottest rims I had ever seen a whip with in a minute. She unlocked the doors and we got in.

"Make sure that you put on your seat belt. I am very serious when it comes to that. I lost my sister in a car accident," she said.

"I'm sorry to hear that," I said as I fastened my seatbelt.

"Yeah, it was a while ago. But, I think about her every time I see that someone doesn't have on a seatbelt."

She handed me a CD case. "Put on whatever you wanna hear. Right now I'm listening to this mixed CD that my peoples hooked me up with."

"That's cool. We could listen to that. I'm real easy when it comes to music. I listen to everything," I said rolling down my window a bit. The bass from "Lean Back" by Terror Squad boomed out of the speakers.

"So, where do you live, Carmen?"

"Oh, not too far from here. About fifteen minutes away in Fishkill. Me, Robert, and Chino share this apartment there." She pulled out of the lot and we were off.

"I know that you're thinking that this is a rowdy place to work at, but it's not like that at all. I just had to get outta there, to clear my head." She lit a cigarette.

"I know that Janet and Jacqueline are probably about to kill each other in there, over some shit that Jacqueline *thinks* happened." She took a pull of her cigarette. "Shit, this store is going to make me lose it."

Being nosy, I asked her "What were they fighting over?"

"Jacqueline thinks that me and Janet are fucking each other." She smiled. "I told her that just because she goes that way doesn't mean that I would *ever* do any shit like that. I am strictly dickly. That's the only way that I roll!"

Now, I didn't know what to think. I knew what I heard in that backroom bathroom. I had a strong feeling that she was lying. Her and Janet were doing *something* in there. But, I would have lied too. Shit, if I had just met someone and I didn't know if I could trust them or not, I wouldn't tell them all my secrets.

We cruised down Route 9 for about ten minutes, and when we got off, we pulled into the parking lot for a place called River's Edge. It was a rental-community made up of a whole bunch of apartments and townhouses. Carmen parked and we hopped out.

"Baby Girl," she asked, "I know you don't smoke bogeys, but do you at least smoke weed?"

"No, I don't," I replied.

"Damn, I wanted you to smoke a blunt with me before we went back to the store." She got her keys out, and we walked to the third townhouse on the left. "It's a little messy in here. I'm usually real clean, but with having Chino here, it's hard to keep shit together."

Knowing how I kept my room, I was not in a place to judge anybody.

"Shit, girl, don't even worry about it." I held her bag while she fidgeted with the lock. "I know how that can be."

Carmen opened the door and she was right, her apartment was fucked up. It was a beautiful place, but she just had shit everywhere. There were little sneakers and boxers all over the floor. I guess that was all of Chino's shit. There were video game instruction booklets and Hustler magazines all over the couch. I didn't even wanna sit down. I looked around through the filth to see if I could imagine how the place looked when it was clean.

Her walls were a pale peach color with eggshell trimming on the moldings. She had a cream-color leather sofa that was pulled out into a bed and she had a matching side chair, loveseat and ottoman. She had hardwood floors throughout the apartment. I was definitely feeling the layout.

"Yo, Carmen!" I yelled. "How much is your rent? This place is flyy ma."

"I pay $875.00 a month. All utilities included!" she yelled back from the kitchen. "You looking for a place?"

I wasn't looking for a place to live. However, seeing how nice the whole area was made me think about it.

"I don't know. Probably soon." I sat down at the dining room table.

"Whatever you do, *do not* rush to move out of your parents' house. Save, save, save!" She walked out of the kitchen.

"Come upstairs. I'm just gonna roll my blunt really quick."

I followed her up the short flight of steps. There were pictures of Carmen everywhere. She really admired herself. Surprisingly, it was clean upstairs. I guess she knew that's what I was thinking because she said, "Robert keeps this part of the house clean. He can't stand garbage."

Carmen took a backwood and a nickel bag of weed out of one of her night tables. She broke the cigarillo open at the seam and emptied the tobacco from inside. She licked it, took one of her many Cosmo magazines and broke the weed up into the dutch on top of it. She rolled it up, lit it and took a long pull. She exhaled very slowly.

"Damn, I have been so stressed lately."

She massaged her neck and pushed her long, curls away from her face. "Does the smoke bother you Baby Girl?" she asked fanning at the rings of smoke beginning to cloud the air.

"No, I'm okay," I answered.

"Janet and Jah-dee probably think that I'm somewhere eating the hell outta your pussy!" Carmen said laughing hysterically. "Shit, if I *was* a fucking lesbian, your shit would probably be the safest to eat outta any bitch's in that store."

She took another long, hard pull from her blunt. "Yo Jaliyah, let me tell you about them in that store."

"They are some scandalous hoes. Jah-dee is cool peoples and shit, but don't let that hoe near your man. She will fuck him quick. Shee-yit, she fucked Robert at Denny's after a store meeting one time."

"Word?" I asked her not knowing if she was bullshitting or not.

"Yeah, that bitch fucked my man. I beat her ass for it too. I stomped that bitch out right in my living room. Then, I let Chino and a few of his peoples run a train on her." She took another long pull of her blunt.

"Oh my God?! They ran a train on her?" I asked dumb-founded.

"Oh yeah! About four or five of them fucked her. I made them all use condoms though. I'm not that grimy."

"She just let that shit happen?" I asked Carmen.

"Yeah, at first she was like, '*No*' and shit, but then she said, 'Well, at least all of y'all look good.'" Carmen rolled her eyes. "She's such a fuckin' disgrace to the entire Puerto Rican race.

"How long have you and Robert been together?" I asked.

She smiled and tapped her blunt out in the ashtray. "Rob? Me and him have been together for like three and a half years. I love him so much. We got engaged a couple of months ago."

I glanced down at her hand to get a closer look at the ring that I had seen yesterday during the interview. It wasn't there.

"Oh, I don't wear it on my finger all of the time. Today I put it on my chain." She reached into her shirt, and showed me. "See."

"It must be nice to be in love and engaged and shit." I said. "When are y'all gonna say 'I do'?"

"Damn, this weed got me feeling nice as hell," she said.

"We haven't set a date yet. After that whole shit with Jacqueline, we just put shit off for a little while. Eventually though, we will."

I looked over at the cable box for the time. It was 5:30.

"I know. Yo, we better get back to the store before Janet pulls some slick shit and calls my District Manager to let her know that I ain't there."

Confused I asked, "She would do that?"

"Yo, that bitch will do anything for the right price. Whether it is weed, E pills, coke, some dick, some money…she does it all."

"Yo, Baby Girl, you sure that you can't come out with us tonight?" She put some gel on her hair and sprayed on some perfume. "I really think that you would have fun." She snapped her fingers and did a little dance.

"Nah, I got a date tonight at um—" I thought about it and pulled out my cell phone that was on silent. Oh my gah! Damn, I had three missed calls!

"Carmen, I don't even know. I gotta call him back!"

She laughed. "Bitch you better call that man back! Go ahead before we leave!"

I selected Quincy's number from my missed calls and hit dial.

I was greeted with an "*Oh*, I was starting to think that you had forgotten about me girl. Where you been?" he asked cheerfully.

"Man, this day has been hectic, and then I had my phone on silent. Just trying to learn the ropes. How are you though?" I asked him.

"Oh, well I'm great now that you've returned my call," he said sweetly. "What time do you want me to pick you up?"

I thought about it. Not too early, but not too late. "I was thinking maybe eight o'clock."

"Eight o'clock is great. You can just text me your address when we get off the phone and I'll search it in my computer and I'll see you at eight, okay," he said.

"Cool. I'll do that and I'll see you at eight."

"Cool," he said. "I'll see you later."

"Bye," I said.

We hung up. I texted my address to him as soon as I got off the phone and waited for his response.

"I hope that you have a good time," Carmen said, her bright, green contacts beaming. "By the time that we get back to the store it'll be time for you to clock out."

"I know!" I responded excited about eight o'clock coming on faster and faster.

"You should bring him by the club. We are heading over to Jordans at about 11:00. 50 Cent is supposed to be performing there tonight."

Now you know that I was game. Back then I was so in love with Curtis "50 Cent" Jackson that I ain't know what to do with myself! "50 is gonna be up here! In that case, I'll see. Maybe we *will* meet y'all there."

"I'ma see if he'll let me fuck him!" Carmen said as she

laughed. "It's just something about him that makes me so fucking horny."

She glanced over at me. "I at least wanna blow him."

"Well," I said shocked and a bit disgusted, "knock yourself out!"

I was noticing that Carmen was definitely a freak for real. All she ever talked about was sex. Damn, at least she was honest with her shit. I didn't feel like I knew her, I just felt like I knew a little more about her than I did yesterday.

I got my text response from Quincy saying that he'd see me at eight, and Carmen and I got our bags and we left. Before I knew it, we were back at the mall and it was time for me to leave. I still had to go inside because I had to buy an anklet and I had to clock out. I had decided that I was going to wear a dress, but it was going to be a simple one. I hated wearing dresses without an anklet or a toe ring. It just felt too plain. We were selling all jewelry for half-price at my job, so I got it from there.

As we entered the store, Carmen said, "If those bitches act funny or say some slick shit to you, curse them the fuck out. Smack them if you want. They ain't shit."

We walked inside and a girl with a pair of fitting-room keys ran up to Carmen.

"Janet left about a ten minutes ago. She said that she was going to your apartment to find you because she knows that you were going to mess with some bitch named Jaliyah. She said that she was gonna fuck you up."

"Okay, first off, Nadia, you're real rude." Carmen picked up a dress off the floor. "This is Jaliyah right here."

"Oh. Hi, I'm Nadia," the girl said avoiding eye contact.

"Hi, I'm Jaliyah." I took a deep breath.

"See Baby Girl, I told you that Janet thinks that I am fucking you." Carmen shook her head in disgust and rolled her eyes.

"Look, Jaliyah, I hope to see you and your friend at the club tonight. Don't worry about Janet. I'll handle everything."

Carmen looked at Nadia and in a nasty tone, she told her, "Go do something."

"Nice meeting you." I said to Nadia.

"Yeah, you too." Then she went back to the fitting-rooms.

"Is everything gonna be cool Carmen?" I asked her walking over to the jewelry section.

"Shit, I ain't stressing Janet. She stays on that bullshit. You would think that me and her were messing around." She picked up a sterling silver, jeweled anklet. "Get this one."

Handing me the anklet she said, "As a matter of fact, I'll put it on my tab."

"Nah, that's okay Carmen. I got it." I told her.

"No, it's a gift. A friendship gift." She flashed a wide smile. "I'll clock you out."

"Okay, thanks so much. That is so sweet!" I looked at the time on my cell. "Ooh, I gotta go. I have stuff to do at the crib before my date!" I put the anklet in my bag and I ran to use the bathroom before I left.

When I came out, I saw that the emergency exit door had a shoebox in the doorway holding it open. I didn't have time to wonder about what was going on.

I really didn't care. If someone came in through the back and robbed them blind, it would not be my problem. By that time, I would have bounced off to wherever. In this case, wherever was on my date with Quincy.

# chapter twelve

"You gon be late Jah-dee! You have been home since six o'clock! How are you rushing right now?" My sister Angela said as she struggled to find the mate to my other shoe.

"You should've had this shit done by now!" she huffed as she rummaged through my closet.

"Just find it!" I yelled back as I fixed my makeup in the bathroom mirror.

"Well, I want both of you to shut up! Y'all are getting on my nerves already. I always thought that the fighting would end once y'all got older. It has only gotten worse. You all drive me crazy in this damn house!"

My father had his little outbursts every now and then about the noise level in my house. Yeah, we are older now, but we are sisters first and sometimes it be's that way.

It was getting closer and closer to eight o'clock and Quincy would be there shortly. Finally, Angie found my shoe and I finished my makeup. Not too much, just enough to bring out my dress. I decided to wear a cream-colored, floral sundress with pink flowers and some pink espadrilles. Between you and me, I hate wearing makeup. I always forget that it's there and I end up smearing it all over my face like a lame. There have been many a time that I've been dancing in a club or just chillin' anywhere, and I just straight up forget that I have on eyeliner or mascara and just smear it down my face. I had to be sure not to smear it tonight. That would be embarrassing.

I checked the clock and it read 7:50. *Cool*, I thought to myself. He should be here in a little while. Just then, the doorbell rang.

"He's here!" I said to Angie excitedly. Nicole came out of her room, then both her and Angie ran downstairs to meet Quincy. My parents were already downstairs drinking wine and listening to old records.

I grabbed my purse and went to open the door. I looked through the panels on the side of my front door.

"I see you peeking through! Is the policeman here yet! Open up the door, we hungry! What y'all got to eat!"

I opened the door to find my Aunt Tiffany and her two sons, Michael and Gary standing on the front porch.

"Hi Sweetie!" she smiled and gave me a hug and kiss. "Your mother told me that you were going out with a policeman tonight who is 35-years-old!"

"Dang Mommy!" I yelled into the kitchen to her.

My cousins, Michael and Gary, took off their coats and went into the kitchen. Tiffany continued, "I gotta see him. Thirty-five *is* a little old. You ain't but twenty-one. You just turned it at that! Let me find out you tryna be grown!"

"Yeah, you're buggin' Jah-dee," my cousin Gary said.

My aunt smacked him in his arm. "I know your black behind ain't talking. She can do what she want! She's grown. Don't nobody say nothing to your black ass about being color struck!"

Now, my aunt always told my little cousin Gary, who was 17-

years-old that he was color struck because he usually only dated mixed-looking, Spanish and Black girls with light eyes.

"Ma, I'm not color struck. I just like girls with a certain look." He said as he went and hugged my mother, my sisters and my father.

"Yeah, certain look my ass!" Tiffany said snidely.

My other cousin Michael had already greeted everyone and was sitting down drinking some Kool-Aid and eating the black-eyed peas and cornbread that my mother had cooked up.

Just then, my father put on, "Soul Makossa" by Manu Dibango.

"Hey! Owww!" she screamed. "Ooohh! Ooohh!" she yelled in a high-pitched voice. "Come on Deena, let's do the bump!"

My mom ran over to her and they started doing the bump.

"Remember when we used to dance at Reesee's parties when she lived over on 169th!" She dropped down to the floor and came back up. "Those were the parties, boy!"

"*Heyyy!*" she screamed again. She danced until she looked across the room into the kitchen and saw Gary and Michael eating black-eyed peas.

"*OOOOHHHHH BLACK-EYED PEAS!*" she screamed as she dashed into the kitchen to get a bowl and began serving herself. "Oh, y'all got the Kool-Aid and the cornbread going on and everything! Heeeeyyyyy! A sista is bout to get her grub on!"

The doorbell rang again. I looked through the panes on the side of the door once again praying that it wasn't another relative. *Jackpot!* It was Quincy. I opened the door, and there he stood with the nicest bouquet of Calla lilies in hand.

"These are for you," he said.

I took the flowers and gave him a hug. "Thank you so much."

I took him by the hand and brought him into the family room/kitchen area where everyone was now partying hard to James Brown's "Hot Pants."

He smiled. "Oh, I see y'all are having a good time up in here tonight." He looked at me and said jokingly, "We should stay here and party!" He did a little two-step.

My father came over and shook his hand. "Hey man, how you doing. I'm Lonnie and this is my wife Deena." My mother came over and shook his hand. My father continued, "The greedy one over there chowing down on those black-eyed peas is my sister-in-law Tiffany, those two are my other daughters Angie and Nicky; and those two over there are my nephews Michael and Gary.

"Oh, well y'all got a full house tonight!" he smiled. "Nice to meet you all."

He waved to everyone. I'm Quincy Chase. You have a beautiful home here Mr. and Mrs. Whitfield.

*Oh snap*, I thought to myself, *he remembered my last name!*

"So you're on the job, huh?" my father asked.

"Yes Sir," he answered, "I'm in the 2-8 Precinct."

"Whooo!" my father said. "I know it gets hectic over there! My brother-in-law used to work over there, but he became a sergeant and they transferred him over to the 2-6."

"Yeah, I know a few people in the 2-6. What's his name?" he asked my father.

"Campbell, Anthony Campbell," my father answered.

"Ohhhhh, yeah! Ant!" he yelled. "That's my boy!" he exclaimed. "Me and him used to hang out all the time! He just had a baby girl! Yeah, I was in his wedding when he got married and everything!"

"Get outta here!" my father said. "Oh, man! What a small world!"

"Deena, call Anthony up," my father called to my mother who was now in the kitchen with my Aunt Tiffany.

"Okay, baby," my mother yelled back.

A half a minute later, my mother brought the phone over and gave it to Quincy.

"Yeah, man. I'm here about to take your niece Jaliyah out on a date." He laughed. "I met her at the mall man. I'm here with your brother-in-law, your sisters and your nieces and nephews man!"

Quincy laughed, "I know, it's crazy!" He smiled, "Yeah, I know, I know. I'ma play the highest note with her. Oh, you ain't gotta worry about that, now!"

I mouthed to him, "We gotta go soon Q!"

He winked at me. "Okay, Ant. Alright, I'm gon put Mr. Whitfield on. Okay. Talk to you later. Okay hold on," then he gave the phone to my father.

I looked at my sisters and rolled my eyes. "Can y'all believe this shit here?"

"So what if he's friends with Uncle Ant. He's fine!" they said whispering and giggling.

"You betta tap that J!" Angie laughed.

"Okay, man. I'll call you tomorrow. Alright. Lata."

My father finished his phone call with my Uncle and shook Quincy's hand. "Y'all better leave man. I can already see my daughter making faces over there and talking to her sisters."

"Quincy smiled, "Okay." He looked over at me, "You ready?"

I smiled. "Yeah, I'm ready. Let's go!"

I kissed everyone in the house, told my mother where I had left the info on Quincy, although she now had a direct line to him through my Uncle Anthony, and I asked her to put my flowers in some water. I grabbed my purse and my cell phone.

"Bye everybody!" Quincy and I said.

"Bye y'all!" they yelled. "Have fun!"

My mother put on, Frankie Beverly and Maze's "Before I Let Go" and Quincy and I headed out the door to go on our much-anticipated date.

# chapter thirteen

I never went out on *any* date without money. My mother taught me that from when I was young.

"Never rely on no man!" she said when I went out on my first date ever. "What are you gonna do if he decides to just leave you, or he tells you that you can't get no cheese on your hamburger because he can't afford it! Hell, that's when you go into your purse and say, I *don't know what you gon' do, but I'm gon' have me some cheese on mines tonight brother!'"*

My mom is always creating these hysterical hypothetical situations. But, it's true, you really cannot rely on any man to do things for you that you should be doing for yourself. I'm teaching my little sister that. She don't hear me though. Angie taught me. She lived, she learned, and she took notes.

We bounced outta my crib at 8:25, and we hit the highway. Quincy drove a silver Infiniti FX35 SUV.

"This is nice Quincy," I told him.

"Thank you," he said. "I bought it last year. I don't drive it everyday though. I drive my Honda Accord to work. That's my beater. Those things run forever."

"Oh, okay. Yeah, I have a Honda too." I told him.

"Yeah, I saw it in the driveway when I pulled up. You got some nice rims on your whip," he told me. "You want me to put on some music?" he asked.

"It doesn't matter," I smiled. "Whatever you wanna do."

"Is Earth, Wind and Fire okay?" he asked me, glancing at me briefly before turning his eyes back to the road.

"Of course. They are more than okay! Put it on!" I told him.

He bumped "Love's Holiday" and we rode out to that until we reached Red Lobster. We got there at a quarter to nine. We were seated immediately although they had a good crowd of people there that night.

"A booth if you have it please," I heard him tell the hostess.

"Right this way," she said, leading us to a section of the restaurant that had a million young couples in it. We sat down.

Quincy wore a pair of dark-blue jeans, with a fitted brown t-shirt, a brown belt, a brown Yankee fitted tilted a little to the side and an iced out pinky ring. On his feet, a pair of fresh, low-top, white Nike Uptowns.

Even though I had been telling everyone about him since the first time we met, I had forgotten *just* how good this nigga really looked. You just don't know. He looked like he had just stepped out of a magazine. His Nextel was clipped to his belt, his Baume & Mercier watch gleamed from under his sleeve and he smelled incredible.

"You're killin' it tonight J!" he told me in a soft whisper. "You almost look as good as me!"

"Aww, see now why you gotta go startin' mess." I laughed. "I'm tryna have a nice evening. I don't wanna end up bustin' your ass on our first date and what not."

"Oh, you gon beat me up?" he laughed. "See, why does it always have to come to violence with y'all ladies. Why can't y'all just smile and laugh and not hit?"

"Nah, I don't be hittin' guys and all that craziness." I lied knowin' that a few of my exes had caught a couple of quick right jabs to the eye every so often. But, I wasn't on that no more. My father always told my sisters and me, "You never see me hit your mother, and you never see your mother hitting on me. If you have a relationship like that, you're a fool."

"Well, that's good. I tell any woman, if you hit me, I'm leavin'. You just won't hear from me no more. I don't even do that shaking bullshit."

He opened up his menu. I did the same.

"I don't even know why I'm looking at the menu when I come here all the time and know the menu by heart."

He laughed. "Okay then, well what do you want?"

I closed my menu and said, "I want the sailor's platter dinner."

He checked it out on the menu. "I think that I'm going to have the same thing."

The server came over and we placed our drink and food orders at the same time.

"I'll have a diet Sprite with lemon," Quincy said.

"I'll have a Shirley Temple please," I said.

He laughed to himself. "You little baby. I used to drink Shirley Temples when I was in little league baseball and we would go out for our end of the season dinners."

I stuck my tongue out at him.

"Ill, so!" I smiled. "I don't drink like that. Only when I'm at home or something and I know that I'm not going out anywhere."

"I drink, but very rarely," he licked his lips. "I gotta keep my body straight and alcohol will pack pounds on you quick."

I loved Q's whole style. His swagger was bananas!

The server brought us our drinks, our cheesy garlic biscuits and our salads. I grabbed a biscuit right away.

"So, do you go to school or did you graduate already?" he asked me taking a sip of his soda.

"Yeah, I finished, but it's only a two-year degree. I just finished my last class a few weeks ago. They told me that I can pick up my degree sometime next week. I majored in Communications. I can't believe that I'm done. I almost gave up so many times."

"A two-year degree is a lot more than many other people can say they have, you know. Have you had any experience in that field?"

"I had an internship straight out of high school at a record company."

"Oh, okay. Internships are good. They will get you far as long as you stay connected to the right people," he said. "I took an internship my freshman year of college and it was hell at times. Yo, I had to do so much fuckin' grunt work. Just bullshit. I wanted to be in the music business at one point."

"Changed your mind," I smiled.

"Yeah, the badge was calling me."

"That's what's up." I said. "So, you like what you do now?"

He took a few bites of his salad. "I *love* what I do now. I work with the little shorties in the schools. I'm a youth officer. Those kids are so cute. It's nice to know that although I won't reach all of them, I will reach a few. You know?"

I smiled at him. "Yeah, I know"

"You know that we're gonna have dessert and all of that tonight right?" Quincy dug into his salad again. "You ain't gonna try and play the shy role tonight."

"And what shy role is that?" I asked.

"You know how some girls say that they're too shy to eat around dudes on dates and just anywhere," he responded.

"Nah, I ain't shy like that. I will kill a plate of food! You'll be like, *Damn, ma, push back the plate!*, I laughed.

"I'll be sayin' that?" he laughed.

"Yes, you will." I answered. "You'll be all embarrassed."

"You lying!" he smiled. "You serious?"

"Yeah, I love to eat pa! It's like my favorite past time." I finished my salad.

"Well, that's good to know. Because we're gonna be hittin' up every restaurant in New York mama!" he wiped his mouth with a cloth napkin.

"You so sure of that?" I asked.

"Do you bring your own cash with you on dates?" he asked.

"Of course. I *never* leave home without money," I responded surprised that he would even ask me that.

"Then, yeah, I'm sure of that."

"Oh, so I'm picking up the check tonight?" I smiled.

"Nah, but what matters is that you could if you had to," he answered back.

"Let's toast," I said. "To….to…um, my Uncle Ant."

He laughed. "Yeah, my man Ant!"

We raised our glasses.

I continued, "And to the fact that he will beat you down if you mess with me!"

"Okay, you got that one off," he said. "He wiped his mouth. I can't believe that you are Anthony Campbell's niece."

"I know right," I smiled.

"I ain't gon' lie J. That has been on my mind all night. I'm still feeling you though."

I laughed. "Well, we'll see how it goes. Y'all cops got unlimited sick leave so if my uncle beats ya ass, at least you'll get paid for it!"

He laughed and imitated Martin Lawrence. "You so crazy! You so muthafuckin crazy!"

I cracked up even more at that. I laughed so hard that I snorted.

"Oh my gosh!" I laughed, "I cannot believe that I just did that!"

"It's okay. Be yourself. If snorting like a piglet is you, then that's cool."

He took a biscuit and dipped it in some of the French dressing that he had left in his salad bowl.

*I do that too*, I thought to myself.

I knew that he was a cool dude. I knew that I liked him. I knew that the night wasn't over yet. Maybe we would hit up Jordans and meet up with Carmen and the rest of the crew. On the other hand, maybe we would just end the night after the Red Lobster and head home. Well, he would go to *his* home and I would go to mine.

So many thoughts swirled in my head. Catching my wandering glare Quincy spoke.

"What's on your mind J?" he asked me.

"Oh, nothing. Nothing at all." I answered. "I'm just having a nice time with you tonight."

The server brought our food.

He looked at my plate. "You better eat all that stuff too girl. I wanna see how much you really *can* eat before you pop out of your cute lil' dress."

"Don't worry about it. I'm good over here. You just focus on what's going on over there with you and yours." I told him as I piled some mashed potatoes onto my fork.

"I-ight," he said.

"I know," I commented.

He smiled at me, I smiled at him and we finished our dinner under the low lights of the Red Lobster.

# chapter fourteen

**Meanwhile at Jordans Night Club…**

"I really and truly don't give a fuck about how you feel about this situation! You can suck my asshole muthafucka!" is what everyone watched Carmen yell in Chino's face outside of the club.

"Yo, you better calm the fuck down! I'm already pissed that we had to leave the crib so fucking early because you ain't want to be turned away at the door! It ain't even ten o'clock yet and we out here waiting looking stupid! I don't give a fuck about that faggot nigga 50 anyway B!" Chino yelled back at her taking a puff of his blunt.

"And Janet, I don't wanna hear *shit else* about me and Jaliyah leaving the store earlier! You say something else I'm gonna slap you right in your fucking throat!" yelled Carmen.

She took a moment to glance at Robert.

"What the fuck are you looking at? I don't need *your* shit too! I told you, we just went to get some ice cream and then we fuckin' walked around the fuckin' mall."

Carmen lit a cigarette. "It's a wonder y'all two ain't see us as much as y'all walk ya fuckin' asses around the fuckin' mall not doin' shit."

She took a long pull from her cigarette. "Why the fuck is it taking so long to get inside of this fuckin' shit!"

Robert adjusted his Yankee fitted. "Look, I'm sick of this shit! All I know is that when I walked up in the crib, it smelled like weed and there was fuckin' seeds and stems in the ashtray! What the fuck was that about?"

"First off, who the fuck are you yelling at like that?" Carmen screamed rolling her eyes. "Huh! Who the fuck are you yelling at you cocksucking, broke-ass, bitch-ass, pussy-ass nigga! I told you," the line moved up, "I was not at the fucking crib! I was in the mall all day. All mutha fuckin' day!"

Robert shoved his hands into the pockets of his baggy jeans. "Yeah, okay Carmen."

"Yeah, okay Carmen." Janet said snidely in her direction.

Carmen sucked her teeth. "Bitch, you can lick my clit on a bloody day!"

A bunch of *"ills"* and *"you ain't have to go theres"* could be heard throughout the crowd waiting in line. They finally reached the entrance.

"Oh, I *thought* that was y'all making all that damn noise but I couldn't tell," a big, tall, muscular bouncer said at the door in a deep-ass voice.

"Look here, I don't want any shit up in here tonight. I swear. I'll kick all of y'all asses out tonight! We got enough drama just havin' 50 here tonight. We got police here and extra security."

"A-ight Tony," Jacqueline said as she walked in without reaching into her purse once. "I got you later papi."

Tony smiled. "Yeah, I'll see you inside girl!"

With that, he stopped Carmen, Janet, Chino and Robert dead in their tracks. "Fifteen cash a piece!"

"Look Tony, how about—"

Before Carmen could even finish her sentence, Tony cut her off, "I said NO SHIT! You wanna get the fuck out before you get in?"

Carmen fixed her lips to answer. "No, cause it's just—"

*Huh, what you say?"* Tony cut her off again, comically putting his hand by his ear for emphasis.

"Damn!" said Chino as he began walking inside, "Janet, you got this right?"

"Yeah J, you got this right," Carmen said as Robert took her hand and they strolled inside together.

"Yeah, I got it," Janet answered hesitantly.

Tony grinned. "That'll be $60.00 cash money even."

"I only have a fifty dollar bill," Janet said sounding sorry as hell.

"Damn, then I guess you can't get in." Tony handed her back a five-dollar bill. "Here's your change."

"Come on T," she whined, "how you gone play me?"

He laughed. "Janet, you still owe me money from last week! You lucky I gave you change back!"

"I had it to give to you until just now! What am I supposed to do?" Janet asked.

"Head to the border!" He pointed to the sidewalk. "People *with money* are trying to get in here. You need to get yourself a backbone girl. That's what."

Janet moved out of the way. "I don't even have my ATM card on me or nothing neither. Shit!"

Janet stormed off to her car. She had driven everyone there and now she was thinking about whether she should leave them there or not. Even thinking about something like that was contemplating suicide. She knew that if she left Carmen and them, she would have a serious ass whoopin' coming her way.

Instead, she just got into her car, lit a cigarette and turned on the radio. Yeah, they would be in there for a good three or four—maybe even *five* hours, but she knew that if they felt like leaving earlier than that and she wasn't there, she would get fucked up.

"I can't wait until I'm the fuckin' manager!" Janet said as she took a long hard pull from her cigarette. "This is bullshit!"

# chapter fifteen

Now, I had always heard that the Velvet Lounge was all that, but I had never been there. The word around town was that they had the best cakes and crème brûlée in the Hudson Valley. When Quincy and I entered the place, the brick walls were lined with picture frames holding photos of musical greats such as John Coltrane, Ahmad Jamal, Nancy Wilson, Billie Holiday and so on.

The vibe was extremely laid back and low-key. There were a few tables, but many of the people there occupied the velvet loveseats and ottomans that the place was named for.

"Jaliyah, are you sure that don't want to hit up Jordans?" Quincy asked softly.

"Yeah, I'm sure. Why, you wanna leave?" I asked concerned that maybe we should have just gone to party it up with G-Unit.

"Nah, but I remember you telling me how much you love 50 Cent."

"I'm fine Q. Trust me." I said smiling at him.

"Oh, okay." We found an empty table and took a seat.

"Yo, what is this guy talking about?" he asked me with a look of confusion on his face.

I hadn't even noticed that anyone was up on the stage because I was so blinded by Quincy's good looks.

"Yo, I don't even know." I answered giving him the same confused look that he had just given me.

"Yo, you flow?" he asked me.

"A lil' shumtim', shumtin'," I said jokingly.

"So, you gonna spit tonight or what?" he asked me.

"I don't know. I don't even know what type of poem or rhyme or anything."

"Say what's in your heart. Speak on what's going on in those thoughts of yours that you are always getting lost in," he smiled at me.

"I'm scared though. I have never spoken in front of this many people." I ushered the server over.

"I'm gonna have the crème brûlée with an espresso," I told him.

Quincy looked at the small menu. "I'm gonna have the vanilla bean cheesecake topped with Oreos and an ice water."

"Okay," said our server, "I'll be right out with your order."

Q looked at me and cheesed. "Back to you though, look here, my girl can't be scared. I ain't never scared, so you can't be either."

I stuttered to place an emphasis on what he had just said. "Your *girl*?" I looked around the lounge playfully and asked again. "Your—your girl? Oh, where she at? I thought that you were single GQ. *Where she at!?*"

He laughed. "Oh, see! A brother tries to make the first move and claim you and what not and you just shut my shit down. Straight knocked my hustle! Okay, I see how you do. That's okay! It's not a problem."

"You damn right," I laughed, "we ain't even a good four hours in! You betta slow down homeboy!" The server brought out our order and set my crème brûlée ablaze.

Quincy continued on. "Yeah, yeah, yeah. I know. So J, you gonna get up there or what? I wanna hear something," he said.

I rolled my eyes and sucked my teeth. "Yes—no. I guess so."

"A-ight then. Let's get it poppin'. Let's go!"

I got up to add my name to the list of performers. Halfway there, I heard him yell, *"And don't be flirtin' with the MC dude either! I can see old boy lookin' at you from all the way back here!"*

I laughed to myself. I ain't even know who he was talkin' about. That was until I got up there. Dude was sooo fine, I forgot why I had went up there.

"Hi, um, I wanna spit something right quick. My name is Jaliyah. Where do I sign up?"

"A-ight. My name is Elliot, and you sign up right here."

Now, Elliot was *gorgeous*. He was about five-feet-ten, with silky-smooth, vanilla-custard colored skin. His braids reached mid-way his back, and his full, pink lips looked so sexy. He had bright, doe slanted-eyes and a thin mustache and a goatee. His smile was adorable. He stopped me dead in my tracks. He wore a simple white tee with a pair of blue jeans and some white Jordans.

"You ready right now?" he asked me as the person on stage wrapped up his poem.

I smiled nervously. "I—I don't know. I've never been here before."

"Well, do you always get nervous about going places that you ain't never been?" he asked, his voice low and raspy, as he licked his lips and winked at me.

"No I—" I couldn't even finish my answer.

"Well, you're next, so get ready. Let's get it poppin'!"

He took the stage and introduced me. "Our next performer is a rookie to the stage. Show some love y'all, for Jaliyah."

Everyone clapped. I did not have a clue about what I was

going to recite. I had written so many poems that I could not choose.

I wanted to recite something that would move the crowd; something deep and inspirational. Something that would evoke the same kind of hope and change back then, that President Barack Obama is always talking about. I closed my eyes, took a deep breath, and I do not know how in the world *this* managed to come out, but it did.

**It's On You**
*What up pa, how you do?*
*Yeah you know who this is*
*It's the chick who works ya dick*
*And will give you the biz*
*I like flyy shit,*
*But ain't no need to be flashy*
*You got doe?*
*Ya' own crib?*
*A sexy nigga?*
*Holla at me*
*I'm bout five-six, a lil' thick in the thighs,*
*Small waist, pretty face*
*Wit' the honey-brown eyes*
*Come and holla at a chick,*
*Call me up or come thru*
*Won't suck, but down to fuck*
*Let me know,*
*It's on you...*

Now, I don't know what in the world possessed me to get up on that stage and recite some trashy mess like that! Y'all, I was so 'shamed! I had not recited that stupid rhyme since I was 15-years-old. I have no idea of how I even remembered it!

Evoke hope and change my ass! I bet Michelle Obama would've slapped my face if she knew that I *ever* put that trashy-ass rhyme in the same *thought* with her husband.

The crowd just kind of sat there, not quite sure of what to do. I spoke back into the mic, "Uh—I'm done."

Then I smiled and nervously turned to walk off of the stage.

You could literally hear crickets.

Elliot came over and took the mic from me. "Let's hear it for Jaliyah y'all. Show her some love!"

All of a sudden, the crowd erupted with cheers.

*"That shit was fire right there!" "Yo, can I holla?!"* I looked through the crowd to see if I saw Quincy. He was nowhere in sight.

*This nigga done left my hot-ass right here!* I thought to myself. *I had embarrassed him.*

Elliot gave me a hug.

"See, that wasn't so bad ma," he whispered in my ear.

"Kind of freaky for what we do here on the nights that I host, but your skills are tight!"

"Thanks Elliot. I appreciate it."

"Yo, take my number. I'm trying to get this poetry shit up off the ground and maybe you would like to be down with it." He handed me a card with his name and number. "Please, feel free to use it ma."

"Okay," I smiled, "will do."

I walked off stage and back to my seat. Quincy was *still* nowhere to be found.

"Okay, I'ma take a quick break and I'll be right back. Holla!" Elliot said into the mic, before he walked off of the stage and over to me.

He sat down. "What's really good ma-ma?"

Damn, now *this* dude looked *so* good. "Nothing, just chillin'. Waitin' for my date."

"Oh, I'm sorry. I don't wanna start shit or nothing like that. You know." He smiled at me. "Y'all first date?"

"Yeah."

"Oh, well, see, I definitely don't wanna fuck this shit up for you. I mean, this could be the night that y'all fall in love and live happily ever after and all that good shit." He laughed, took my right hand and kissed it.

"I'm about to get back up there, but I hope to be talking to you real soon ma. Real soon." And with that, he walked back on stage to host some more.

I was about to call Quincy's ass up on his cell to find out where the hell he had dipped off to when he emerged from the crowd looking a little out of it.

"That food is fucking my stomach up—bad. Yo, I was in the bathroom taking a shit, I actually had my cheeks on the seat and everything—that's how bad it was! Now, I'm gon' probably get hemorrhoids and shit." He laughed a little.

"Oh no! Well, what do you wanna do? You wanna go home?" I asked him with concern.

"Yeah, I think that I'ma skate off. I don't wanna leave though. I'm having such a good time with you."

*He didn't hear my rhyme*, I said to myself. *He was in the bathroom*. Crisis averted.

Jokingly I said, "Well, like Robin Harris use to say, '*You gotta go, you gotta go.*'" Then we both smiled and said at the same time, "*But after you finish your homework!*" throwing in a quick reference to *House Party*.

"You like *House Party* boy! Let me find out!" I said rubbing the top of his hand and gently squeezing it to reassure him that I was fine with us leaving.

We got up and walked out of the lounge into the warm, night air. We got into his car, and drove back to my house to the sounds of the Isley Brothers.

We pulled up to my house and he walked me to the front door.

"Look Jaliyah, I'm sorry that this has to end like this," he said to me looking totally out of it.

"What's ending? It's cool. Just make sure that you call me between tonight and tomorrow night, okay." I hugged him.

"Okay," he said in my ear as he kissed me softly on my cheek.

I waited for him to get into his car before I went inside, and he waited for my mother to open the door for me before he drove off. He rolled down his windows and yelled out, "Goodnight Jaliyah. I'll call you when I get home. *Oh,* and your rhyme was off the meter!"

"Oh my gosh! You heard that!" I screamed as I laughed and playfully hid my face behind my hands.

"Yup!" He backed out of the driveway slowly, honked his horn and drove off.

My mother greeted me at the door. "That brother *is* fine Jaliyah. You ain't lie about that. You know your uncle ain't having it though, *right*?"

I smiled, "Yeah I know."

She closed the door. "You're back kinda early."

I went into the kitchen and grabbed my car keys off the key hook. "Yeah, I know. Quincy's stomach started bothering him so we called it an early night."

I smiled at her. "But that's why I'm about to go back out and see my husband, Curtis Jackson, perform down at Jordan's. Holla!"

Her face lit up with excitement. "Fiddy!" She did a little dance before giving me a kiss.

"Okay, have fun, and be careful. I'll let your father know. Call us and let us know where you are though, okay."

"Alright ma," I headed out the front door, "I'll call you when I'm on my way home."

Then I hopped into Pearl, and headed to Jordans.

# chapter sixteen

The line was long as hell when I got there. People were circled around the block. I found a parking spot halfway down the block, and I trooped it back up to the club. Girls were showing their asses for real. This one chick had on a lime-green thong and a pink, fishnet skirt with a black halter-top and some white jelly-sandals with glitter. I would've preferred to have on a pair of jeans. I hadn't even thought to change while I was home. The line moved up a little.

"Jaliyah! Baby Girl!" I heard someone calling from behind me.

I turned around and guess who it was y'all. It was Janet, the assistant manager from DIVAS. Now, I ain't know what the fuck this bitch wanted, and I ain't know why the fuck she wasn't inside because I know that Carmen had told me that she was tryna get there early and they were *all* rollin' together. I'm not the type to bite my tongue, so I asked her, "What are you doin' outside the club?"

She laughed. "Oh, it's a funny story. I didn't know that it was fifteen to get in tonight and I ain't have enough."

"Oh, really. How much do you need?" I asked her.

"Oh, like ten cash. I promise I'll pay you back if you loan it to me Jaliyah!" she begged.

"Oh, you are *definitely* gonna pay me back! Yo, you only brought five dollars with you to get up in Jordans? It's usually ten, you know that. Don't you always be up in here?" I asked her still not knowing the whole truth.

"Yeah, I don't know what I was thinking!" she laughed as she gently took the money out of my hand.

"Why didn't Carmen or Jacqueline give you the ten dollars? Y'all came here together right?" I asked her looking into my compact mirror.

"Yeah, but they trippin'. How was your date?" she asked changing the subject.

"It was good for a bit, then he got sick and shit."

"Did you fuck him?"

"Nah, nothing like that." I answered her. *"Didn't you hear me say he got sick?"*

"Did you brain him?" she asked me smiling as she took her fists, stacked them on top of one another, and moved them up and down in front of her mouth to simulate a blow job while poking her tongue in her jaw.

"Nah, I ain't do that either!" I snapped, annoyed with her stupid questions.

Her smile turned to a frown and she sighed with relief. "Good, I am so sick of that shit. That's all that goes on here. This one is fucking this one and this one is sucking that one."

"Oh, that's all that goes on here?" I asked her, frustrated with the length of the line.

"No, it's not *all* that goes on, but it's a pretty good piece of what does go on here. Do you know that Carmen once gave the old Guyanese man in the Sunoco Quickmart some head for a pack of Newports?"

Now, I was listening to what Janet had to say, but I ain't really feel like hearing it. She seemed cool up until she thought that I was fucking with Carmen, then I became *"a bitch named Jaliyah"*. I know that *she* was the one who I had heard in there earlier. It sounded like some serious shit was going on in there for real.

When I finally tuned Janet back in we were at the club entrance. This big, tall, black dude was standing there. He looked like the big dude from *Baby Boy*. You know, the one who was butt-naked in the crib drinkin' the Kool-Aid. Dude was big like that.

"I don't remember ever seeing you here before," he said to me as I handed him my money.

"That's because I don't really do the club scene up here too much," I answered politely.

"Ten dollars for you because you're cute, he said as he put out his hand to accept the money.

"Thanks. How about my girl right here? She's just as cute as me. What can she get off?" I asked him pulling Janet close to me.

His smile faded as he looked at Janet. "Oh you back again? You know, your friends ain't even come out and look for you once. They been inside shakin' they ass since you paid for them to go up in there!"

"Yeah, well—" Janet said in a serious tone, "I'm gon' handle that shit once I get inside there."

"Now look," he said, "I done told you that y'all best not start any shit up in here tonight. These doors are closing in a few minutes because the fire marshal done drove his nosy ass past here twice already, and I know that he is just looking for a violation so he can hit me with a fine. I ain't havin' it tonight. Y'all better not start nothing."

"Fine Tony!" Janet said. "I hear you. Damn!"

"Don't damn shit. You just want to go up in there and start something because you know that we gon break it up. I told you, if you really want to fight Carmen like that, just drive off up on a hill somewhere away from everything and y'all can just bang it out!"

Tony looked at me. "I'ma let her in for ten dollars too, but you better not let her fight in my club." He winked at me playfully.

"Don't worry, I got you!" I told him. "Thanks again."

"No problem," he said.

"Thanks Tony!" Janet said.

"Mmm, hmm," Tony said half-heartedly.

"I can't stand his ass!" Janet leaned in and whispered as we walked in.

"Yeah well his *ass* just let you in for ten cash. I want my money back too." I said to her.

"Yeah, I got you Baby Girl," she said as she started dancing to Nina Sky's "Move Ya Body".

The aroma of weed and spilled liquor filled the air. Yo, the club was *on* that night! DJ Whoo Kid was on the ones and twos. There were so many cuties there offering to buy me drinks, that I ain't know what to do. It was times like these when I wished that I drank. Whenever I went out with my peoples in Mount Vernon, I would give them all of my drinks. I'm cool with soda or some cranberry juice.

I got drunk on liquor *one* time, and that was enough for me. I was so fucked up that somehow, I wound up in Cheyenne's bathtub with her high school graduation cap and gown on and a bedroom comforter wrapped around me while freezing cold water from the shower head ran on top of me. Don't ask me how.

I ordered a Sprite from the bar, then I stepped back and just looked around observing everything and everyone around me for a minute. I checked for all of the exits because I knew that I was chancing it going to see 50 Cent in a local spot like this. I wanted to be prepared just in case some shit broke out somewhere and I had to dip.

Chicks were shakin' their asses all around. Just wildin' out. Drinks were splashin', phone numbers were being exchanged, and then, in the middle of everything, there was Carmen giving this nigga a lap dance in the middle of the floor. She had on a pair of tight, black stretch pants and a gold glittery halter-top. Her rolls were falling out everywhere. She was flinging her long, curly ringlets all around the place.

Carmen had the guy seated in a chair while she gave him the most in-depth dry hump that I had ever seen in my life. She raised her top up a little, and dude immediately took her left nipple into his mouth and began devouring it. He then grabbed her right breast and began sucking on that one too! Mind you, this is happening in the middle of a nightclub. I could not see who the guy was because she was so in his face. I couldn't get a closer look because the crowd was lovin' it and them niggas wasn't *hardly* trying to let me through.

I turned to walk away, and I stepped on a dude's foot by accident.

"Damn shortie, watch where you're going!" a deep voice yelled over the loud bass.

"I'm sorry," I said not even looking up at him.

"Yeah, you best be sorry. I should fuck you up P-Puff!" he said back to me.

I looked up and saw no one other than Mos, Trey and a couple of my other boys from the Ville.

"What the fuck are y'all doing up here?" I asked surprised before giving each of them a hug.

"What you think nigga?" Trey said. "We came to see my nigga 50 and to check the honeys!

He pushed me. "What you doing here? I thought that you don't fuck with clubs up here?"

Now, that was true, but I ain't want to get into too much detail about my date with Quincy. Therefore, I just said, "I'm out with some of my girls from my new job."

Trey nudged me, "They look good?"

"What, nigga they look a-ight. Why?" I asked annoyed because I knew that he was hollering at my girl Alicia back home.

"Shit, nothing! What the fuck you getting so amped about nigga?" he asked me. "You ain't never given a fuck about who I was layin' the pipe to. Shit, you the one who tells me what to say to get the pussy half the time."

Whoo Kid threw on Nas and Ginuwine's, "You Owe Me" and the crowd went nuts.

"Takin' it back real quick!" *Whooooooo Kidddddddd!* His signature drop boomed over the speakers.

"Yo, Jah-dee, I ain't even feeling the vibe that you giving off to me right now!" Trey yelled as he took my hand and said, "See, we gone have to dance until you ain't mad at me no more!"

Me and Trey found a spot on the floor and we went to work.

"So, I take it that nosy-ass Cheyenne told you about me and Alicia?" he asked me. Then he said, "No, you must've got it straight from the horses mouth because Shy don't know yet. Am I right?"

Unsure of how to respond I said, "No…Yes…Maybe…Yeah T, Licia told me." Then I turned to face him.

"What's good with y'all two? You feelin' her or what?"

He smiled. "Maybe."

I rolled my eyes. "Maybe muthafucka?!"

"You know me and you go back like seatbelts and fuckin' spinal cords. We been through some shit." He spun me around. "I just don't know how I feel just yet. Nah mean."

"Yeah, I know," I said.

We were about to dance to the next song when Mos came up behind me and said, "Oh, now you know we all waitin' for a dance with you, so you gone have to leave this nigga right here. Come on ma!"

"A-ight. Yo T, I'll get up a-ight!" I called to him as Mos pulled me over by the bar.

"Yeah ma, okay." Trey said as he grabbed another girl and started dancing with her.

"What chu want?" I asked Mos.

"Nothing, I just ain't want y'all talking about him and Alicia," he said taking a sip of his bottle of Henny.

"Look at you, drinking all that shit. I hope that you ate something fool." I said while doing a cute little two-step.

"Don't worry about me. Are you good with what you're drinking Puff?" he smiled.

"Yeah," I took a sip of my Sprite, "I'm cool."

"A-ight, then keep the heat to ya self tonight." He took another sip from his bottle. "Yo, Jah-dee, the girls up here is right. Ma, why you ain't tell me?"

"I don't know. I ain't tryna look at none of these bitches up here." I snapped at him, taking another sip of my Sprite.

"Yeah, well I know that Cheyenne would want to know about the chicks up here. I gotta put her on when I go back home tomorrow." He took a sip of my soda.

"Tomorrow? Where y'all gon' stay at?" I asked him curiously.

"Your crib." He smiled.

"Y'all ain't stayin' at my crib. What the fuck, nigga you buggin'!" I yelled over the music.

"*Ill*, what you getting all like that for? I already called up Mama Whitty, and she said a-ight. So you can just chill, and calm down with all that heat my G." He took another sip of his bottle, before taking his pointer finger and *booping* me on the tip of my nose.

"Whatever Mos. Look, next time y'all need to let me know something," I told him.

"Well, we did call you but Angie said that you were out on a date with some nigga named Quincy Jones. Speaking of that nigga—" he looked around suspiciously, "Where is he? I would like to meet him."

"Well, he ain't here. And his name is Quincy, but it ain't Quincy Jones smart ass," I shot back at him.

"Where is he then?" he asked jokingly.

"Look, that ain't none of your business stupid ass!" I yelled.

Then I mumbled quietly, "He got sick."

"Aww P-Puff," he said. "Is he a chill nigga tho?"

"He's real cool. I like him," I said.

"Well that's cool," Mos said. "But yo, I'm bout to go holla at these hoes. I'll get up Puff!"

He took another sip of his Henny and then he bounced to go dance.

# chapter seventeen

"**B**aby Girl, you made it! How long have you been up in here?" Carmen screamed as she hugged me.

"Who are your friends?" Jacqueline asked wiping the perspiration off her forehead with a napkin.

"Oh, these are my boys from Mount Vernon. This is Shawn, Trey, Wes and Myles." I said pointing to each one of them.

"What up, I'm Jacqueline but you can call me Jah-dee." Jacqueline said smiling.

Trey laughed. "Well, Jaliyah is Jah-dee so I'm gon' call you Jackie ma-ma. Is that a-ight?"

She played it off. "Yeah, that's a-ight. It's cool."

"I'm Carmen. I'm Jaliyah's boss at DIVAS." She hugged them all. "Nice to meet y'all."

"What up, I'm Janet. I work at DIVAS too," Janet said taking a toke from Chino's blunt.

"Did I say that you could puff on my shit bitch?" Chino snatched the blunt back from her.

"Yo, what up. I'm Chino, and that's my nigga Rob," Chino said. "Yo, you wanna burn this shit down yo?" he asked the group.

"Nah, we're good son. But that's peace of you to offer my nigga," Myles said.

"When is 50 gonna show up?" Carmen asked impatiently. "I can barely keep my thighs together," she laughed.

"Soon ma," Jacqueline said. "I can hardly keep mine together either."

They both laughed.

Just then, Tony, the bouncer approached our group and pulled Jacqueline aside. They talked for a little bit, then him and Jacqueline disappeared somewhere towards the back of the club.

Usher and Lil John's "Yeah!" began.

"Oh, this is my shit!" Carmen screamed. "Come on Janet! Let's get busy, baby! I'm so glad you finally got inside! I was worried about you! I came out looking for you, but I couldn't find you anywhere!" Carmen lied as her and Janet danced like there was no tomorrow.

About five minutes later, a giant, double-sided screen came down out of the ceiling. The music stopped and Whoo Kid spoke on the mic once again.

"Okay y'all, turn your attention to the screen so we can see what's going on live in the Champagne Room!"

It took a couple of seconds, but just like that, up on the screen popped a room full of girls dressed from head to toe in next to nothing. They were sitting on the laps of the various "ballers" who were in attendance that night. They were getting down for theirs too. Some of them were just talking, but the majority of the girls were kissing each other, sucking each others nipples or fondling each others pussies. It was gross.

Then there were the girls who weren't into the other girls and were just focusing on the men. They were giving head and hand jobs like they were going out of style. Some of them were even fucking! The camera panned the room and I could not believe my eyes! There was Jacqueline sitting on one of the couches talking to Tony the bouncer.

"Yo J, ain't that ya girl that was just here?" my nigga Wes asked me shocked as hell. Now that nigga was higher than a fuckin' light bill, but he knew that was Jacqueline's silly ass up on that screen.

"Yeah, that's her!" Carmen said laughing. The music started up again and Sean Paul's "Get Busy" blasted out of the speakers. The crowd got amped but no one could really dance because they all wanted to see what was going to happen next.

"I know that she ain't bout to let that nigga beat!" Trey said pointing up at the screen with a perplexed look on his face.

Jacqueline and Tony continued to talk and then, just like that, it went down. Better yet, *she* went down. Jacqueline got down on her knees, unbuttoned and unzipped Tony's jeans, took out his dick and commenced to suckin'.

She took off her shirt and moved her thong to the side under her skirt so he could play with her nipples and finger her clit. Yo, that was one of the nastiest things I had ever seen. This pretty-ass girl fuckin' and suckin' dick just so she didn't have to pay fifteen cash to get in a club. *Come on now!*

After about ten minutes, Tony got to shakin' and he busted all in Jacqueline's mouth. It was a lot too. It looked like he hadn't cum in *years!* The crowd exploded with shouts of *"Oh No!"* and *"Ill"* and there were even a few of them asking, *"Yo, where that bitch at?"*

It wasn't over yet though. Jacqueline tried to spit out her mouth full of jizz, but Tony would not let her. He gently grabbed her face and mouthed to her, *"Swallow that shit baby."*

She shook her head no, but she ended up swallowing. He even made her open up her mouth to show him that it was all gone.

"Yo, that is a nasty bitch. J, these are the chicks that you be spending your time with when you ain't with Licia and Chi-Town?" Mos asked me disgusted, yet amazed.

"Pa, we ain't all like that. I'ma tell you just like I told Baby Girl when I hired her, Jacqueline is a disgrace to the whole Puerto Rican race of people. She makes me wish I was Mexican." She laughed.

"And Carmen fuckin' despises Mexicans," Chino said laughing. "All Mexicans except Rob of course."

"Yo, I ain't Mexican nigga!" Robert snapped.

"A-ight chill!" Chino said softly. "I was just fuckin' with you! Calm down."

"Yo, I don't give a fuck what none of y'all have to say because I don't even know what the fuck I'm talkin' about!" Jacqueline came over laughing with a martini in her hand out of nowhere.

"Where were you?" Carmen asked her in front of everyone.

"I was…uh," she began to speak.

Janet put her ring up to her nose, snorted what appeared to be coke out of it, and said in a nasty, harsh tone, "Bitch, you were sucking dick! We fuckin' saw your nasty cum-slurping ass on the big screen like five minutes ago! You're busted!"

She sniffed a little more, then pinched her nose with her fingers.

"I told y'all that she was back there sucking his dick a few months ago!" Janet said as she dipped the tip of her pinky into the ring and rubbed some coke onto her gums.

Jacqueline did not respond. All I know is, before I knew it, Jacqueline was punching Janet in her face with her left hand and choking her out with the right. Fists were flying everywhere. Janet grabbed Jacqueline's hair and wrapped it around her hand. Immediately, she began jerking Jacqueline's body all over the dance floor. When she finally managed to make her fall down,

Janet took off her right shoe and began to attempt to hit Jacqueline in her face with it, as if she were trying to smash a bug.

*"That's right; fuck her up for fucking your man! Yeah bitch, she seen you sucking her man's dick all on the big screen!"* Carmen lied in an attempt to stir up the crowd even more.

*"Yo, that's that white girl's man yo! That bouncer nigga who was getting his shit sucked on the big screen shit! That's why they fighting!"* is what echoed throughout the crowd.

Finally, the bouncers arrived and broke the fight up. I don't know where Janet was hitting Jacqueline because when she got up she only had a few scratches on her. They both ended up being thrown out of the club and that was the end of that.

"Yo, let me find out that it's poppin' in upstate New York!" Mos laughed.

It was 1:30 in the morning when 50 finally hit the stage. That shit was wild though. The show was live. When it was done, I was ready to go home and knock out. We all left the club at the same time. Myles and Wes decided to drive back to Mount Vernon, so only Mos and Trey were coming back to the crib with me.

"Nice meeting all of y'all," Carmen said as she headed towards Janet's car with Chino and Robert.

When they reached her car, I couldn't believe it. There in Janet's car, were Janet and Jacqueline turning up to 50 Cent's CD. They were laughing and having the best time. I couldn't understand how they could be so cool after the fight they had *just* had with each other. I was not in the mood to ask any questions.

"Yo, neither one of those bitches better call out tomorrow. Both of them have to be at the store by 8:30 in the morning for inventory."

Carmen smiled. "Goodnight Baby Girl!"

Then they all piled into the car and drove off to wherever. Together.

<h1 style="text-align:center">chapter eighteen</h1>

"Yo, those are some wild chicks that you working with up at that store! Coked out, blunt smoking! Sucking dick all crazy! What the fuck Jah-dee! I haven't been entertained like that in months!" Trey laughed as he poured himself a glass of soda and took a bag of Lays salt-n-vinegar chips out of the cabinet. We arrived back at my house at about 3:30 in the morning.

"Hell fucking yeah!" Mos said. "Your boss kept grabbin' my ass and shit when her man had his back turned. I was like *chill ma, ya man is right there*. She said, 'He doesn't have to know.' Or some slick shit like that."

"Word?" I asked him taking the bag of chips from Trey. "I ain't surprised."

I went and got a bottle of water.

"Oh shit, y'all got bottled water and shit now. Suh-ditty muthafuckas! What happened to just runnin' your lips up under the faucet my nigga? Too good now?" Trey asked me drinking his soda.

"Shut up." I said. "Yo, do y'all remember after the prom when we were talking about how we were gonna always meet up when we got older and chill?"

"Yeah, I remember that shit," Trey said as he sat to the table.

I continued my sentence. "I don't think that I want to anymore. Y'all niggas make me sick!"

Trey made the ugliest face. "Your ass *better* do that shit. Or else I'ma fuck you up!"

"Hell yeah, we gon fuck her up if she try and play us like that. I don't give a fuck if you married or whatever. You are comin' to check us right?" Mos asked.

"Yeah, I am. I just wanted to make sure that y'all still knew. You know how y'all be actin' all funny style when y'all get girls and what not. Be walkin' past and not speakin and what not." I said looking in Trey's direction.

"Damn J, that was one time and it was in the eleventh grade!" Trey yelled at me.

"So! I don't give a fuck if it was in nursery school nigga, you shouldn't have done the shit!" I snapped at him. "You better not reach for no more of my chips neither! I'm mad about that shit now!"

"Anyway," he said taking a chip out of the bag and crunching it loudly in my ear.

"Anyway," Mos said, "what happened on this date of yours tonight ma?"

"That brother is finer than frog's hair! We had to end it a little early because he got sick from the food." I drank my water.

"And," Mos said.

"And what black ass!?" I yelled.

"And what else happened?" he asked me.

"Nothing. We kissed and we said goodnight." I told him.

"Kissed where?" he asked.

"He kissed me on the cheek." I smiled.

They started laughing. "That's nigga's pussy! I woulda fucked you right on your front porch!"

I rolled my eyes. "You're an asshole. What the fuck do y'all niggas know? He's grown. He don't do dumb shit like that." I said snidely.

Trey rolled his eyes and rubbed his hand across his edge-up. "Oh yeah, how grown nigga?"

I paused briefly. "Thirty-five."

Mos's face dropped and so did Trey's as they said simultaneously, "Thirty-five!"

"Y'all better shut up all that damn noise down there!" my mom screamed from upstairs.

"Sorry Mama Whitty!" Trey yelled up the stairs.

He looked at me. "Yo J, seriously, you OD'd. For real. *Thirty-five?* You need your ass kicked for that bullshit."

"I don't know. Like, I ain't know that's how old he was when I met him. He told me over the phone when I spoke to him that night." I told him tryna get some sympathy.

"You going out with the nigga again?" Trey asked me.

"Yeah, probably. Just do me for a minute. Ya know!" I said, giving him a kiss on the cheek. "It's so sweet that you worry about me though pa-pa. Thanks."

I gave Mos a kiss on his cheek, cleaned up their little mess and I said, "Let's go up to my room and go to bed. One of y'all can crash on the floor and one of y'all can sleep with me. I don't care which one. Just make sure the one who sleeps in the bed with me is the one who washes his ass."

I laughed. "I don't have to work tomorrow, so we could do something."

We all went upstairs, took turns showering and went to bed. Trey slept with me. I plugged my phone into the charger, turned it off and then said, "A-ight. Love y'all."

"Love you too J," Trey said.
"Love you Puff," Mos said.
Then it was lights out.

# part three
# sunday

# chapter nineteen

At about 8:30, I woke up to the sound of the house phone ringing. I was so tired from the night before that it had to ring a couple of more times before I realized that it wasn't a dream, and it was ringing for real. Somehow, I managed to roll over to the side of the bed where my nightstand was and I answered it.

"Hello," I said in a groggy voice.

"Hi, Jaliyah, this is Jacqueline. I'm at the store."

Now, you *know* that I was thinking *what the heck does this chick want?*

She continued on, "Sorry to wake you but Carmen needs you to come in right away to help with inventory," in a believable, yet non-believable voice.

"Really? But she told me that I was off today," I said sounding a little annoyed.

She laughed snobbishly. "Yeah well she asked for you to come in this morning so make sure that you're here by ten o'clock. The store is closed today just for this."

"Look, I got company over. I told them that I would drive them back home. They live all the way in Westchester County. I can't come in." I was more awake now and I felt my heart beginning to beat faster and harder because she was pissing me off.

"Well, let me—" she started to say.

"No, let me call up Carmen and find out what's good." I said sternly, displaying the exasperation in my voice.

"Look, just wait a second. I'm sure that she can get someone else to come in and do the inventory. Calling her ain't even necessary like that," she said in a calm, playful voice. "I'm sorry that I woke you. Go back to sleep."

"I'll do that Jacqueline." I retorted pissed as hell.

"Oh, Jah-dee, tell your friends that it was nice meeting them." Then she hung up.

Now, I was surprised as fuck that this bitch had just called me Jah-dee. Usually, she went out of her way to call me Jaliyah or Baby Girl. Nah, shit ain't seem right. I wasn't going to call Carmen right then because I knew that it was still early and they were all probably still asleep at her crib. I was definitely going to call her later on though to find out what Jacqueline's early morning phone call was all about.

I ain't wanna even think about it. I closed my eyes and before I knew it, I had fallen asleep again. This time, it lasted a little longer than five hours.

When I woke up, it was close to two o'clock in the afternoon. I looked in the fridge and saw that we had a whole bunch of chopped meat and salad. So, I threw together a quick little barbecue for us. By the time they had waken up and got dressed, everything was ready.

"See Jah-dee, that's why we love you. You always take care of us!" Trey said getting his plate.

I flipped the burgers over. "True story. I gotta take care of y'all since it's been made clear to me that I can't get rid of ya!"

I looked over at Mos. "So Mr. Mos," I said, ready to start

some shit, "I like how you was all in *my* business last night. But uh…what's good with you and yours brotha?"

"What chu' talkin' about girl?" he said piling relish onto his hot dog. "What business? I ain't been doin shit."

"Ain't no need to get all defensive. But the business that I'm talking about is you havin' a girl. As a matter of fact, I heard that Cheyenne even beat her ass once."

"Ha, ha, ha, oh shit!!!" Trey burst out with laughter. "Yeah, that was funny as shit!"

Mos gave Trey a look, but Trey ain't care. "Yo J, look, you better go head wit' all of that bullshit ma!" He took a bite of his hotdog. "Who told you that anyway? Cheyenne?"

Now, I could have said that Alicia told Cheyenne who told me, but that would have blown up Trey's spot and I knew that eventually I would need some more information out of him. If I put the shit on Shy, she wouldn't care. She says whatever she has to say to Mos and vice versa.

"Maybe," I answered covertly.

"Yeah well, she don't know what she's talking about. She needs to stay out of everyone else's B.I. and get her shit right."

Trey stopped chewing to say, "Very true my nigga, very true."

I shot him a look just to let him know that I knew that *he* was the one who told Alicia. That ended his commentary for a while.

Mos spoke again. "I don't give a good goddamn what she said! She don't know what in dee-hell she talkin' about!"

"Fine Mos. Why you gotta get all country on me and what not!"

"COUNTRY GOTCHA CRAZY!" Trey started singing playfully.

"Yo J, remember that song ma? Them chicks that used to be dancers for MC Hammer. Fine as hell? What were their names?" He tried desperately to remember. "Juicy". Or somethin' like that."

"Nah, their names was like, "Inglewood 2-1-0" or something like that," I said polishing off my second burger.

"Damn you greedy!" Trey said rudely. "Eating all them hamburgers like that is really fucking unattractive."

"Kiss my ass T!" I sucked my teeth and took another bite of my burger. "*Anyways*, their name was Inglewood 2-1-0!"

"Word, oh a-ight. Inglewood 2-1-0 my nigga! See, J you stay on your toes! Just up on em' like this!" He stood up on the tips of his Timbs. "I say like this!" Then he did it again.

I fell out laughing. "Yo, I know. I know. That is how *I* do it! That's how *I* remember the thing! Ya know!"

Fed up with hearing *both* of our voices, Mos interrupted and yelled, "Oaktown 3-5-7! Okay! "Juicy Gotcha Krazy" is the song that y'all are singin' wrong as fuck—and y'all are puttin' the word *country* where *juicy* should be! Inglewood 7-3-4 is some bullshit! Damn yo! Shut up!"

"It's Inglewood 2-1-0," I said quietly.

"I don't give fuuuuuuck!" he yelled. "Just shut up!"

Now don't you know that me and Trey looked at each other and said all kinds of "*Who he think he talkin' too's*" and "*He's trippin's!*"

Now, the only reason he *did* flip out like that is because he knew that he was busted and his spot was blown up. He had a girl. He had somethin'. I couldn't worry about it though. He would need some advice sooner or later about his *non-existent* significant other. Then, all the information would come out. At that moment, he was just upset because I had let the horse out the closet on his ass.

Now, I had to make peace because I ain't want him all mad at me and shit. I said, "Mos baby, you need a hug or something?" I smiled and walked over to him and gave him a hug.

"*And baby…*," I continued.

"Yeah," he responded.

*"Don't you be yellin' in my backyard no more*. I'll knock your ass out!"

He laughed and pointed to his food. "Good, good, good, very good!"

I looked down at my cell and I saw that I had two voicemail messages. "Yo, what time y'all wanna roll out?"

"What time is it now?" Trey asked eating his fourth or fifth hamburger.

"It's like almost three."

"A-ight then, we could bungee after you clean this shit up." Trey said as if he had just said something good.

Stuck for a minute I said, *"Y'all gonna help my black ass!"*

I ran into the house to listen to my voicemails.

Quincy's voice sounded so sweet.

*"Hi Jaliyah, it's about 10:45PM, and I just got home a little while ago. I guess you're already asleep. I am definitely on my way there. But, I'll leave my phone on just in case you wake up and wanna give me a call. I had a great time with you. Your uncle called me on my way home and I told him what a great girl you were. Okay then, I'll talk to you later. Goodnight."*

Oh, now y'all know that message made my day, right? I called him back, but I got his voicemail. I left him a message though.

*"Hey Quincy, it's Jaliyah. I hope you're feeling better. I got your message. Sorry I'm just getting back to you now. I actually did slide through to see 50 Cent at Jordans. Call me when you get a chance. Lata."*

Once I hung up, I remembered that I had another message. I redialed my voicemail.

*Damn*, I thought. *Where would we go on our next date? When would it be?*

Before I could answer any of those questions, my voicemail said, **Next message.**

*"J, this is Uncle Ant. How you doing sweetie? I know that*

*you're out on your little date or whatever wit Q, so I'll keep this short.*" He said calmly in a deep, but rugged voice sounding just like DMX. Then, yeah, y'all know it. He brought the crazy!

"*Yeah J, uh...so you and Q—NOT HAPPENING!*" he hollered loudly. "*THAT SHIT IS DONE. DEADED! YOU HEAR ME!*"

Then he went off on a tangent, ranting and raving until my voicemail stopped recording.

"*You know...Lonnie told me that they was gon' come for me. Shee-yit! I got like a year left to retire and these muthafuckas tryna get me to catch a body! They want me to commit murder. They want my black ass to do twenty and out like a muthafucka! And they done stooped so fucking low. This da real bullshit here! They done stooped so low, that they done gon' and recruited my little niece to help do my black ass in! Ain't that about a bitch! The NYPD is full of some grimy ass muthafuckas! Damn, what part of the muthafucking game is this? Q betta step the fuck off! That's what! I can't believe this shhh....*"

Then all I heard was a lot of scratching and banging until I think that fool broke his damn phone.

**End of Messages.**

Well, there was the answer to my many questions right there. Q and I were over before we started. I could not have my uncle bugging out like that. *Come on now!*

However, I *did* save the message, and I still have it to this day! That shit was funny as hell!

I went back outside to see Trey gathering up the remaining burgers and hotdogs. "Shee-yit, I'll take these leftovers to the crib wit' me. That's about it. I ain't cleaning up though. I don't even know where anything goes!"

After about ten minutes of arguing back and forth, I just gave up. I realized that it wasn't gon' do me no good. I took everything back inside and I washed down the grill. Trey went inside to get some foil for his food. He was good until my sisters came home and thugged him for half of it. He must have yelled *"Yo, what the fuck son!"* about a thousand times. He bitched about that up until it was time to go.

Finally, we were ready to leave. The two of them claimed that they were scared to have me drive them into the city, so I agreed to let Trey drive. There wasn't a whole lotta traffic and the way he drove, I swore that I was on a freakin' G4 jet plane. It takes a good hour and fifteen minutes to get to Mount Vernon from Poughkeepsie. I swear this to you, we left out at like 4 o'clock, maybe a little bit after four. We got down to Mount Vernon by 4:45. That's crazy right there.

So anyway, we got downtown, and we dropped Mos to his crib first, and then Trey drove himself home. He hopped out and said, "Call me when you get in to let me know you're good," with an empty piece of aluminum foil in his hand. He ain't even wait to eat the leftovers. He ate them, *while driving,* on the way home. He didn't share shit.

I got back home at around 6:30. I called Trey and told him to let Mos know that I was in the crib. I stood around for a while trying to remember what it was that I had to do.

Oh yeah, I had to call Carmen and find out what Jacqueline's morning phone call was all about.

# chapter twenty

"Carmen, this is Jaliyah. How you doing ma?" is what I said when Carmen answered her phone.

"Hey Baby Girl, what's up?" she said sounding even more vibrant than usual.

"Nothing much." I switched the phone to my other hand. "I just came in from dropping my peoples back home to Mount Vernon."

"Oh, yeah, Jacqueline was fuckin' talkin' about them the *whole* ride home. About how she wanted to do this and that with them."

She laughed. "Can you believe her last night? Suckin' Tony's dick like that all on the fuckin' widescreen and shit! That bitch is disgusting!"

"Yeah, that was crazy," I said. "But uh, actually, I was calling you because Jacqueline called me this morning."

"For what?" she asked in a way that let me know that it was news to her.

"She told me that you said that I had to come in and do the inventory."

"No I didn't. She probably just ain't want to bring her tired ass in to do it. She *is* management you know. But uh, I told that hoe about throwing my name around *here and there* just so she can get what she wants done."

"I knew that you ain't say that shit because when I started to press her about it and what not, she got all defensive and was like, 'Oh, I'm sorry. Go back to bed'." I told her getting tight that Jacqueline had just lied like that.

"Yeah, that shit is crazy. She's a fuckin' liar!" Carmen said exasperatingly. "What time did she call you?"

"Um, about 8:30 in the morning," I answered.

"Did she call you from home or from the store?" she asked me.

"She said that she was in the store," I remembered and told her.

Carmen sucked her teeth. "That bitch was in her damn bed. She probably called you from her house." She exhaled. "Do you have Caller ID mami?"

"Yeah, I do," I answered.

"Can you go and check it and see if it says Marte on it?" she asked me.

"A-ight, one second." I ran downstairs to see what the Caller ID said. Campbell, Young, a 1-800 number, and sure enough, at 8:32 am it said *Marte, Esteban.*

I ran back to the phone. "Carmen, yeah she called from her crib."

"See, that bitch was supposed to be in that fuckin store at 8:30 this morning. I'm gonna beat her ass!"

She yelled to Robert. "Baby, guess what! Jacqueline tried to be on some slick shit to get Jaliyah to come in for her this morning. Remember when I called the store at like 10 o'clock and I asked her what time she came in and she said 8:30? That trick was still in her fuckin' crib!"

"What, that's shady," I heard Robert say in the background.

"Yeah it is," Carmen added, "And I bet she put down 8:30 on her fucking timesheet too."

"What are you gonna do?" I asked her.

"Nothing right now," she said. "I'll keep it in my mental Rolex though. "You can believe that."

"Okay." *Rolex?* I thought to myself. "Well, I'm about to go. Um…what time do I work tomorrow?" I asked her.

"You can come in from three to close. Those are the hours that I'm working so it'll be fun," she said joyfully.

"Okay, so I'll see you then." I told her.

"Oh…I almost forgot," she said, "there is a store meeting tomorrow morning at 8:00 in the store. I have something important to talk to you girls about. Okay."

"Cool," I said.

Carmen was cool and *such* a sweetheart. I was beginning to see why she was the way she was with the girls. They *were* a handful. I didn't know how she did it. I looked at the time. It was almost 8 PM. I noticed the little purse that I had carried on my date the night before laying on the floor. I had all of my shit in there. My license, my money. I just wanted to switch everything back into my DIVAS bag so I wouldn't be assed out tomorrow.

I poured everything onto the carpet in my room, and Elliot's card came out along with it. I had forgotten about Elliot with his fine ass. He seemed sweet, and since Quincy was a done deal, I figured, *why not*. He probably wouldn't even have remembered who the hell I was. *But maybe he would.* What the hell? I decided to give him a call. The phone rang and rang and rang some more. Finally, his voicemail picked up.

*Get money! Get money! Whatcha say uh! Whatcha say, whatcha say uh!*

Yo, my man had taken it back with the Junior Mafia voicemail. I was open; I had almost missed my cue to leave my message. His message was the typical: "Yo, this is Elliot, leave it. One!"

So all I said was, *"Yo Elliot, this is Jaliyah. We met last night at the Velvet Lounge. You know, the chick with the rhyme skills. Anyway, I was just callin' to see what was good with you. Hit me back when you get this."* I left my number and I hung up.

He called me back within minutes on some, "Your number came up private so I ain't wanna take no chances and have it be my ex-girl. Me and her ain't on good terms right now."

"That's cool," I said. "You still feelin' her? You still in love?"'

He laughed. "Noooo. Absolutely not! That has been done wit. For a minute now."

He sounded believable, but it was entirely too soon to tell.

"So, what's good ma? What's going on with you? Honestly, I thought that you would *never* call me." He laughed on the phone.

"Nah, I was cleaning out my purse and I found your number so I called you up," I told him.

"Oh, so you had forgotten that it was even in there." He laughed. "Oh, see, I see how you do me. That's okay though. You know you just broke my heart right?" He said playfully.

"I'm sorry! I ain't mean it like that," I said.

"Nah, I know. I'm just fuckin' with you." He took a bite out of something that was crunchy, as I don't know what.

"*Ill*, you eating in my ear all crazy! What is that?" I laughed.

"Pork rinds," he said. "I'm sorry ma!"

"You better be. Shee-yit don't be crunchin' all in my ear like you ain't got no goddamn sense."

"Oh word? You gonna try and order me around and what not?" He laughed.

"Yeah!" I yelled. "No doubt!"

"Okay, I see how you roll. But uh, where are you from? I ain't never seen you anywhere around here before," he asked me. "You from up here?"

"No," I said. "I'm from Mount Vernon, down in Westchester."

"Oh, with Heavy D and Ben Gordon," he said all excitedly.

"Yeah, Denzel Washington. All of em."

"Yeah, your high school had the nicest basketball team. Yo, they beat our asses every time we played them." He crunched another pork rind.

"Yeah, well go hard or go home, right," I laughed.

"Yeah, y'all were good, but your school is ghetto as hell. The girls were all rude when we walked out onto the court and what not. Someone threw a bottle and shit."

"Whatever, you a hater like Starr and Buck nigga! My school was the shit!" I said snobbishly yet jokingly. "I should hang up on your ass, tryna play my school and shit!"

"Oh, damn ma. I'm sorry. You know that I don't want that." He began to laugh. "So, what's good for Saturday? Are you working or anything? Maybe we could go and catch a flick or something."

"Well, I just started a new job and I don't know my hours for the week yet. But uh, when I find out what's good for Saturday, I'll let you know. It might end up being late. Like around ten because I may have to close. I'm sure that we're going to be busy that day."

"Okay, well as long as you let me know. That's peace," he said.

"A-ight, cool," I responded.

"Yo, so ma, I'm about to take my moms to the Chinese restaurant to pick up her food and shit. They don't deliver but that's the only place where she likes the food. She could drive herself but she just wants to be difficult."

"I know how that goes," I responded.

"So, I'll call you tomorrow, a-ight," he said.

"Cool, tomorrow," I answered back.

We said, "One" and hung up.

I remembered that I had that early meeting tomorrow morning. I stayed up for a minute thinking about what it was going to be about. Maybe Carmen was gonna give someone else the ax. *Chile*, you never knew when it came to these people. I took my shower, washed my hair, set my alarm clock and hopped into bed. No sooner than I cut off my light, my cell phone rang.

"What up, it's Quincy," he said. "What's good J?"

"Oh, what up pa? You finally hopped up off the toilet and decided to call a chick back?" I asked laughing.

"Oh, okay, you got jokes. Oh, a-ight. You probably was on the toilet too." He laughed.

"*Ill*, no I wasn't!" I yelled.

"Yup! You probably were holding onto the toilet paper holder for support and all of that. Panties were probably all down around your ankles! Shee-yit, you probably had to step out of em'!"

I fell out laughing. "Nasty!"

He continued on, "Shit, I know that I stepped outta my draws. I was butt-ass on the toilet clenching my teeth and all of that!"

I laughed some more. "This whole story is totally just stank and trashy! I ain't *hardly* feeling it!"

"Yeah, I'm good now though. But what's good with you? So you went back out last night, huh?" he asked. "I knew you were gon' go back out even before *you* knew that you were gon' go back out."

"How'd you know?" I asked him.

"Because," he said, "I know women—I know them, but I'll be damned if I understand them. But you, you probably said to yourself, *"I look too good tonight to be goin' home so I'm goin' out to shake my ass!"*

He was so funny. He said it in the same stank-girl voice that he had used the day that I first met him.

"Well anyway, if you must know, I went to Jordans and I

chilled. I seen a few of my peoples from the Ville, and we just kicked it or whatever back at my crib afterwards."

I sucked my teeth and whispered jokingly under my breath, but loud enough for him to hear me, "Nosy muthafucka."

"Oh, see, now I ain't gon' be too many more names! You gon' get your soul clapped messin' with me!" He laughed.

"Whatever, ain't nobody hardly scared of you!" I rolled my eyes. "Please believe me!"

"Okay, sleep on me then! Sleep!" he barked into the phone playfully.

"That's what I was about to do before you rang my phone off the hook and what not."

"Oh, so it's like that, huh?"

"Yeah, it's like that. What's up?" I asked him, a hint of seriousness in my tone.

"Nothing much. You were just on my mind so I wanted to call you up and see what was good with you."

He paused. "I thought that *maybe* we could go out again and do things up the right way this time. I was thinking, Saturday."

"*Oh*, let me stop you right there playboy," I interrupted. "Let me be honest with you. Boo, me and you are not going to be able to go any further than last night."

He got quiet and exhaled deeply. "I had a feeling that you were gonna say that to me."

"You did?" I asked him.

"Yeah, when I told your uncle about what a great girl you were, I could have sworn that he was talking to me through clinched teeth."

I laughed.

He continued. "Plus I heard your little cousin say, *"Daddy, if you go to jail for killing Uncle Q, can I still get my Barbie car for my birthday?"*

Shocked I said, "Word? Oh my goodness!" I started to giggle.

"Yeah, I know." He sounded a little upset. "Well, we tried. But you gotta respect his wishes, and so do I. That's my man. You know."

I agreed. "Yeah, I know."

"But you're a good girl. You'll make some lucky young man really happy one day," he added.

I smiled to myself. "Yeah, that's what they all tell me."

He laughed. "Awww, it's the truth."

I decided to end the conversation before it got any more painful for me. "Well, all the best and I really did have a great time with you Q."

He sounded cheerful. "Me too."

"Okay," I said. "Take care, then."

"You do the same," he replied.

"Goodnight Q."

"Goodnight J."

We hung up, and I immediately dialed my Uncle Anthony.

His cell went straight to voicemail. I called the house and my Auntie Kima answered the phone.

"Hey Auntie Kima, it's Jaliyah," I said once she answered the phone.

"Giiiiiiiiiirrrrrrlllllll—" she said sounding like she had been going through it, "you done ran up your uncle's blood pressure. That fool done broke his cell phone, a glass, kicked over the damn barbeque grill on top of my flowers and burnt them shits the hell up, overfed and killed one of Amaya's goldfish, went out of the house wearing a high-top sneaker and a flip-flop, and pulled out one of my damn tracks last night while we was getting busy!"

I laughed hysterically. "Whuuuuuuuut?"

She laughed quietly. "It ain't funny. It ain't hardly funny."

I laughed some more before she asked me, "Did you end it with Q? Lord, *please* tell me you did."

"Yeah, I did."

"Good gracious," she said. "I know it liked to killed you though, right?"

I laughed. "Mmm hmm. Auntie, you seen him!"

She laughed. "Mmm hhmmmm. Whew Chile! I'll get your Uncle. Hold on a minute."

"Ant," she yelled, "it's Jaliyah! She ended it with Q!"

After a couple of seconds, my uncle picked up the phone.

"Bye sweetie," Kima said before hanging up the phone.

"Bye Auntie Kima!"

"Hello?" my uncle said pitifully.

"Hey psycho!" I said.

"Awww…Jah-dee," he said. "I was just looking out. I could not have my little niece going out with a dude like that. That nigga is my boy and all, but he's not for you. I know these things. I'm Uncle Ant. I come to you only with love and caring. I love you J."

I smiled, and then laughed. "Unc, I can't believe you! Going around breaking up stuff and what not. Did you hurt yourself?"

"Hell yes," he said calmly, but you could tell he felt like an asshole. "I'ma be out for two weeks on sick leave. I got some glass in my shooting hand from squeezing my glass of water and breaking it. It hurt like a bitch! Kima was pissed too. And J," he whispered, "don't tell her I told you, but I pulled out one of her tracks last night while we was getting busy."

We both laughed.

I shook my head in disbelief. "Well, get better. And calm down. You don't have to worry about me. Little Amaya and Jade will be plenty to worry about in about ten to twelve years. Ya heard me!" I laughed hysterically.

He just got quiet. "Not funny J."

"Bye-eeeee, I love you," I said.

"Love you too J."

Then we hung up, and I went to sleep.

# part four
# monday

# chapter twenty-one

### The Meeting

Before I knew it, it was time to get up. I threw on a pair of sweatpants and a white tee. Nothing spectacular. It was just a meeting. I guess they had a lot of things to talk about with me being hired and Michelle being fired the other day. I didn't know what to expect. I thought about calling Carmen to ask her if she had spoken to Jacqueline about the phone incident. Even though Jacqueline had lied, I didn't want Carmen to blow up her spot in front of everyone. I knew that was *just* what she wanted to do though. I suddenly felt a little bad about telling her.

When I got to the store, the gate was pulled down and locked, and all of the lights were turned off except for a very faint one in the backroom.

"Yo, anyone in there!" I yelled through the gate. "Yo!"

The door opened, and Carmen shut off the light, before walking out.

"Yo Carmen!" I yelled again.

She looked towards the gate. "Baby Girl! I'm coming out right now!"

Carmen locked up the backroom, unlocked the gate, lifted it up and said, "What up ma?"

"What's up!" I yelled to her and smiled. "Where's everyone at?"

She rolled her eyes. "Those bitches got greedy and decided that they wanted to have the meeting at Friendly's instead. None of them wanted to wait for you and shit. I had a few phone calls to make, so I told them that I would wait."

"Are you done with your calls?" I asked her.

"Yeah, I'm good. You all set?" she asked me.

"Yeah," I answered.

"Well, let's bounce!" Carmen shut the gate and locked it. "You wanna take your car or mine?" I asked her.

"We're gonna have to take yours because mine is with Chino and Robert. They went somewhere last night, and they ain't come back yet. Janet had to give me a ride this morning."

"What? That's some shit right there," I said to her. "Well, we can take mine then."

"Okay, cool," she said.

We walked outside to the parking lot and I let out a huge yawn.

"I'm so sleepy right now!" I whined playfully.

"Well, you don't look it. Look at me!" she laughed. "I stayed up all night stressin' about where them niggas went!"

Now, to me, she looked much better than I did at that time. She was wide-awake, and her makeup was just right. She wore a pair of Baby Phat, faded-blue jeans, a black shirt and her black Timbs.

"Let me find out that you're fishing for compliments Carmen." I smiled at her as I clicked my car alarm to unlock the doors.

"Nah, nothing like that." She laughed. "It's just that lately I've been feeling real insecure and shit. Like about me and Rob and everything. It just feels good to have somebody say nice things every now and then."

I started the car and Mariah Carey's "Thank God I Found You (Make It Last)" Remix with Joe and Nas exploded from the speakers.

Carmen smiled and began to dance in her seat while rapping Nas's verse. *"You taste like banana cake, you shaped like the number 8, and you my number one candidate!"*

"Nas is so muthafucking sexy! Oh my Gahhh!" Carmen said excitedly, as she rolled down her window.

I rolled my window down as well. "Yeah, that's my husband right there, girl! Oh, the things I would do to that man! What!"

"Mmm, that's my husband too, girl!" Carmen laughed. "Baby Girl, you coming outta that shell, huh?"

I laughed. "A little something, I guess."

We pulled up to the restaurant and the parking lot was ridiculously crowded.

"Damn, this place is packed as shit!" I said to her.

"Yeah, I knew that it was gonna be like this. I told them to hold down a table so we should be good." Carmen said.

We locked the car, got out and walked into the restaurant.

"I hope that we're in the smoking section" Carmen whispered, "I need a bogey bad!"

"Over here! Jaliyah, Carmen!" is what we heard as soon as the waitress was about to say, "It'll be a wait."

We went and sat down with the rest of the girls. Carmen lit a cigarette, and smiled at the group.

The restaurant manager came over to the table. "Miss, there's no smoking in here. Please put that out."

Carmen rolled her eyes and put it out in Janet's orange juice. "Fine."

Janet just shook her head in disbelief and yawned. "It's too fucking early for this bullshit."

"Yo, we packed like a dick in this bitch!" Jacqueline laughed.

"Yeah I know, but it's—" before Janet could finish her statement, Carmen interrupted her with, "Damn, can we eat already!"

"Yeah!" they all screamed.

The waitress came around and we all ordered. I ordered toast, home fries, two scrambled eggs and a large apple juice.

I just wanted the meeting to begin, so it could end. I wanted to go home and get back into my bed. We chatted about a whole bunch of nothing until the food came.

"Okay so, as you know I called you all here for our monthly meeting. As you also know, Michelle is no longer with us, so that gives us an opening in management."

She looked at me. "Say hello to your new head cashier, Jaliyah! She begins training today when her shift starts at three o'clock."

*Now*, I was speechless. I didn't know what to say. I knew that although I took a few classes in business management at school, I didn't know a damn thing about *being* management. I mean, I had just learned how to work the register two days ago. I just looked at her and said, "Carmen, are you sure that you want me to be the head cashier. I mean, I still don't know too much about anything yet."

She just laughed and took a sip of her soda. "You'll be fine. I have faith in you."

I sighed with a smile. "Okay, then. Cool. Thank you!"

The waitress brought our food, and just as I was about to dig in, Nadia exclaimed loudly, "JANINE WAS SUPPOSED TO BE HEAD CASHIER!"

*"Excuse me?"* Carmen said, angrily cutting her eyes at Nadia.

Nadia lowered her tone. "I mean, I thought that Janine was

supposed to be the head cashier of the store when Michelle got fired."

Carmen regained her poise and smiled. "Well, there's been a change of plans. I believe that Jaliyah is more qualified for the position. Plus, she's older and she can work later hours. It'll be good. Trust me."

Carmen closed her eyes and quietly blessed her food.

"Okay, everyone eat, and we can discuss all of the things that are being said about us *divas* throughout the mall this month." She took a bite of her eggs. "Who wants to start?"

Janet tapped her new, butt-less glass of OJ with her fork to get everyone's attention. "I'll start. This girl from The Sunglass Hut came up to me and said that she heard that someone was having sex in the back parking lot of the mall. She said that it was one of us because it was *right* behind the door where we receive our shipments."

"What? Who's having sex in the parking lot?" Carmen asked inquiringly. "First off, is someone here having sex in the back parking lot?" she asked.

All of the girls laughed and gave her questioning looks. Then Janet spoke again, "I told her that no one here is fucking *anyone*, *anywhere* around the store."

Carmen laughed. "So, that's the big one of the week huh? That we are fucking and sucking random guys in the back parking lot."

"Oh and there's more!" Janet waved her hand excitedly. She didn't say that it was just *a* guy that was being fucked." Janet laughed. "She said that it was a girl, a guy and *another girl*."

"Oh, so now we're having threesomes in the back parking lot!" Carmen yelled loudly.

All of the talking in the restaurant ceased for a minute and all of the customers stared at our table.

Carmen looked around at the crowd. "It's not true!" Then she smiled.

The table erupted with laughter. "They're gonna ban us from here now too probably." Carmen laughed. "We're not allowed in Denny's *or* the diner across the street before 9:00PM anymore because of the *content* of our discussions."

Jacqueline laughed. "One time, Carmen was showing Michelle, you know the girl who got fired—she was showing her how to suck dick and where to put her hands and all of that! For some weird reason, Janet had a dildo in her purse and Carmen was *actually* showing Michelle *on the dildo* how to do it. It was so funny!"

"Yeah, I had forgotten all about that!" Janet looked at Carmen. "You are a *nasty* bitch!"

Carmen started laughing, pretending to be offended. *"I can't believe that you just said that to me!* Well, your mother was a whore and she liked it!"

"*Ohh*...!" we all laughed.

"Anything else?!" Carmen asked.

"I overheard the girls from Rainbow bragging about the new space they're moving into downstairs in the mall. It's huge—and it's been *completely* remodeled!" Cordelia said while taking bites of her Moons Over My Hammy sandwich.

"Oh, they are the ones who got that new space? Who cares. They think they're the shit because they have more stores than us —so what—our clothes fall apart after *one* wash, and theirs fall apart after *two*! Who gives a shit!" Carmen laughed and rolled her eyes as she went to light up again before quickly remembering that she couldn't.

"Okay, okay, we have some *real* store business to discuss too." Jacqueline said.

"Okay, what needs to be done in the store?" Carmen asked.

"Everything," Janet answered. "We need to put up new

displays. We have to do a thorough cleaning of the store. At inventory, so many clothes were missing. It was insane."

"Okay, well, we have to pick a day where we can all come in, and stay late cleaning up and straightening. I'll get approval from the District Manager," Carmen said. "We'll wear jeans and order pizza. It's gonna be fun!"

She looked around. "Are there any other grievances from anyone?"

It was quiet, and then Nadia, spoke up again. "Well, me and some of the other girls who don't smoke wish that you wouldn't smoke in the bathroom."

"We spray air freshener though!" Carmen yelled jokingly.

"Yeah, but it's like, 'Whoa!' when we go in there after you," Nadia explained as she fanned the air for emphasis.

"Look, Nadia, I need to smoke a cigarette when I'm in the bathroom." She lowered her voice. "It helps me to take a shit."

"No, Carmen, that's all in your mind. Can y'all just go outside and smoke?" Nadia asked politely.

"What about when it's busy? Can we smoke then?" Carmen asked.

"Yeah, that's okay." Nadia smiled at her.

"Cool." Carmen went to light up another cigarette before putting it away, remembering that there was no smoking in the restaurant. "We will *only* smoke in the bathroom when it's really busy in the store."

"Cool," everyone said.

I really didn't care one way or the other. The smoke didn't bother me. But, I was surprised with the way that Carmen handled the whole situation with Nadia. She was respectful of her wishes and she was considerate. I was also surprised that Carmen was about to wrap up the meeting, and she hadn't mentioned anything to Jacqueline about calling me.

Carmen said, "The meeting is done then!" She looked at

Jacqueline. "But, before everyone goes off to wherever, I need to let y'all know that when I ask one of you to do something, it means that I want *you* to do it and no one else. Do not throw *my* name around when *I* am *not* around—Jacqueline."

Jacqueline froze and stared at Carmen.

Carmen spoke again, "I need management to stay, and everyone else to leave."

"Can we stay...*please*?" Nadia begged. "This is so fun."

"Bounce! You wanna fuckin' complain about cigarette smoke and now you're tryna stay. Leave! Get the fuck outta here!" Janet yelled with an attitude.

"Janet, don't start your shit!" Carmen said to her. Then she looked at Nadia. "No, sweetie, these are things that just involve the management staff. I'll be in later though okay."

"Okay," Nadia said. "Well, here's our money for our breakfast." Then she turned and exited the restaurant with Cordelia.

"Damn, finally!" Carmen said. "Okay, Jaliyah, I have to introduce you to the new co-manager that's coming in. Her name is Tina. She's like maybe in her late twenties, early thirties. She's from Atlanta or North Carolina, hopefully, she'll be of more help to us than the *last* co-manager was."

Janet smiled at me. "Congratulations!"

"Thank you!" I said to her. "Is Janine gonna be upset when she finds out that I'm the new head cashier and not her?"

"Oh please!" Jacqueline said. "She's not even here right now. She's in California on vacation. We'll just tell her that Michelle got fired sooner than expected, and we really needed to fill the position."

"Okay, I need a favor from one of you girls." Carmen said to us.

"Yeah, okay," Janet said nonchalantly.

"No, I'm serious, it's important." Carmen said.

"What is it?" Jacqueline asked.

Carmen lowered her voice and leaned in close to the group. "Okay, it's like this. You know that Chino is living with me and Robert now because of whatever reasons."

"Yeah, okay," we responded with no clue of where she was gonna take this.

She continued, "Well, lately, Chino has been saying some really slick shit to me about how he wants to put his tongue in my pussy and eat me out and how he wants to fuck me and shit."

"*What?!*" Jacqueline blurted out in a disgusted tone.

Carmen looked over at her and said, "Well, he has been."

Then she continued, "But see, at first I was like whatever. But lately, I have been wanting to fuck that little nigga like nobody's business. He has been lookin' so good to me lately. Last week, in the backroom, I was opening shipment and I had on my jean dress and my open toe shoes. You know the one with—"

Before Carmen could finish her sentence Janet interrupted her by saying in a malicious manner, "Yeah, I remember. The one you told me that *I* couldn't wear to work and then you showed up in it the very next day!"

"Yup, that's the one bitch! How many goddamn times are you going to bring it up?" Carmen retorted sounding happily psychotic.

"Any who," she continued before clearing her throat, "like I was saying, I was bent over separating the clothes and Chino snuck up behind me, moved my thong to the side, and slipped his fingers inside of me.

"*What!?*" I exclaimed surprised that she was telling this story to all of us in a family-friendly restaurant let alone, in front of his ex-girl.

"Yeah," Carmen said. "I swear on everything I love."

"So what did you do?" I asked her.

"I busted all over them!" she laughed. "For real!"

Unimpressed and hardly moved or surprised by Carmen's story Janet asked, "So what does this shit have to do with us?"

Carmen stopped laughing and got serious. She took a deep breath.

"Look, I need one of you to…um—I need one of you to step up and fuck my man this weekend."

# chapter twenty-two

I could not believe what I had just heard. I could not believe that Carmen had even formed her lips to ask *me* some bullshit like that. How are you really going to ask someone to fuck your man? Like, that is so gross. I wanted to think that she was playing, but I knew that she was dead ass.

The only thing that I could say was, *"Nah, Carmen, I respect you too much as my boss, I respect myself too much and now I respect you too much as my girl to even do some shit like that."*

Before she could even respond, Janet blurted out, "I'll do it!"

I couldn't believe that shit either! She sounded like she had been waiting forever for the chance to get to mess around with Robert.

Jacqueline shot her the nastiest look ever and then said, "I was thinking that, um, maybe I would do it."

Completely ignoring Jacqueline's statement, Carmen said, "So, it's settled then. Janet will fuck Robert this weekend."

Still not believing that all this bullshit was being discussed I just sat there. Eventually, so did Jacqueline.

"You know how it is though, right J?" she asked Janet. "I just don't want it to look like I just wanted to fuck Chino and what not. I don't want to make myself look bad and shit. I figure this way, he's fuckin' a bitch and I'm fuckin' a dude."

Janet smiled. "You don't have to explain. I understand completely. I would love to help you out. C'mon C, you're my girl."

Carmen looked at Janet. "We'll talk about the details later." Then, she looked at me, "Baby Girl, can you drop me home?"

"I can!" Janet said enthusiastically.

Carmen sucked her teeth. "I don't want you to slut. Your passenger seat is full of cum stains."

Janet got quiet, then grabbed her purse.

Now, I *really* didn't feel like driving Carmen to her house, but you know, she had just hooked me up with the promotion and all.

"Yeah. It's nothing." I told her.

"A-ight, cool," she said. Then she took the money that Nadia had left on the table. "I'm gonna go and pay the bill, okay."

Now, the way they do it in Friendly's is the waitress gives you the receipt and then you take it up to the counter and pay it. Now, I saw Carmen walk towards the counter, but I didn't see her stop at all. She walked straight out of the door. It was so busy, that they didn't even notice. I paid my portion of the bill just to be on the safe side. I even left the waitress a tip. I wasn't gonna play her like that.

When I walked out of the restaurant, I found Carmen standing by my car smoking a cigarette.

"I knew that you wouldn't go for that shit," she said taking a few more quick pulls from her cigarette and then flicking it to the ground.

I unlocked the car doors. "What are you talking about?" We both got into the car and I started it up.

"The whole shit with me wanting one of y'all to fuck Robert," she told me.

"So, you *don't* want Janet to fuck Robert?" I asked her.

"Nah, yeah I do. I know that he's not going to go for it though. You know," she said.

"He would want to fuck someone like you. He knows about all the shit that Janet has done. He likes nice girls. You know."

"Yeah," I said thinking to myself, *well what the fuck is he doing with your trashy ass then?*

"I'm glad that you said no though," she told me. "It's so cool to be around someone that's not out of their minds around here. "It's hard tryna keep this shit together by myself."

I switched the track on the CD, and Pharell's, "Frontin'" began."I feel you."

Before I knew it, we were pulling into Carmen's apartment complex. "My car still ain't here." She sucked her teeth. "They get on my last nerve with this shit!"

She wrestled her keys out of her bag and got out of the car, closing the door behind her. "Thanks for bringing me home. I'll see you later on at the store okay."

"Okay," I said as I backed out of the parking spot and made my way back home so that I could catch a few more hours of sleep before I had to go into work at 3.

# chapter twenty-three

On the way home, everything that we discussed at the "meeting" was on my mind. I could not believe it. I could not believe this store. Yeah, we *did* discuss some things that had to do with the store, but most of it was bullshit. It was as if Carmen had herself fooled, and she *actually* believed that she was doing work. I wasn't gonna concern myself with it. Whatever they did outside of DIVAS was not my business. I had my own shit to worry about.

When I got back home, it was about 11 o'clock. I figured that if I slept until two o'clock, I would be good for the day into the night. I turned on the television and I saw that channel 9 was running an *A Different World* marathon. I knew that I wasn't gonna get any sleep now. *A Different World* was my shit! I ran downstairs to the family room to see if I could find a tape to record over. I found one with some old episodes of *Columbo* on it. My pops wouldn't miss it. I got some chips, some Kool-Aid and I ran back upstairs to watch as much of the marathon as I could before I went to work. I would just tape the rest of it.

"How was the meeting Jaliyah?" my mother asked me as she passed my room and headed into hers.

"Ma, I don't even wanna talk about it? I ain't never met stranger people in my whole life!" I laughed. "If you knew the things that went on up in that place you would want me to quit!"

"Well, stick it out and mind your business. You may like it," she told me.

"No ma, I like it. It's cool." I took a sip of my Kool-Aid. "Oh, I'm a manager now!" I yelled to her as she entered her room.

She peeked back into my room. "What? How did you pull that off so quickly?"

"Well, the other day, Carmen fired this girl and she was the head cashier. So, Carmen chose me to replace her." I laughed.

"See, and there you were talking about the woman and she done made you management already." She threw a piece of paper at me. *"And clean this room!* You ain't got to be to work until what time, 3 o'clock? Girl, you better at least vacuum or something!"

"Okay ma," I said knowing that I wasn't going to do anything.

Yeah, my moms was cool and everything, but I wasn't about to tell her about *everything* that was going on in that store. Not yet anyway. She would have flipped if I had told her about the proposition that Carmen had made us along with *all* of the drama at the club the other night.

I got up off my bed and went to look in my closet for something to wear. It was going to be extra nice out, so I chose a nice cream-colored pantsuit. I was management now, so I had to look the part.

"Nicky!" I called to my little sister, "how does this look?"

"You look like a butthead," she said.

That was her way of saying that it looked nice. I hung my outfit on the outside of my closet door and I went back to watching my show. I could not believe that I was going to get my raise already. I didn't know how much of a raise it would be, but I knew that it would be more than the $8.00 an hour that I had started at.

I was so into the marathon, that I hadn't even noticed the time. When I had picked out my outfit and everything, it was nearing twelve o'clock. Now, it was almost *2:30*, and I still wasn't dressed yet.

I threw in the tape that I had stolen from downstairs to finish taping the marathon, and I ran into the bathroom to shower. I got out, dried off, got dressed and ran out of the door.

I got there at exactly three o'clock. Of course the music was blasting out of the speakers, spilling out into the mall when I walked in the door. This time Jay-Z's "Encore" was playing. I could tell that it was going to be hard for me to contain myself from dancing like I was at the club every now and then. None of that mattered at that moment. I had to get myself trained for my new position *and* still learn my old position at the same time.

Janet came up to me as soon as I came in and said, "Carmen wants you to start on the training manual. Whenever you finish a chapter, I need you to take the test at the end and sign off on this sheet. Tomorrow, Tina, the co-manager is going to give you a key quiz so you can get your key to open and close."

I smiled at her. "Well, *hello* to you too!"

She laughed. "It's been so busy in here and I'm so tired. I can't wait until you are trained completely so you can start helping me out around here because Jacqueline ain't good for shit."

She looked around. "I'm gonna go in the bathroom and sneak a cigarette before Nadia comes back from her break. Jacqueline told me that Nadia told her that she was gonna complain to the District Manager about us and shit if we didn't stop smoking in the bathroom."

I looked around. "Well, hurry up."

"Yeah, I know right." She ran to get her purse. I'll be back."

Janet handed me the manual and the sign-off sheet and ran to the back get her smoke on.

*"Oh, y'all, she ain't up in here today! Just them other lame bitches and that new one! Yeah, come on! Hurry up!"*

I turned around to see Jameka and his entourage coming into the store yet again. This time he wore a bootleg Burberry bikini top, a pair of white, pleather pants and some pink slip-in shoes that I had spotted in the Payless window earlier in the week.

He looked me up and down. "You think you cute huh— Miss Bitch? What chu' lookin' at?"

I rolled my eyes and began to approach him. "Yeah well if you see a bitch, then slap a bitch! Bitch!"

"What!" he yelled. "No this bitch didn't. No, this John Travolta, Saturday Night Fever, suit-wearing heifer didn't!"

"Yes, I did!" I yelled back, sick of his shit. "And who *you* callin' heifer with your nasty, ashy corned and crusty big-ass, size 14 feet, hooker!"

"Ohhhh girl! This bitch done gone and said it now!" Jameka began to charge towards me, so I threw the handbook on the floor and my hands up in the air and got ready to whip his ass.

His friends held him back. "Jameka, she ain't even worth it! You gon' mess up your probation for this bitch?"

Just then, Nadia came back from her break and went straight into the backroom. About a half-second later she came out and said, "I just called security so y'all better leave!"

"Jameka, you better read that bitch!" one of the girls in his entourage said as she snapped her finger in Nadia's direction.

"Fuck you, you Kung Fu, Sum Dum Goy Bi-yotch! You betta chop-chop your holy-ass up outta my face like Bruce Leroy! I *know* that I can whip *your* weak-ass for sure bitch!" Jameka hollered referring to Nadia's Asian and Black heritage.

He continued. "You think you all that? Who you think you

are, Lucy Liu? You ain't cute! You ain't hardly cute! You look very stank! Very stank and very, very ugly!"

He then put on the nastiest, *fake* British accent I have *ever* heard in my life and yelled loudly, *"Scratch your minge and sniff your fingers —FISHHHHH!"*

Jameka kept talking his shit until the security guards came. When he saw them his voice automatically lowered to an angelic whisper and he said, "They stay harassin' me up in this store. I have money to spend in here. I show them the *utmost* respect. But what do they do? These young ladies show me *no* respect. I mean, all I want to do is shop just like everyone else. They say I steal. They—"

He was so calm. You wouldn't have thought it was the same fool that had just walked up in there poppin' mess a few minutes before. *Well*, that was until one of the security guards said, "Cut the bullshit James!"

Oh, now that was it! He spazzed out for real. "Don't be fuckin' callin' me James! My name is Jameka muthafucka! *You* should know the shit because I have had *you* callin' it out plenty of times! Don't front!"

With that final outburst, the security officer grabbed him up, and ushered his whole crew out of DIVAS.

Jameka and his entourage were gone—yet again.

"What just happened?" Janet said catching the tail end of everything that had just went down.

Nadia rolled her eyes. "While you were in the bathroom *smoking*, we almost got hit again by Jameka and his crew. He was about to fight Jaliyah when I came in from my break!"

"First off, I was not smoking I was taking a shit! Secondly, go hang up those ten boxes of clothes until it's time for you to leave, and third, watch your tone when you're talking to me. I don't go to high school with you sweetie."

Janet looked at me. "Oh, let me set you up in the backroom. The television and the videos are all set up."

We walked to the back and she cleared off Carmen's desk. "You can sit here. There are your videos. If you need me, call me."

She walked out and shut the door behind her.

*Damn,* I thought. I hated orientations. They didn't do anything else by the book, so I wondered why they were making me do *this* nonsense. The videos didn't have any sort of labels on them telling me which order they should be watched in, so I figured that I would watch them first and then read the book afterwards.

I put in the first video and the DIVAS logo appeared on the screen in bright, rainbow letters. The videos consisted of a bunch of role-playing and then I had to mark off what I would do in each scenario, on my answer sheet. It was *so* boring. I couldn't stomach another video right after that one, so I decided to read the manual a little.

It dealt with the basic dos and don'ts of the retail industry. It explained that as a manager, I had access to confidential personnel files and such and such. I read about six of the twelve chapters that I had to read and I skimmed through the other six. The answers were in the back of the book.

It was time to watch the next video on customer service. I put the tape in expecting to be welcomed by the DIVAS logo in rainbow letters, but to my surprise, I was welcomed by Carmen servicing someone, who was *not* the customer. Shockingly, it wasn't Janet, Jacqueline, Chino or Robert either. I couldn't really see *who* it was. That was until I fixed the tracking on the VCR.

The girl getting ate out and finger popped was Sabrina from the Gold and Go counter out in the mall.

"What the fuck?" I asked myself. "Is Carmen fucking *every-body* in this damn store? Betta yet, in the damn mall?"

I shook my head in disbelief. "This bitch really *is* off the hook."

# chapter twenty-four

I didn't know *what* to think about the whole situation. It wasn't my business. I didn't know how long ago this happened. I couldn't say much. I turned the video off and I put it back with the stack of videos in the drawer next to me. I wasn't going to say anything to anyone about what I had seen. I didn't want to drudge up anything that was meant to be forgotten or kept on lock. I was not one for putting people's business on front street.

About an hour passed, and I finished answering all of the questions and filling out the paper work necessary for the promotion. It was now about 6PM, and the store didn't close until 9:30. I put all of my papers in order and I got ready to leave the back-room when Carmen came in.

"Jaliyah baby, go and take your lunch. When you get back, we'll discuss your pay rate and all of that. I put in a good word for you with the District Manager, so she's agreed to be flexible with the pay scale." She smiled and then picked up the phone and began dialing someone. "Here are your register over-ride keys. I'll see you in forty-five."

"Okay thanks," I said.

I went and got my bag from the locked cabinet under the register. I had my own key to unlock it now, and I was a little gassed, I can't lie. I could not seem to shake what I had seen on the videotape. Maybe they had some sort of relationship together. Maybe she accidentally took the tape from home and it somehow was mixed in with the training videos. Maybe someone planted it there on purpose.

Either way, the shit had gone down and it did not concern me. I was hungry. I walked around the mall for what seemed like forever, but when I looked down at my Virgin Mobile cell phone, only ten minutes had passed.

"Damn, I got thirty-five minutes to go," I said to myself.

I ended up in a small pizza shop called Papa Giorgio's. I didn't want anything heavy, so I ordered a small, Caesar salad with a medium fruit punch and extra croutons and dressing. I sat down at an empty table and waited for my food. When it arrived, they had put grilled chicken in it. I didn't complain though. It costs 3 bucks extra for the chicken and *I* had already paid. It was their bad.

I dug into my salad and mid-bite, I heard a dude say, "Can I have some?"

I didn't even turn around. I just said, *"no"*, rudely, rolled my eyes, and continued eating my food.

"Please?" he asked again.

Agitated, I said, "Look nigga I said—" I stopped mid-sentence. It was Elliot from the poetry spot. He was looking fine as ever. He had on a red and black Bulls throwback jersey, a red and black Bulls fitted cap with a pair of blue jeans, and a pair of red and black 16s.

He laughed. "Look at you ready to fight a nigga and what not." He imitated me, *"Look nigga I told you I said no!"*

"Shut up!" I said. "My day has been kinda hectic."

"I ain't know that you worked up in here," he said.

"Yeah, in DIVAS."

"Oh, you work up in there. I heard about how they get down in there. My niggas go in there like twice a week tryna holla at that Jacqueline chick. She be deadin' em' though." He laughed.

"What chu' doin' up in here?" I asked him.

"Ain't shit. Shoppin'. I need some new gear for this last month of summer school, you know." He held up his many bags that I had failed to notice.

"Damn. Since when niggas been dressin' to impress in college and shit? What happened to the fuckin' white tee and some Uptowns?" I asked him.

"Well, I'm still in high school right now, so you know how that goes. It's a fashion show all the time." He smiled.

I was shocked. "Pa, you still in high school? Damn yo, I thought that you were like the same age as me." I took another bite of my salad. "Well, what were you doin' in the Velvet Lounge?"

"Oh, the night you came was teen night and anyone fourteen and up could get up in there." He licked his lips.

I figured that I should ask his age since everything thing else was out in the open. "Well, Elliot, how old *are* you?"

He laughed. "I'm 17, but I'll be 18 on October 22."

*I can't believe this shit. They are either too old or too young,* I thought to myself.

I laughed. "So where do you go to school?"

He smiled. "I go to Poughkeepsie High School."

"Ha, ha, ha…You must know my little sister then because she goes there too and she's the same age as you!" I laughed.

"Who's your sister?" he asked, his mouth wide open.

"Nicole Whitfield," I drank some of my juice and smirked at him.

"Ohh shit!" he yelled, "Nicky is your sister!"

"Yup!" I answered.

He sat down at my table. "So hook me up with her! What's good?"

I rolled my eyes playfully. "Boy please! You was just tryna get with me and now you tryna kick it to my baby sis? If you don't take your young, Lil' Fizz looking behind up on away from this table!" I laughed.

"Oh okay, okay. I see how you do." He got up and looked at me with a sexy stare. Then he licked his lips. "Y'all are both fine as shit tho!"

I smiled. "That's just how we do. Ain't no other way!"

He laughed. "I can't believe that Nicky is your little sister. Wow!"

He looked in the direction of his friends and he saw that they were half way down the mall. "I gotta go and catch up wit' my niggas, but for real Jaliyah. I'm a good dude. Could you at least put in a good word for me with Nicky?" he asked.

I finished off my salad. "First, I gotta see what she thinks of you." I wiped my mouth. "I got your number so I'll call you this weekend and I'll let you know. Depending on her answer, I guess you can take it from there." I smiled. "Cool?"

"Yeah," he cheesed crazy, "real cool!" He turned to leave, but then he turned back around and looked at me again. "I can't believe I didn't know that. Y'all look just alike. Damn."

Then he left with his friends.

I looked down at my cell. My forty-five minutes was almost up. I cleaned up the area where I had eaten, ran to the CVS to buy some gum and then I headed back to the store.

# chapter twenty-five

"Okay, Baby Girl, we're going to start you at $12.75 an hour. Now Jaliyah, you *cannot* tell *anyone* how much you're making. Not Janet, not Jacqueline, not anybody. The only way that they'll find out is if you tell them or they sneak and look into your personal file." Carmen spoke quietly in the backroom with me. "Which they will probably do anyway."

"For real Carmen, $12.75? That's great!" I smiled.

"Since I didn't send off your paperwork yet, the hours that you've already worked will be paid to you at the $12.75 rate instead of the $8.00 rate. Okay." she whispered again.

"Cool. Thank you so much Carmen!" I hugged her. "I really appreciate all that you've been doing for me."

"It's nothing Jaliyah. You're a good person. I saw that when I hired you. Good people deserve good things."

She took me by the hand. "Come on up front, and I'll explain everything to you and walk you through the store. You're here til close so that's good. We have time."

We left the backroom and went out onto the sales floor. The store was packed. The fitting-rooms were constantly being occupied. The registers racked up the sales and the music pumped throughout the night.

As B2Ks "Bump, Bump, Bump" boomed in the background, Carmen explained the different zones that the store was split up into. She showed me what each key did and told me what I was in charge of.

Now that I was management, I had the authority to write people up, make up schedules, open and close the store *and* deal with *all* of the bullshit that the customers had to offer. And trust me, there was a lot of it. In the next few months that followed, I would have about forty more run-ins with *Jameka,* and countless episodes of people stealing. People *love* to steal.

Carmen finished explaining the daily operations of DIVAS, and at the end of the night, she had Jacqueline show me how to count down the register and secure the nightly deposit. We had pulled in a little over seven-thousand dollars and it *all* had to be counted by hand. We didn't have one of those fancy money counters. Nah, we had to do it straight old-school style. I was ready to leave once the money was counted and the store was straightened, but to my surprise, Carmen turned the music *back* on and blasted Teena Marie's, "Square Biz".

"It's Square Biz time—and y'all know what *that* means!" she yelled loudly, "It's time to try on clothes!"

All of the girls began jumping up and down in the air and squealing excitedly. They went to the racks and began picking different styles of dresses and jeans in their sizes. Then they opened up the fitting-rooms and began trying on their outfits.

All I could hear were a bunch of, "That looks cute on you, girl!", "That is fierce!" and, "Oohh, maybe that is not your style!" coming from the back. I stood by the register, with my bags in hand because I was ready to go.

"Baby Girl!" Carmen yelled. "Try something on!"

I made a face. "No, I don't want to," I said, as I shook my head no.

"Girl come on, you got that cute little shape and I know that you have been eyeing some shit up in here." She went to the rack, and pulled a short, tight fitting dark-blue and white, tie-dyed dress. She held it up to my body. "This looks like it's about your size. Try it on!"

I took the dress from her and looked at it. "Well it *is* cute." I smiled at her, and then ran towards the fitting-rooms. "Okay, I'll try it on!"

I went into the fitting-room, put on the dress, and looked in the mirror. It was really nice. It *was* a little short, but overall, it looked good. I thought to myself that the shoes out there on the rack would be *perfect* with this outfit. Just then, two shoes flew over the fitting-room door. One almost hit me on top of my head, and the other one landed in front of me, just missing my toes. I looked at them.

"Wow," I said to myself. "These are the shoes I was just thinking about!" I checked the size, "I wear a size 8!"

"Those are an 8 and a 1/2 because they run kind of small!" Jacqueline shouted from outside of the door.

Suddenly, I heard Carmen yell, "Get out here girl! Let us see!"

"Yeah, bring your sexy ass out here!" I heard Janet yell.

"Fine!" I yelled from inside the room. "I'm coming out!"

I slid my feet into the shoes, which fit perfectly, and I opened the door and walked out.

"Oh, go head girl!" Carmen shouted.

I smiled and did my *signature* runway walk as Bobby Brown's "My Prerogative" began.

"Ouch!" Janet shouted. "You look hot!"

*"Yes you do,"* an unfamiliar, masculine voice co-signed.

"Thank you," I said as I turned to see who had said it.

When I turned around, there was a tall, extremely handsome

white dude who looked to be my age standing inside of the store with Robert and Chino.

He stood about six-feet tall and had a chiseled jawline and high cheekbones that accentuated his handsome features. He had a low-cut caesar, with a perfect edge-up, and piercing, gray eyes that complemented his sexy smile. He had a scruffy, dirty blonde goatee/mustache combo, a diamond stud in each ear, and a gold hoop in his left nostril.

His build appeared to be athletic, lean and well-toned. He wore a pair of loose-fitting jeans and a baggy, yet slightly-fitted white tee. On his feet, a pair of loosely laced, wheat, nubuck, Timbs. His yellow-gold Jesus piece sparkled under the store lights.

He smiled and said, "If you don't buy it, I'll buy it for you."

I looked at him unimpressed, with an attitude and said, *"Who are you?"*

He smiled and said in a typical *white-boy-trying-to-be-hood* accent, "I'm a friend of a friend sweetheart." It was very MC Serch-ish with a hint of Michael Rapaport in *Zebrahead* and a twist of Marky Mark when he used to roll wit' the Funky Bunch —maybe some Eminem too.

I rolled my eyes. "Well, I ain't been working up in here long enough to have many friends, so you can't be a friend of a friend of mine, feel me."

Chino and Robert laughed uncontrollably. "Oh, my nigga, she played you!"

I walked into the fitting-room and changed back into my clothes. Of course, he was still there when I came out. I gathered my things and got ready to leave. He slowly walked over to me. "I'll walk you out shortie. I'm leaving right now too."

I looked up at him. "Look, um—," I said not knowing his name.

"Dominic," he said.

"Dominic." I said finishing my thought. "I don't even know you. You see me trying on a dress, you compliment me and I'm supposed to let you walk me out. I don't think so boo."

"You forgot that I offered to buy it," he said.

*"Whatever,"* I said as I headed towards the door.

"Come on Jaliyah, let me walk you out," he said smiling.

I looked at him surprised that he knew my name.

"Oh see, you didn't think that I knew your name. I know your name. I know more about you than you think," he said.

I exhaled deeply. "Well, do you know that my mouth is filthy, my attitude sucks and my patience is thin?

"I have a million nieces and nephews so my patience is never-ending," he smiled as he reached over and gently removed my cell phone from my hand.

"What are you doing?" I asked irritated as shit.

"Here, I'll save my name and number in your phone. *You wanna do something,* give me a call."

Right off, I knew I did *not* like this dude. He was too cocky and he was tryna be too smooth in front of everyone. I was tired of tryna let him know that I wasn't interested, and I was ready to go home, so I just said, "Okay," and dipped.

# chapter twenty-six

When I got home, I was exhausted. I felt like I had worked a hard-ass day, because I had. I ran a hot bubble bath and played a slow jams CD that I had made back in the twelfth grade with all of my favorite old school love songs. Keith Sweat's "I'll Give All My Love To You" set the mood as I lit some candles, slid down into the tub, and zoned out until the water got cool. I decided to wash up quickly before I fell asleep in there.

I got out and dried myself off. I put on a tee shirt and a pair of boxers. I hopped in my bed and looked at the clock. *10:43PM.* My phone rang. I looked at the display to see who it was.

*Dominic M.* showed up.

*Dominic M.* I thought, *who—*

*Damn it*, I thought. *It was the asshole from DIVAS.*

My first thought was not to answer. But my second thought was to answer and curse his simple ass out for being sneaky. So I went with option 2.

"*Hello*," I said with major attitude.

"*Jaliyah,*" he spoke smoothly, "what's goin' on sweetheart?"

I sucked my teeth before answering. "What's goin' on is that I told you that I ain't wanna talk to you. How did you get my number anyway? I thought that you said that you were gonna give me your number and wait for me to call your ass?"

He laughed. "Yeah, that was my intention, but I realized that I had my cell phone in the car, so I dialed my number from your phone *before* I programmed my number into it."

"My number is private," I said annoyed.

"Yeah, well I figured that, so I dialed *82 to unblock it beforehand. Look at your recent calls when you get a minute. You'll see it there."

I was pissed. "*Real fucking clever*," I said as I shuffled uneasily underneath the covers. "I hate when people acquire things of mine under false pretenses."

"I'm sorry, I'm sorry, I'm sorry," he apologized. "I just thought that you were so goddamn beautiful when I saw you that I *had* to talk to you on the phone and get to know you a little better."

I yawned deeply. "Well tonight ain't the night fool. I am tired. I've been working all day, and all I am thinking about is hitting these pillows, ya heard. So I'm about to get off this phone before I get nasty and say something rude."

He laughed. "I think that you are half past nasty and a quarter past rude sweetheart. But okay, I can respect that," he said. "I can respect it as long as you promise to call me tomorrow and we can talk for a little while then."

"Look, I don't make promises that I have no intention of keeping," I told him half-heartedly.

"Why are you so mean?" he asked. "You're causing frost and icicles to form on the end of my receiver as we speak."

"Look, I'm not mean. I just don't like when people don't listen to me. If this is how you're starting out already, I can't see no good coming from anything that could *ever* come of me and you." I yawned again. This time quietly so he couldn't hear it.

"I understand Miss Jaliyah," he said, his voice now devoid of all cockiness. He sounded a little more genuine.

He was attractive. But I didn't know anything about him. I didn't want to deal with someone who chilled with Chino and Robert. That *probably* meant that he was mixed up in all of the bullshit at the store in some way, shape or form. It probably also meant that he had fucked a few of the girls at DIVAS as well. I decided to ask him a few questions before I hung up with him just to see where his head was.

"*So,*" I started out, "how do you know Chino and Robert? Those are your friends?"

He laughed. "No, they are kind of friends of a friend. I get weed from them sometimes. They saw me in the Friday's restaurant downstairs and I asked them if they were holding or whatever. Robert said that his girl had some on her that he could sell me, so that's how I ended up there."

"So you smoke then," I said.

"Just weed every now and then. I use to smoke cigarettes, but them shits will kill you, you know."

"I wouldn't know. I don't smoke either."

"Oh, word. That's good then." He said. Girls shouldn't do those types of things. They should leave shit like that to the fellas. You know. Well, at least *my* girl shouldn't. Well, not without *me,* anyways."

He paused briefly. "Is smoking a problem?"

Not caring either way I said, "If you can function and you don't lay up and not do shit, then it's cool with me. I don't really care either way. As long as you ain't sniffing coke and smoking crack, and I don't have to give you any money for it, do you by all means."

"Okay, so what *do* you do?" he asked me. "You drink?"

"I'm a party chick, but I'm not a *party* chick. Get it?" I said to him. "I'd much rather be at home under a blanket watching an old movie. I am very simple when it comes to things like that."

"Oh, so you're a homebody. I like that," he said. "I don't do the party scene anymore.

"Oh, okay. You live by yourself?" I asked him becoming a little more interested in him.

"Yeah, I own a little two-bedroom townhouse in Chelsea over by Wappingers Falls. It's good enough for me."

"Well, what do you do?" I asked.

He laughed. "You know, for someone who was ready to hang up on me like five minutes ago, you sure have changed ya tune!"

"Shut up!" I laughed. "What do you do?"

"My family owns a construction company so I do that full-time, and I am a part-time freelance writer."

"You write," I asked him. "Like what about?"

"I'm really interested in politics and the state of our country so I write about that type of stuff, you know."

"Wow, I expected you to say that you freelance for like *King Magazine* or *XXL* or something like that." I told him feeling bad for pre-judging.

"Well, you can't always judge a book by its cover now can you?" he said. "Now you know a little about me, but what do I know about you?" he asked me.

Being honest, I told him, "Look Dominic, you are the third guy in three days that I have talked on the phone with, gotten to know and had shit not work out for one reason or another."

I laughed. "I just *can't* go there with you right now. Tomorrow though, I'm working until about seven, and I will *definitely* give you a call once I get home. Okay."

"That's fair enough," he said. "So until then."

I laughed. Yes, I'll talk to you tomorrow. Goodnight Dominic."

He laughed. "Goodnight sweetheart."

Then we hung up.

Before I fell asleep, I thought about the day's events. I thought about the videotape of Sabrina and Carmen. I wondered if Jameka would bring his broke-down ass in and steal from us tomorrow. I thought about Dominic, the construction working, weed smoking white boy from Chelsea. I had never *seriously* dated a white boy. I had gone out on a few dates with a couple of them, but they always turned out to be Looney Tunes. Whatever. Me and Dominic needed to learn more about each other.

I closed my eyes to take that trip to Dreamland and *guess what*? Yeah, you guessed right, the phone rang. This time it wasn't another dude, *thank the Lord*. Nah, this time it was my girl Alicia callin' me to let me know what was up with her and Trey.

Now, I really didn't give a shit because I was tired, but she just needed someone to talk to and I knew how that could be.

# chapter twenty-seven

"Hey girl, what's goin' on ma?" I said trying to sound as awake as possible as I sat up in my bed and cut on the lamp on my nightstand.

Alicia sighed deeply. "Nothin'."

I sucked my teeth and let out an irritated groan. "What did that muthafucka do now?"

She immediately broke down in tears.

"Jaliyah, do you know how many bitches that Trey has fucked with?"

"Yeah, that's why I ain't never fucked wit' him," I said with a loud yawn. "Yo, Alicia, what happened between y'all two cause I gotta take my black behind to sleep soon or else I'm gon' be looking a hot-ass mess come tomorrow?"

She blew her nose loudly into the phone and regained her composure. Then she began to speak. "You know how Trey tells me everything and he feels that he can talk to me like I'm his nigga and what not."

I got up out of my bed and started pacing the floor in an attempt to keep focused and not fall asleep. "Yeah, I know that y'all are real cool."

She sniffled. "Yeah, well now that we're talking, he shouldn't be telling me the shit that he used to tell me when we were just friends. Don't you know that every time we walk down the street or we're riding somewhere he *always* sees a chick that has given him head or he's fucked, or whatever else!" She blew her nose again. "I can't take this shit J! I'm about to knock his ass the fuck out!"

"Well, *don't* do that because that nigga's crazy, and there is no guarantee that he *won't* pop yo' ass right back!" I looked at the clock. It was a little after 12:30 in the morning. I had to get her off the line quick.

"Look Alicia, just hang in there. You knew how Trey was before you started talking to him. Yeah, that nigga has fucked a lot of girls. So what. Many niggas have fucked a lot of girls. Yeah, it's fucked up, but that's the way the shit is. You just gotta decide if you want to deal with it or not. Feel me?"

She took a deep breath. "Yeah, I feel you. But J, I just don't know. Yo, I like him so much. Nah, fuck like, I love that nigga. I've been knowin' him forever."

Now her saying *that* woke me up. "*What?* You love *that* nigga? You *in love* or you love him like—because he's your peoples?"

"Like, I'm in love with him." She paused briefly. "J, I think about him all the time. I catch myself daydreaming about him when I'm supposed to be focusing on other things. It's crazy."

I thought about what she had just said.

*"You got it, you got it bad!"* I sang jokingly before sucking my teeth. "Damn, for Trey? I can't believe that you even gave that nigga some pussy."

I went downstairs to the kitchen to get something to drink. "Was he good? Like was he *big*?"

Alicia started laughing. "Yeah, surprisingly, he was. Like all that shit that he used to talk about just getting his nut off and all of that shit," she paused for a bit, "yeah that shit was all true. It took a while for me to learn him girl!" She was beginning to sound more upbeat now. Good, I could get her off the line and take my ass to sleep.

But, there was one more thing I had to ask her. This was something that I had to know. *"Did he eat your pussy, girl?* Cause you know that he said that he would *never* do that shit. Remember Trey always said, '*Eat to live, don't eat to beat!'*"

Now do you see what I mean? Trey was a silly-ass nigga. I mean, he looked good as shit. But he just *wasn't* the boyfriend type. I admired Alicia for takin' that step with him. She was like a little lab monkey. She was *actually* taking it there.

"Girl, he gives this pussy a spit shine like I ain't never had before!" She laughed. "You can see your reflection in this pussy after he's done!"

"Alright now!" I had to hold in my laughter because everyone was asleep. "I hear that!"

I got back into bed. "Well, let me just tell *you* that I met this new dude who seems like he could be really cool tonight at work."

I heard her toilet flush. "What happened to the other dude?"

"Long story that I don't feel like getting into right now," I told her.

"Oh, okay," she said.

"Were you just peeing?" I asked her.

"Nah, I was taking a shit, but it was a quiet one," she answered.

"Oh, okay," I said as my track of thought was interrupted by a wave of sleepiness.

"Girl, I'll tell you about it tomorrow. I'm tired."

"Okay then," she said. "Love you mama."

"Love you too Alicia."

We hung up and I prepared to go to sleep, but Trey called as soon as I pulled the covers up to my neck. The conversation was short, and it went like this.

"Yo J, what up? I know that Alicia called you on some bull-shit. Yo, she think that I'm gonna play her and shit just because I fucked around with madd girls and this and that."

He sighed. "That's why I ain't want to catch feelings for no chick. I ain't want a girl because this is the type of shit that you have to deal with!"

I finally got a chance to get a word in. "Well, what did you tell her? Nah, first off, what did she ask?"

He laughed. "She asked me how many girls that I had fucked. Then she asked me how many girls that I had gotten head from or whatever."

"So what did you tell her?" I asked him.

He laughed. *"The truth."* He paused for a minute. "Hold up, I'm lightin' a bogey."

"Nigga, since when you started smokin' bogeys?" I asked him curious as hell.

"Since I stopped smokin' weed when they started piss testing us at my job!" He laughed and took a quick pull from his cigarette.

"You know the only time black niggas smoke cigarettes is when we in jail or when we quit smokin' weed. We just don't fuck with the cigarettes right away and shit."

"Yeah, true that. True that." Then I remembered that he hadn't told me what he had told Alicia yet. "Nigga, what's the truth?" I asked him.

"Oh, yeah. I told her that I had fucked maybe 70 to 80 chicks so far and that I had gotten so much head in my lifetime that I couldn't even remember."

He took another pull from his cigarette. *"What the fuck?* I care about her. That's why I told her."

Now, he had a point, but he could have sugar coated that shit just a little bit. I knew about a lot of the girls that Trey had gotten down and dirty with, but it never bothered me because I wasn't tryna start no relationship with him. I was ready to go to bed, so all I could tell him was, "Look, I respect the fact that you care about her and all of that, but the first rule in the early stages of a relationship is that you *never* tell the whole story. Pa, sometimes, you have to lie a little. Feel me?"

"Yeah, I feel you. But she needs to stop trippin', for real. I ain't on that shit no more. I gave up all the titties J! *All* of the titties and *all* of the ass, for her *little* titties and her *little* ass! And ya girl's a skinny broad, B! That gotta be worth somethin'!"

He laughed. "You know how much I like doin' me. I like doin' me as much as you like doin' you!"

I laughed. "Yeah, I like doin' me but the only difference is, me doin' me, doesn't mean that I have to do *everyone* else too."

I laughed. "Trey, you really have been with a lot of girls. Damn, I'm surprised that you ain't caught nothin' yet. I'm surprised that your dick ain't fall off with some of the bitches that you've fucked around wit'."

"Never that. I wrap my shit up every time. I put the jimmy on extra tight like Caine in *Menace II Society* my doogie! Yo, I ain't watch BET all them years and not learn nothin'! I used to dance my ass off to "Let's Talk About Sex" back in the day *and* the "Aids" remix! Fuck outta here with that! Plus, I get tested like twice a month even though I wrap my shit up every time."

He laughed. "Nah, I need my shit. I love life. I love me. I love my dick. I ain't tryna do some shit to make it fall off! How would I fuck!?"

"Well at least you're all set in that area. That's good. But um, on the real, you and Alicia need to work this thing out. Tell her not to ask questions that she doesn't really wanna know the answers to because you're going to always keep it real!"

I rolled my eyes. "She knows how truthful you are. That shit actually boggles my mind how truthful you are for a man."

"Nothin' but the truth ma. Nothin' but the truth." He exhaled deeply.

"Well, let me call her ass up and see what the fuck she's talkin' about now because I *know* that she called you right before I did. Right?" he asked.

"Yeah, you right. But, y'all just need to talk. Communicate a lil' bit. Y'all will be a-ight." I yawned. "But pa, I got to get to bed. I got work in the morning and shit."

"Oh, with them freaky hoes? The baby swallower and all of them? Well, don't be chillin' wit them bitches too hard. They nasty as shit."

"Bye Trey," I said.

"And you best not tell Shawn that I told Alicia about Lena and shit.

"Bye Trey!" I yelled this time.

"A-ight nigga, Bye!"

part five
# tuesday

# chapter twenty-eight

The next morning I woke up with Dominic on my mind. I couldn't get over how wrong I had been about him so far. I couldn't get *too* ahead of myself too soon though. All I could think about was how good he looked when I first met him. He was a fuckin' dime. Maybe after a few more phone conversations we could set something up. I still really didn't know that much about him. I would call him later on that night when I got home from work. Maybe at like 10:30 or 11:00 since I knew that he had to go to work in the morning.

I got up, got dressed and headed out the door. The drive to work was always cool because it gave me time to think about what I had to do for that day. I was opening with the new co-manager Tina, and I had no idea of what to expect. Maybe she would be crazy just like the rest of them up in the store. Maybe she would be the one who kept everyone in line. I really had no idea of what to expect. I made sure to be there on time though. I wanted to make a good impression on her.

I pulled into the mall parking lot and took a minute to apply my lip-gloss. I was so busy thinking about that morning that I had forgotten all about my face. All the girls at DIVAS wore tons of makeup. Even the young ones. They thought that they were so grown. I just stuck with my lip-gloss and clear mascara.

I got to the store and the lights and everything had already been turned. I had to take a minute and look at the time to make sure that *I* wasn't late. Nah, actually, I was a little early. Fifteen minutes early to be exact. I went to lift the gate up to get in, but it was locked.

"Hello," I yelled. "Can someone come and unlock the front gate?" There was no answer. I took out my cell phone and called the store.

"*DIVAS*, Tina speaking," a woman with a bright, southern accent said on the other end of the phone.

"Hi, this is Jaliyah. I'm opening with you this morning. I'm outside of the gate." I said in a voice as vibrant as hers.

"Oh, I'm sorry. I'm coming to open it right now." She hung up.

The back door opened and a young, slim-thick, light-skinned black woman came out of the backroom and walked down the middle aisle to unlock the gate. She wore an aqua pants suit, with tan and rhinestone, Enzo Angiolini, strappy sandals. She had big brown eyes like Mya's, and her hair, which was about five inches past her shoulders, was light-brown with chunky-blonde high-lights throughout.

Her earrings were large, silver hoops. Her nails were French manicured, and her middle fingers were adorned with rings that resembled diamond and platinum wedding bands. Around her neck, she wore a necklace similar to the one Ashanti often wears —a platinum chain with a diamond-encrusted heart pendant hanging just above her navel. I noticed her navel was pierced, because the tight-fitting shirt she wore with her suit showed it clearly.

"Hi, Jaliyah I'm Tina the new co-manager here," she said as she opened up the gate and lifted it.

"I'll help you girl," I said lifting the gate up the rest of the way and closing it back.

"Well, how old are you Ms. Jaliyah?" she asked me as she bent down and locked the gate back.

"I just turned 21-years-old," I told her.

"Oh, well, I'm 31-years-old and I was the manager at a DIVAS in North Carolina. It wasn't anything like this one though. This one is a whole lot larger. I peeked in last Saturday night and it was a madhouse in here. I don't know if I'm prepared for this. But, I'ma try."

She smiled at me. "We just have to work together as a team. You know. It's Carmen, me, Taylor, Janet, Jacqueline, and now you."

She smiled again and then she asked, "Why are we standing here talking? Girl, we got work to do before the store opens."

I liked her style already.

"What do we have to do?" I asked.

"Well, we have to get these mark downs done. I was in the back looking for Carmen's mark down sheets and inventory lists before you got here."

She rolled her eyes up in the air. "It's a mess back there. There is so much shipment that hasn't been opened yet."

"Well, just let me know what I have to do and I'll start," I said excited to *finally* have someone around who was actually interested in the store.

"Okay, cool," she said. "I hope that all of the girls are this responsive." She handed me a few sheets of paper with some numbers and descriptions of some of the items of clothing on it and a marker.

"I don't know. I can't promise you anything, but you should be okay." I said trying to give her some encouragement. I knew that they weren't gonna like her though. I think she kind of knew it too.

I went to the first four-way with the jeans on it and began marking away at the tags, changing the prices to match what they said on the sheets of paper.

"So, what do you all do for fun out here in Poughkeepsie?" she asked me. "I just moved up here and I don't really know anyone. I have some family scattered around, but no friends really."

I was surprised. "You must really like working for DIVAS to move and leave everything behind for it. I would have been like, y'all betta find someone else! Forget that!"

"Nah, I just broke up with my fiancé and I just needed a change. Corporate said that I could always go back and work in North Carolina if things didn't work out here." She came over to me and leaned in close, "They even paying for my rent here."

"Holla!" I yelled.

"Okay!" she said. "Don't tell anybody though. The only person who knows other than you is Carmen."

I smirked. "Well, then they know already. Trust."

She looked confused. "Why would she tell them that?"

Now, I ain't just wanna come right out and be like *they nosy and they will talk your business*, so I said, "Well, I have only been here for a few days, but I've noticed that they treat each other like sisters. They are extremely close." I lied.

"Oh, well then I guess *that's* okay since she didn't tell em' for spite. I can't stand spiteful and malicious type people. You know. I hate backstabbing and all of that crap." She smiled at me. "Well, we got about twenty minutes or so left so let's just finish up what we can of the markdowns and then we can open up."

"Sounds good. Let's go." I clicked my marker, and got back to work.

Those twenty minutes passed like nothing, and before I knew it, it was time to open up.

"A new CD, finally!" I heard Tina yell when she went to put the music on.

"Do they have the same CDs for all of the DIVAS stores?" I asked her curiously.

"Yeah, they do. We can get written up if corporate comes in and we're playing an out-of-date CD."

"*Word?*" Tina seemed to know *a lot more* about DIVAS than Carmen did. "Well, what's on the new CD?"

"Um, lemme see. Oh, that new Christina Milian song is on here. And, um…what else…" Then she jumped up and down and started screaming with excitement. "My J-Kwon joint is on here! That's my shit!"

"*Yeah! Everybody in the club gettin' Tipsy!*" I sang while doing a little two-step.

She laughed. "Let's stop playing around and get this store opened."

She popped the CD in, and J-Kwon boomed throughout the store. It was slow at first, but soon the customers began filing in.

"Okay, Jaliyah, why don't you do the fitting-rooms and the register since they are right next to one another until Nadia comes in at 12, and then you can take your first break." Tina said, while taking down a camo display to put up a white and pink one. "This is just not summer-like enough. I hope that Carmen doesn't mind."

"Nah, Carmen is not like that." I smiled at her. "It looks really nice so far."

"Oh, well thank you girl!" She looked around the store. "We got customers."

"Okay, I'll be over there if you need me. Like I said, I've only been here for a little while, but I'll help you out when I can." I turned and walked over to the register.

It got a little hectic at one point, but it was nothing that I couldn't handle by myself. When the time arrived for Nadia to come in, I had returns and layaways down cold, let alone running the register. I can't front though, I was glad as hell when she walked her ass through that door. I told her what was goin' on and what she would be doing during her shift.

"It feels good to have some kind of order around here," Nadia said to me as she went to let a few customers into the fitting-rooms. "Tina seems like she is really nice. She is so pretty. *I know that Carmen is gonna hate that.*" She looked at me mischievously.

"Why do you say that?" I asked her even though I already knew the answer.

She leaned in close. "Look, I'm surprised that you and me are even working in here. They are so fucking jealous up in this place that sometimes I don't believe the shit myself. Just because I'm a minor, I don't get to hang out with them after hours, but I know what they do and I am *always* hearing stories throughout the mall."

I got quiet. "Well, I'm just here to do my job."

Nadia smiled. "Yeah, well it's kind of hard to do your job when you don't have anyone helping you. I already learned that if they don't wanna work, then the work is just not going to get done. You're gonna get pissed after a while."

I looked down at my watch. "I'm gonna take my break okay." I smiled. "I'll be back in fifteen. Oh, and Tina is really nice. Just make sure that you let them all know that before they start up okay."

Nadia smiled back. "Okay."

I got my bag and I headed out of the door on my first break. In the back of my mind, I was hoping that the day would be slow paced and trouble free. Yeah right.

# chapter twenty-nine

y fifteen-minute break wound up being twelve minutes of waiting in line at the CVS down the way. I raced back to DIVAS to use the bathroom quickly before I was due back on the sales floor.

"Jah-dee's on the phone in the back so just knock before you go in. I think she's talkin' to her baby's father," Nadia said when she saw me approaching the backroom on my way in from my first break.

Surprised I said, "I ain't know that she had a baby."

"Yeah, his name is Ricky. He is the cutest little boy ever!" Nadia said smiling.

"Wow," I said.

"I gotta pee though. I'll be right back." I rushed towards the backroom.

I waited for like three seconds and then I knocked twice and opened the door. Jacqueline was sitting at Carmen's desk wiping tears from her eyes.

"What's wrong?" I asked her.

"Nothing," she said. "Just man issues, that's all. I'll be a-ight."

"You sure?" I asked her. "We can't have one of the most beautiful girls here sobbing and shit. That shit can't rock ma!" I smiled at her and rubbed the top of her head.

"Nah, I'm cool." She smiled back.

"A-ight, then," I said.

Then she asked me, "Jah-dee, why in the world are you shaking like that?"

Not realizing how obvious I was I said, "Cause I gotta pee really bad!"

She laughed. "Girl, go ahead and pee! You crazy?"

"Thank you!" I said as I ran into the bathroom and half shut the door.

While I was peeing, I thought about why I had just been so nice to Jacqueline. I mean, she was a-ight as a person, but I don't know. I guess it was just one of those things. I don't like to see any girl in tears.

I finished using the bathroom and I flushed the toilet, washed my hands and came out. Jacqueline was getting her make-up together and fixing herself up. Tina walked into the back.

"I was wondering where the two of you were?" She smiled. "Y'all just left me and Nadia out front by ourselves with all them evil-ass New Yorkers? Y'all New Yorkers up here are mean, but y'all ain't as mean as them ones down there by where a few of my cousins stay. Down on St. Nicholas Avenue in Harlem."

She cut her eyes, "Now them down there, oh Lord chile! Rude and just don't care!"

She put her hands on her hips, "Y'all better come on here now! Let's go!"

"She is too cute with her accent and everything!" Jacqueline said as Tina walked out of the backroom and back onto the sales floor.

"I know," I said in agreement.

"Jah-dee," Jacqueline said, "I apologize for calling your crib that morning. I was just really tired and it's not that I wasn't gonna come in, I just—"

I cut her off.

"It's cool," I said. "Don't worry about it." Realizing that she had called me Jah-dee, I said, "Oh, lemme find out that you calling me Jah-dee and shit now? What happened to Baby Girl?" I asked her sarcastically.

"Oh, I'm off that shit. Honestly, I don't mind a bitch as cool as you seem to be sharin' the same name as me. You's a *young gunna* tho, so as long as you know that I had the name first and shit, it's cool." She laughed.

"*Ill*, anyways," I said playfully rolling my eyes at her.

"Okay cool," I said. "We can both call each other Jah-dee. It's nothing."

"Todo esta bien ma-ma," she said.

"A-ight then," I responded while opening the door to the sales floor for the two of us.

"Déjeme descubrir que usted sabe hablar español chica?*," she said comically.

"Sí, he hablado español desde que era bebé. Mi niñera era una señora puertorriqueña muy linda y mayor que vivía en mi edificio cuando crecí. Ella solo hablaba español, y me enseñó, † " I answered.

She smiled. "Oh okay. See now, sometimes you can come and chill at my crib. I live with my grandparents and they only speak Spanish."

She moved her bangs off her forehead. "Not to say that you couldn't come and chill without you speaking Spanish, but some

______________

* Let me find out that you know how to speak Spanish, girl?

† Yes I have been speaking Spanish since a baby. My babysitter was a cute, old Puerto Rican lady who lived in my building growing up. She only spoke Spanish, and she taught me.

people get uncomfortable when they come around because that's all we speak in the house."

"Yeah, that'd be nice." I smiled.

She laughed. "Good thing I wasn't talking shit about you! You would've beat my ass!"

We headed back out onto the floor.

"Girl, wait until you have to count down those registers tonight. You gonna be goin' outta ya mind! I'll help you though. Either Janet or me will. I think that Tina is still gonna be here too, so you should be okay."

*Now*, it seemed like Jacqueline had done a complete 180. I had forgotten that this was the chick who gave the bouncer at the club a blowjob just so she didn't have to pay. Right there, at that moment, I wasn't thinking about all of that.

Honestly, it didn't seem like she was being phony. She sounded very genuine. Whatever the reason was, I liked her this way. All I could hope was that she stayed like this when Carmen came around.

# chapter thirty

"That nigga just don't be hittin' my spot like the way Reggie used to. He don't even get my pussy wet. I told him that he got to lick in and *all around these sugar walls*, but he don't listen! He talkin' about he don't do that! *Shit*, he betta stop playin' wit' it and eat this pussy!" a girl trying on a million different outfits said to her friend who was standing outside waiting for her while handing her clothes back and forth.

She stood on her tippy toes and peeked over at me. "Ain't it the truth? You would want a nigga you been fuckin' wit' for six months to eat ya' pussy, right?"

I laughed. "It depends on whether that's his style or not."

"*Shit*, fuck a nigga havin' a style! I know that plenty of times suckin' dick wasn't my style, but a bitch was on her knees holdin' shit down. I held down the dick *and* the balls! Feel me!" She began to laugh and a few girls in the other fitting-rooms chimed in.

"That is so true! Damn, I feel like I been doin' that shit all my life," she went on to say. "Do you know how many times I wanted to just be like, *Fuck this bullshit!*, but I couldn't. Don't even get me started! You get on your knees. He grabs your hair and fucks your face pretty much. You gotta have your gag reflex together; you gotta make sure that your teeth don't get in the way. You gotta work your hands. Shit. Like my homegirl Samantha Jones said on *Sex and the City*, *'They don't call it a job for nothing!'* Sucking a dick is hard work! Not to mention how your jaws hurt the next day.

Girl, you do not know *how* many times I have been at work at my desk typing, filing and wondering why my jaws feel so sore and swollen. Then after some time, *it hits me*. I remember that I was sucking dick the night before."

"Girl, I thought I was the only one!" another customer said from inside of her fitting-room.

I could not contain my laughter. A couple of teenage girls headed towards the back of the store.

"Look y'all, we got young ladies on the premises. We gotta shut this conversation down."

"I hear that!" Carmen said as she approached the fitting-rooms with an armful of dresses and jeans. "What up Baby Girl!"

"Chillin'," I answered still blushing from the conversation that had just taken place.

"Oh, Joy and Shauna always come up in here with their man problems and they end up having a big-ass discussion and everyone in the store joins in. I always shut it down though once we get the young girls in here. I do have some morals."

She smiled. "So what's up for today? Are you feelin' Tina and what she has to bring to our store?" She asked very calmly.

"I like her a lot. I can't believe that she came all the way up here from North Carolina. That shit trips me out," I said as I unlocked a fitting-room for a customer.

"Her outfit is flyy too! I know you feelin' that!" I said smiling.

Carmen glanced at Tina, lowered her voice and said, "It's okay. I just think that it's a little too much for a fuckin' teen clothing store and shit."

With that comment, I just looked at her. I guess she could tell that I was like, *"Okay—"* because right after that, she looked at me and smiled.

"I'm just kidding! Girl you should have just seen your face. You was looking at me like you was gonna whoop my ass!" She shut an open fitting-room door. "Her suit is hot as hell!"

I wrinkled up my nose. "Nah, I ain't mean to look at you like that. I'm sayin', she looks really cute." I laughed. "I was just thinking like, *Wow! I can't believe that you don't like her outfit.*"

"I know, I was just playing though. Tina looks hot. That's what we need in our store. I tell Janet all of the time about coming in with all those fuckin' cheap looking club outfits."

"Well, to each her own, ya know what I'm sayin'. We do have the club goers up in here too," I said picking up a pile of fitting-room returns to be put back on the sales floor.

"Yeah, I know Baby Girl, but it's just that sometimes she comes up in this piece looking so fuckin' tacky. A lot of the time, she don't even wash her face, let alone her funky-ass pussy after doin' only God knows what at the club."

Carmen leaned in closer and lowered her voice. "I've heard that the bitch drives straight into the mall parking lot after she comes from the club and sleeps in her car just so she can be here on time. So you *know* that bitch ain't washin' shit. Stanky-ass hoe!"

She rolled her eyes, sucked her teeth and leaned in *even* closer. "You know what she told me once? She told me that during her period, she doesn't wash, that she only keeps changing the tampon and shit. It has something to do with her Wiccan religion."

I thought about what Carmen had just said. She was such a liar. Janet didn't even get her period because she was getting Depo Shots on the regular. That was one of the first things she told me on my first day at DIVAS. I just smiled at her and said, "TMI Carmen."

I began to walk away.

She laughed. "No wait, where are you going? Wait a minute." She pulled me back. "That's why I don't pay none of them up in here no mind when they be like that me and her are fuckin' each other because I know just how funky and nasty that bitch really is. Plus, I ain't into that shit. Dicks only! And even *they* can't be too little."

"Well you know, I don't trust anyone's info but my own. And I ain't one to gossip. But—" I said stretching out the word.

"But what?" she asked dying to know what I was going to say.

"But—*please* lemme put away these heavy ass clothes before my arms fall off!" I yelled laughingly.

"Oh okay!" she laughed. "I'm sorry. Girl, I thought that you was about to tell me some exclusive shit! Take your ass on and put those clothes away!"

Finally, she let me go. I wasn't one to take what others said about others and form opinions based on bullshit. And I was beginning to see that Carmen was full of it. I always observed shit for myself.

I went and put all of the layaway returns back where they belonged and then I straightened the things that were out of place on the clothing rounders and four-way displays. In the process of doing this, I found five empty hangers, meaning that we had unknowingly *(like always)* gotten hit with theft *again*. I also found a few little kids playing hide and go seek in between the clothes as usual.

"Y'all can't be playin' in between these clothes," I told them. "You'll hurt yourselves."

"Okay!" three little boys said in unison with giggles in their throats.

I guess their mother heard me because right after I told them that they couldn't play in the clothing racks, a woman's voice exploded from one of the fitting-rooms. "Rashad, David and Kimari! Y'all had better get your asses over by this door before I come out there and whip all of your asses in this damn store in front of all these pretty girls! You hear me?! I don't want any more shit! Get on over here right now for I break a bone and slap fire!"

Them little boys raced over to the fitting-rooms and occupied three of the six chairs that sat opposite the fitting-rooms so fast!

That was a good thing. So many mothers had no control over their kids and would always come up in the store and let em' just wreck shit.

A customer looked at me and laughed. She was a short black woman with a nice short haircut.

"See, that's the way you gotta have they lil' bad asses. A threat of a good ass-whoopin' works every time."

"Always worked on me," I responded thinking back to all the ass whoopins that I had received growing up.

"Well, *I* think that hitting your children is a terrible thing to do," a middle-aged white, female customer on her way to the fitting-rooms remarked.

The black woman's smile turned to a frown. She rolled her eyes and tightened her lips. She went up to the white woman who had just commented and said, "Well, I think that *you* should mind your own damn business cause wasn't nobody talking to *your* nosy ass!"

"No, I will not!" the white woman shouted, "It's terrible the way you people beat on your kids!"

The black woman, now enraged went off. "*You people!?* You would say that! You white women walk around here lettin' your children raise all kinds of hell, and then you don't wanna reprimand them for it. *Beat em'! Whoop they asses!* You keep sticking your nose in my business and I'm gon' end this conversation by whoopin' on you!"

"Oh, I don't think so!" the white lady retorted, refusing to back down against everyone else's better judgment.

"You ghetto, black women hit your children and then they turn around and hit society! They rob, and steal, and kill and fight authority figures! So don't you go tellin' me anything!"

"Oh, you bitch! Don't say you ghetto, black women anything! Talkin' about us *ghetto,* black folks. You in here shoppin' with your daughter, right?! I seen you come up in here with her! And where is she? Huh?"

The woman pointed across to the other side of the store. "She has her lil' hot, fresh-ass over there talking to *my* son! My *ghetto,* black son according to you!"

Now the people who were listening, including the white lady getting screamed on, turned around to see a tall, lanky white girl with dark-brown hair, wearing a pink, terry cloth sweat suit and some white, shell-toe Adidas leaning in and smiling all *up* in the face of the woman's son completely oblivious to the screaming match currently in-progress between their mothers. They both looked to be about 15 or 16-years-old.

The white woman gasped in disbelief. "Megan Amanda Guglielmo come over here right now!" the woman yelled.

The short black woman continued on, "Yeah, you better go and get her fresh, hot-ass away from my goddamn son! And do not *even* try to come back with, '*Oh! Well he's talkin' to her too!* Because a hole is a hole and your daughter's ain't no different than none of these other lil' fast-ass girls round here! *When a man wants to sharpen his pencil—he's gon' sharpen his pencil!*"

"Listen now you—" the white woman tried to interrupt, but the other woman was on a roll, and a crowd had begun to gather.

"No bitch, now you listen! Y'all white women walk around as if y'all are *so* goddamn better than we are. But as soon as y'all get the chance, y'all go chasin' after *our* men and have a bunch of babies whose hair you can't comb! Poor babies be out here looking a mess!"

She got up in the woman's face. "But you know what, by the way things are lookin' right now, seems like you are gonna be blessed with a few mixed lil' *ghetto* grand-babies. And believe it or not, no matter how many drops of white blood they may have in them, the public is gonna judge them the way you are judgin' our young men right now." She turned and began to head towards the register. "Now that's some reality for yo ass!"

The crowd erupted with cheers and laughter. Women were giving each other high-fives and running up to the register to tell the woman how good she told the woman off.

The white woman's face was red. She left her clothes on a nearby rounder, and called out, "Megan Amanda Guglielmo!" about two more times, before she left out of the store with her daughter trailing behind, still oblivious to what had just occurred.

The black woman finished paying for her clothes and headed towards the store exit.

"See you later Miss—," I said struggling not because I forgot her name, but because I never knew it.

*"Nancy,"* she smiled.

*"Miss Nancy,"* I continued.

"And your name?" she asked me.

"Jaliyah," I said.

*"Jaliyah,"* her son smiled and said to himself.

She looked at him. "Yeah Victor, and she ain't interested in your young behind!"

We laughed and he said, "I may be young but I—"

She cut him off in mid-sentence, "Watch ya mouth ya hear! I'ma pop you!"

He laughed. "A-ight momma, but why you always gotta result

to violence? That white woman was right about y'all black women! He laughed. "Just violent and angry for no reason."

She rolled her eyes at him. "Boy, bring your ass on!" Bye Jaliyah baby." Again, she turned to walk out the door.

"Bye Miss Nancy," I said, waving.

Her son, turned back, smiled at me and whispered, *"I'll be back"*.

*"You promise?"* I asked flirtatiously just to tease him.

"Yeah," he said, "I—"

"Boy, leave that girl to her job and come on!" Miss Nancy yelled laughingly.

"A-ight!" he said as they both walked out the door.

She gave him a soft punch in the arm and I heard her voice trail off as she said, "And what chu was doin' up in that lil' white girl's face and you seen me yellin' and fussin' at her simple momma!"

"Lord these people done went madd up in here!" I thought to myself.

Just then, Jameka and his entourage steadily sped past me and out of the door with three *large* Old Navy shopping bags.

*"Bitches!"* he shouted as they turned the corner.

I didn't even care to respond. I shook my head, chuckled at what had just gone down, and headed back to the fitting-rooms.

Nadia walked past and held up a handful of empty hangers. "Never a dull moment," she whispered. *"You havin' fun yet?"* she asked with a huge grin on her face.

Right then, I thought about Jameka's three, big Old Navy shopping bags (that were probably filled with stolen shit from our store and others in the mall), the pink, pleather, "gator-skinned" jump-suit short set that he had on, and the matching flip flops that he was sportin'.

And you know what? I wasn't even thinking, *Yo, I can't believe that they stole madd shit from us again!*

I wasn't thinking, *Yo, he looked a hot-ass mess in his outfit!* either.

I was thinking, *Yo, he really just walked past me, called us all bitches, and I wasn't in the mood to say anything back.*

I was really beginning to feel at home on this job. The drama was becoming routine to me.

Now *that* was some shit!

# chapter thirty-one

Four new messages, two saved messages. First new message:

*Yo, yo Jah-dee wut's good it's Shy! I'm guessin' you got your phone off cause you at work and shit right. Anyways, that ain't even the reason for this call. Yo, um trick, lemme find out that you workin' wit' some nasty, grimy-ass bitches up there at that store J? Oh, and hoe, lemme find out that there are some fine-ass bitches up top where you stayin' at too! Oh, and skank, what the fuck is this shit about that Quincy nigga bein' fuckin' 50-years-old and shit bitch!? Yo, hit me up when you get this message slut! One!"*

**Next new message:**

*Yo, Jaliyah, what's up, this is Dominic. Hey sweetheart, I'm on my lunch break right now and I was thinking about you so I dialed you up. I know you said that you would call me tonight, but I couldn't wait. I just wanted to hear your beautiful voice. I guess I'll have to settle for the voicemail though. Until tonight sweetheart, be safe, and enjoy ya day.*

**Next new message:**

*Jah-dee, it's Nicole. You met Elliot Jacobs from my school. Oh my God! I cannot stand his dumb ass. He is too cocky. He told me that he almost tried to talk to you. That shit is funny as hell. He is such a player. I'll talk to you about it later. Love you. Bye.*

**Next new message:**

*What a gwon bayaby? It's ya bwoy Trey,"* he said channeling his inner patois, courtesy of his Jamaican pops. *"I'm just playing. Yo, it's Trey just callin' you to let you know that ya girl is trippin' on some bullshit again J! She tryna make me throw out all my old shit from the bitches that I was cool with before her! She fuckin' OD'd already! She tore up about five or six of my pictures that some chicks had given me. And the flix weren't even from chicks that I fucked. They were some shits from like graduation or some shit. Anyway, yo, talk to ya girl. You better cause I'm gettin' ready to not even fuck wit' her no more. I don't need this shit. If I did, I would've had a girl since waaaaaaay... back my nigga! Hit me up tonight J! One!"*

**End of messages.**

*Oh Lord,* I thought to myself, *here we go again.*

# chapter thirty-two

I had checked my messages and the day was not even half over. Being management and working all day was crazy. Dominic's message was adorable. I wondered what he was doing. I thought that maybe I would call him on my lunch break. Speaking of which, *when was I getting my lunch break?* I had been in since before ten this morning and it was now going on three o'clock.

Back to Dominic though. I would just wait until I got home to call him like I said. I didn't want to seem too eager. I was in the middle of daydreaming when Tina storming past me and out of the front door abruptly interrupted my thoughts.

"I'm gonna take my lunch," I heard her yell to Carmen behind her.

"Well, you do that then Tina," I heard Carmen yell back right before she went into the backroom and slammed the door.

Jacqueline walked over to me. "Jah-dee, why don't you take your lunch too? You have been here since this morning. We got this."

"Okay," I said. "I was wondering when I was gonna be able to get some food. I'm starving girl."

Jacqueline laughed. "Crazy girl, you should have said something. Don't just wait until Carmen or someone tells you that you can go. It gets so hectic in here sometimes. It just slips our minds."

I walked over to the cabinet behind the register and unlocked it to get my bag. Jacqueline came up behind me.

"Oh, make sure you clock out for lunch in the back and then clock back in once you come back. Corporate wants us to do it to make sure that we are taking *exactly* forty-five minute lunch breaks."

"Okay," I said.

I headed towards the backroom to clock out for lunch. Carmen was back there with Janet ranting and raving.

"That fucking bitch hasn't even been here for a whole day and she's tryna fucking change everything! Dumb country-ass bitch!" Carmen yelled as she took a long pull from her cigarette.

"I bet this is just corporate's way of checking up on me. You know. Checking up on this store!" She rolled her eyes and looked up at me. "Can I help you sweetie?" she asked me, calming down slightly.

I reached over to the other side of her desk to get my punch card. "Jacqueline told me that corporate said we need to clock in and out for our lunch breaks now."

She put out her cigarette. "Yeah, okay. Go ahead."

I went to punch my card, and Carmen blocked me with her hand. She looked me in my eyes and said, "I fucking hate that new bitch Tina. She is so fucking by the book that it's driving me crazy. Another fucking Claudia."

"Who's Claudia?" I asked her.

"Oh," she said, "Claudia was the former co-manager who felt she was *all that*. She was so *perfect*. She had the *perfect* shape and the *perfect* life and knew *all* of the rules and followed *all* of the rules."

Carmen laughed to herself. "She had a perfect little cocaine habit too. Once I found that out, I made sure that she always had *all* that she needed. Her ass was fired in a little over two months."

Carmen stared straight into space as if she was possessed and then said calmly, "Stupid fuckin' cunt."

Of course, Janet was there to do her job of co-signing. "Yeah, she is another Claudia. I don't like her either."

Carmen looked at Janet, "I know right. Who the fuck does she think she is? Coming in and changing all of my displays, and shit like that. Telling me that we need to be more *organized*."

Carmen folded her arms in agitation. "Like *she's* our fucking saving grace! I was about to tell that bitch to get the fuck outta here and take her lunch if she hadn't of left outta here on her own! I don't play that bullshit!"

"Did y'all get into some kind of fight or something because Tina seemed a little upset just now when she went to take her lunch?" I asked Carmen concerned.

Carmen shook her head. "I ain't do nothing to that girl."

"Yeah, you may not have done anything to her, but I could have felt the attitude that you were throwing her all the way from Miami ma," Janet said laughing.

Just then, Janet went over to Carmen, stood behind her and began massaging her shoulders. "Don't worry about it baby. You know we got that thing going down tonight. Don't stress anything that could fuck up your mood."

"Bitch get the fuck off of me!" Carmen yelled as she jerked away from Janet. "You can't wait to fuck my man!"

Carmen stood up and stepped to Janet. "Ever since that day when you caught me and him fucking—"

"Do you really have to get into this right now C?" Janet asked, embarrassment all over her face.

"Oh—why stop now?" Carmen asked, amped and upset.

Feeling my stomach growling, I said, "Um, I'm just gonna clock out and I'll be back in forty-five."

"No, Baby Girl, you can hear this. It will only take a second. You need to know what kind of trash is working in this store," she responded.

Carmen continued. "After Rob busted his nut or whatever, and left out of the room, Janet walks in. I tell her about what had just happened between me and Robert. I tell her about how I love it when he cums inside of me, but I hate how it feels when it drips out."

Carmen looked over at Janet. "And what did you say you *nasty* bitch?"

Before Janet could say anything, Carmen said it for her.

"You said, *'No, don't let it drip out.'* Then you came up to me, got down between my legs and you sucked and licked up every drop of Robert's nut straight outta my pussy. Did you not, you nasty bitch?"

Janet did not say a word.

"Yup, and from that moment on, since the day you tasted his cum, you have been creaming and dreaming about fucking him. Am I right, or am I right bitch?" Carmen asked staring at Janet like she wanted to kill her.

"I—I guess so," Janet said hesitantly.

Suddenly, a big smile crossed Carmen's face. "So make sure you fuck his brains out baby! Drain him!"

Relief washed over Janet's face. "You bitch!" Janet yelled laughing before clutching her chest.

Carmen laughed so hard. "You should have seen your face! You was scared as shit. Baby, you know I love you. Come here." Carmen ushered her over and gave her a hug and a kiss.

*"So, that was all bullshit?"* I asked wondering what the fuck was going on.

Carmen looked at me, and then took my card from me and

punched it in the machine. "No, um, that really happened, but it didn't piss me off. It kind of turned me on."

She put my card back in the holding slot.

*"She's kidding!"* Janet screamed, then chuckled uneasily. "Aren't you hungry? You better get going. The clock is ticking."

I looked down at my cell and saw it was already a minute past my clock out time. "Yeah, I'd better go. I'll be back y'all."

"Later," they said in unison.

On my way out of the backroom, I could hear Carmen say, *"Bitch, who the fuck are you to say that the clock is ticking?* You better fall back and play your muthafucking position! You know you just wanted her to leave because ya spot was blown up…"

Her voice trailed off, I had left the store, and I *needed* to eat something before I passed out.

I walked past Papa Giorgio's, McDonald's, Burger King and the Chinese Restaurant where they hand out the little samples. I ate about three samples, and then kept it moving. They were pissed. I eventually decided on Wendy's. I got my food—a chicken nuggets kid's meal, and then I looked for a place to sit down and grub in peace.

There were no empty tables. However, I did see Tina sitting down finishing her food and reading that day's paper.

"Anything good," I asked her smiling.

She looked up at me and smiled. It wasn't as bright of a smile as she had given me when we first met earlier.

"Hey girl," she said, "take a seat."

"Well I don't mind if I do Lady T. That's what I'm gon' call you, 'Lady T' like Teena Marie!" I said enthusiastically.

She laughed. "Girl you are too cute!" She sipped her soda. "I remember when I used to be like you. So happy all the time. So full of life. So young and optimistic."

"Wait, wait, whoa," I stopped her. "You are still all of those things."

I took her hand. "You know what T, my Auntie Tiffany always tells me, 'don't let *nobody* steal your joy'. Don't let them girls up in DIVAS steal your joy. You were so happy this morning. What happened?"

"Well, I approached Carmen and told her about my ideas, and she shot down every single one. She had a *why not* for each of my *whys*." She folded up her newspaper. "I don't think that this thing is gonna work out."

"*Come on now T*," I said as I dipped a chicken nugget into some sweet and sour sauce, "you cannot just give up after one day. You're stronger than that. I know you are. I mean, you've been wearing what five, six-inch heals all day, and you ain't wobbling or nothing."

She began to laugh. "Girl you stupid!"

"Come on girl. Get it together. You're from the south. My family comes from the south. Me and you. We gon' get through this—together." I smiled at her. "You better get back though."

She looked at her watch. "Oh yeah, I wanted to stop by the candy store and buy some Jolly Ranchers. I love those thangs. Apple and Cherry."

"Girl, me too!" I laughed.

"Well, I'll pick you up some too!" she said as she got up from the table.

"Okay, thanks T," I said.

"No thank you J," she threw her napkins and sandwich wrapper into the garbage. "You really cheered me up just now. I was feeling really down."

"Don't let nobody steal your joy girl," I waved goodbye to her.

"I'll see you later," and she left.

I watched her as she walked away. *Damn*, she was *wearing* those heels! It made me think about the time when those Manolo

Blahnik, high-heeled construction boots were the thing. Remember the ones that JLo and Beyonce used to rock.

Well, I could *not* afford Manolos, so I wanted the next best thing which were the Steve Madden knock-offs. This was all before Jay-Z dissed them in the "La-La-La (Excuse Me Miss Again)" Remix.

I think they were like a hundred or a hundred and fifty dollars. I was going to spend my *own* money on them and everything. When I told my father about them, he said that it was a fad, they were a waste of money and that I could not get them. I went into hysterics! I started crying; I screamed, *"This is not fair!"* Yada, yada, yada. It was all very Brenda Walsh from *Beverly Hills 90210.*

Then, one day I was in Manhattan in Union Square, and I came across this *huge* shoe store. So I am in this store, and they have a pair of Steve Madden knock-offs. Wait, let me be clear. The shoes were *not* Steve Madden, they were *knock-offs* of the Steve Madden knock-offs. They were not made of nubuck, suede, or any other type of leather. They were made of a dull mustard-yellowish colored rubbery type of material. The heel was straight up black, hollow and plastic. When I think back, I don't know what I was thinking.

So, I see these boots in this store, and I want them immediately, if not sooner. The price was right. Something like $29.99! So, I call up my father and I tell him, oh my god, they have the boots and I want them and I tell him how much they are, and he says okay.

I bought the boots and I brought them home.

My sisters said that they were cute.

My mother just shook her head, turned up her nose up at them, and said in her infamous southern drawl, *"You ain't gon' be able to walk in them shoes. Them thangs cheeeeaaappppp! They gon' kill your toes!"*

Then she began to laugh uncontrollably, like always.

I didn't pay any attention to my mother. She was a hater like Starr and Buck. I was happy. I went and got my Timberlands out of the closet, and I took the little metal tree emblem that goes on the laces in the front off of them. I put it on the front of the laces of my fake Manolo-Steve Maddens. I tried them on with the outfit that I was going to wear to my classes the next day. Straight fire! It was flyy!

I decided to wear a dark-blue jean, tight-fitting stretch jumper like the ones that JLo used to wear. I had the boots barely laced, and my pant legs were tucked into the top of the boots. I was lookin' too ca-yute!

The following morning, my father dropped me off at the college shuttle bus because I didn't have a car then. Listen, when I got outta the car I was strutting. I was the bomb y'all! I got on that bus and walked down the aisle to the back of the bus and everyone was sweating me!

I took the half-hour ride to school. Got off the bus, and I was still strutting. I went into the cafeteria and everyone was sweating me!

*"Where did you get those? Those are hot!"* The compliments were flowing like champagne at a wedding honey! So, I'm just a strutting. And I'm walking and stalking. Flowing with it. From one class to the next. I mean, I heard Jay-Z and Beyonce's "03 Bonnie and Clyde" *everywhere* I went that day. Well maybe up until about 12:00PM.

When it got to 12:00 noon, the music started slowing down a little bit, and so did my swagger. Just a little bit though y'all. Then 1:00PM came. The music got even slower, and so did my swagger. Y'all, by the time school was over at 4:30, that damn song had slowed down so much in my mind that it sounded like it had been chopped and screwed for a remix. Real slow, like an old

Mike Jones song! I was dragging my feet. Oh, Lord. My feet hurt so damn bad!

I was too happy to get on that shuttle bus and head back home. At 5:15PM sharp, my father was there as soon as the bus pulled up. I was the last one off the bus, because I didn't want people getting pissed because I was walking so slowly. My pops even called my cell to see if I had missed the bus. I *finally* got off the bus, and I slowly headed towards my father's car.

Now, I don't know if you remember when Michael Jackson played the scarecrow in *The Wiz*? Okay, well if you do. Do you remember when they took him down from that pole, and he tried to walk for the first time? Well, let me just tell you, he ain't have *nothing* on my black ass that day!

Oh, my feet were dragging every witcha way! Lord Jesus, my feet hurt so damn bad! Oh, they like'd to kill me! I was pigeon-toed, knock-kneed, bow-legged. My ankles had given out. I was sweating and greasy. Somehow, my hair had gotten all fucked up. It was terrible y'all. I was a hot ass mess! Literally!

As soon as my father spotted me, he laughed like fool. He had to have laughed non-stop for about a good ten to fifteen minutes before he even pulled out of the parking lot! He thought that I was the funniest sight in the world. He still tells that story.

I can't do anything now but laugh. But, then, oh I was burning mad. I gave them boots to the Good Will. That was the only time I wore em'. My father was right. They were a total waste of money.

# chapter thirty-three

I finished eating and headed back to the store. Mary J. Blige's "Real Love" was playing on the stereo.

"Tina, can you hand me that cream-colored shirt and those white khakis?" I heard Carmen ask just as polite as she wanted to be.

"Sure." Tina handed her the outfit, "Here you go, hun."

Tina glanced at me and winked.

I guess my pep talk had worked. Because there they were, working side by side and not fighting.

I walked towards the backroom to clock myself back in. On my way there, I noticed that the whole vibe of the store was more calm. Nice and serene.

Believe it or not, the vibe of the store stayed like that the entire night. Not one problem. No stress.

I rode home to the sounds of the radio. That was until I remembered that I had to call Trey back and see what he was hollering about earlier.

*"Damn,"* was the first thing he said when he answered the phone, "you sure took *your* sweet-ass time to call a muthafucka

back! Long time no hear from nigga! Where you been all day, laid up with dat old nigga?"

*"Um, no. I've been, like working. So, like, just take it down 1000 dude."* I responded in my best Valley Girl impression. "What's up?" I asked.

"So what's up with you and the old nigga?" he asked.

"First off, his name was Quincy," I told him.

"Was?" he said prying for more info. "My dude, you *do* know that was, means the past right?"

"Duh asshole, that's why I said it!" I yelled.

"Alright, okay. What happened?" he asked.

"My uncle knows him. They're boys. He was in my uncle's wedding and everything."

"Word J," he asked. "Uncle Ant or Uncle Smitty?"

"Uncle Ant," I answered. "Yeah, I guess I didn't notice him because I was um, what 10, 11 when my uncle got married!"

He started to laugh. "That is some funny shit. Now, you know that *cannot* go down. No one wants his boy tappin' his niece's little puss! That shit can never go down!"

"I swear I can't stand your ass!" I laughed. "So, what's up with you and Alicia? Y'all worked it out?"

"Yeah we did. That chick is crazy though. Like, all chicks are crazy, but that chick is *craaaaazy*. I love her though. She gon' be my wife."

I could not believe what I had just heard. *"She gon' be your wife? When?"*

"Calm down," he laughed. "Not right now, but I just know that I'm gonna marry her. I was sick all day today. I felt like shit. She came through to the crib and took care of me. I'm still a little sick, but just the fact that she stopped what she was doing to come through and take care of me. Yeah, I'ma marry her."

I smiled. "Awww Trey. I can't believe what I'm hearing. You've had an epiphany. Wow. Awww, boo."

"A-ight, a-ight. Again, calm your little face," he said.

"Okay," I smiled again. "Aww...."

"A-ight, see now I'ma hang up!" he said with a playful anger.

"Okay, okay, okay!" I said laughingly.

"I don't play that shit. I don't tell everyone my feelings like that. This is new for me. You gotta calm down them, *Oooooohs* and *Aaaaaaahs* and *Aaaaaaws*. I'll hang up on your black ass. I'm not fucking around, nigga!"

"Done. Finito." I said.

"Okay," he paused, "so what's going on with them broads up in that store. Dem in there are some *freaky-deaky* hoes."

I glanced into the side view mirror as I switched lanes. "Well, we have a new girl, well, woman, working with us named Tina. She is so nice. She's southern. I think that she is going to be a big help. She was a manager at our store in North Carolina."

"She got a fatty?" he asked.

"I don't know nigga!" I shouted. "What happened to being in love and marrying Alicia?"

"I still got eyes and an imagination," he laughed.

"Well," I said, "I haven't looked at her booty."

"Oh, okay," he said. "Well look at it tomorrow and get back at me and let me know."

"Fine Trey."

"A-ight Jah-dee, I'll holla."

Then we hung up.

"Hmmm," I thought, "who else had called me?" I remembered that I had a message from Cheyenne. I dialed her up.

*"Hey Boobie,"* is how I was greeted.

"Hey Ma-ma," I said back. "What's good?"

"No bitch, the question is what's good with your hot ass?" she said comically.

"*Ill*, listen to you. Just kee-keeing all crazy. Well, I'm gonna assume that you are referring to the gentleman that I went on a date with who was significantly older than me?" I said.

"Yeah bitch!" she said. "You know that's what I'm talking about! Now what happened Jah? That nigga was really 50-years-old?"

"No," I said.

"Oh, thank goodness. Cause I know ya peoples would have been trippin'," she added.

"He was thirty-five."

"Oh, wow that's *so* much better," she said sarcastically. "So is he nice? How was y'all date?"

I smiled thinking about our date the other night. "He's nice and the date was really fun."

She got quiet. "So—are y'all gonna go out again? Why are you being so secretive?"

"No, we're not going to go out again. He turned out to be one of my uncle's best friends. He was in his wedding and everything."

"Smitty or Ant?" she asked.

"Ant."

"Damn," she said, "weren't you at that wedding? Didn't I go too?"

"Yeah, we were both there."

"Oh, that's why. Me and you were like 10-years-old. That nigga was already twenty-plus and shit." She paused. "Oh no, fuck that. Nobody wants their niece sucking and fucking their boy's dick and shit. That's just wrong! *Plus*, you know how *you* get down for yours once you're in a relationship."

She laughed hysterically.

"Shut up hooker!" I laughed. "I know what you're saying though. Trey said the same exact thing. I called Quincy up the other night and I ended it before it could begin."

"Oh, Jah-dee, that's too bad. Are you upset?"

I smiled to myself. "Nah, I'm good!"

"Okay, I'm not following. You said that dude looked like Stringer Bell from *The Wire*. You *love* him! You damn near left a wet spot on my sofa the last time we watched that at my house!"

"Oh, see now your mouth is trashy just like Trey's! *I did not!*" I could not believe her mouth!

"Okay, so why are you, *"So Good!"* she said imitating my cheerfulness.

"Because bitch, I met another dude the other day and I think that he might be alright. I don't know. We just started talking on the phone. It's still too early to tell. I'ma call him tonight."

"Damn, girly. Drop one, pick another one right up." Then she started up with her, "Hey, good for you girl."

She stopped. "Ooohhh, J, is he cute? What he look like? Who he look like?"

"Um, I don't know. He is about six-feet tall. Beautiful, gray eyes. Earrings in each ear. A nose ring. Nice little mustache/goatee. A crazy, cool swagger. Nice lips. Real cute."

*"Who does he look like?"* I repeated trying to imagine who I could compare him too that she would know.

I thought for a second then it came to me, *"David Beckham."*

"Yeah, but David Beckham is white. There ain't no brotha's who this dude favors?" Shy asked confused.

"No, because he's *not* a brotha. He is *white*." I confirmed.

*"A white boy,"* she asked, "what the fuck?"

"Yeah, he's white. I don't know what. Not Italian. Maybe like Irish or Polish or some shit like that."

"Well, go head Jah-dee. Taking a walk on the wild side with the white boy. Goddamn."

She laughed. "I done been there and done that. Girl, you know they crazy, right."

"Girl, be quiet and let me go on inside of the house seeing as how I have been home and sitting in my driveway for ten minutes now talking to you," I told her.

"Oh, you've been home? I'm sorry!" she said. "Girl take your ass in the house. You been working all day and what not. I'll call you tomorrow. You work?"

"Naw, I'm off."

"Okay, love you girl," she said.

"Love you too."

Then I headed into the house.

Once inside, I was greeted half-heartedly with a round of weak and tired hellos.

My mother and two sisters were gathered in the family room sitting on the couch watching Diahann Carroll in *Claudine* as if they had never seen it before.

"I hate this movie," Nicole said as she reached for a Twizzler. "She is such a little slut. How are you just gonna get into a bubble-bath with bubbles made from dishwashing liquid at some garbage man's house you *just* met and leave your *six* kids in the crib alone?"

My mother laughed. "Mommy used to do it. We used to be home watching ourselves. Then she would bring the man home and be like, *"This here is your new daddy!"*

"The hell you say!" my mother laughed with us all joining in.

My mother, aunts and uncles always had the funniest stories about my grandmother. My grandmother had some funny stories too. She would always, *and she still does,* talk about all the things she used to do *before* she got saved. How she used to play numbers, drink and smoke cigarettes. Go out dancing with this one and that one.

My mom always says, "Don't listen to your grandma's stories. They terrible chile! When someone says that *the world don't owe them no change back*, then you know that they done did some thangs in their lifetime! And don't get her started on them grand-daddies!"

We all continued to laugh hysterically. Now, my grandmother always calls Daddy Long Leg spiders, "Grand-daddies" and she is scared to *death* of em'. Let her get to being rude and surly; we just tell her that there's a *grand-daddy* behind her. She'll run right outta her church shoes!

I had endured *such* a long day at the store. I was so exhausted and tired. The only thing that was on my mind the whole ride home was: taking a long, hot bubble bath, talking to Dominic and then going to sleep. All of those thoughts disappeared once I got home though. We were all having such a good time laughing and listening to my mother's old stories.

I sat down next to Angela and asked her to hand me the popcorn. I took a sip of her Pepsi and finished watching the rest of *Claudine* with them. It was nice.

That's the best thing about family. They are always there. Whether you have a good day or a bad day, you can always count on them to make you smile at the end of it.

# chapter thirty-four

After I got out of the shower and had Nicole talk my ear off for half an hour about *Elliot Jacobs*, I was ready to settle into my bed and call up *Dominic M*. I looked at the clock. It read 9:57. Okay, I would call him now. I didn't want to wait until 10 o'clock on the dot. That would be corny. No, I would call him now.

*"Hi, Dominic,"* I said once he answered the phone.

"Jaliyah, hi, how you doing sweetheart," he said coolly.

"I'm good. I got your message. It was very sweet."

"Oh, I thought that you would be pissed off and be like, *this is one hard-headed muthafucka. He doesn't listen to shit!"*

I laughed. "No, it made me smile."

"Okay," he said. "I'm still sorry though. I just wanted to hear your voice. I thought about you all day. I have like a million and one questions to ask you."

"Well, I have a million and *two* to ask you," I said.

"Oh," he said, "I see how you get down. Competitive, huh?"

"Why you say that?" I asked him.

"Come on J, a million and two? Oh, may I call you J?" he asked.

"Yeah, J is fine. And yeah, I am quite the competitor."

I looked at the clock. "So, let's get started with all of these questions you got."

"Oh, okay," he said, "Well, are you in school and if you are, where do you go? DCC? OCCC? RCC? Marist? Vassar? The Mount?"

"I go to Dutchess. I just finished. I majored in Journalism and Communications."

"Oh, so you do a little writing too, huh. I have my Bachelor's in Journalism and I'm working on my MBA right now. I want to own my own business someday."

"Wow, well go ahead with ya bad self then Dominic. Your MBA, wow! At times, I felt like I wasn't gon' never finish school. It always got so boring and frustrating."

"Yeah, I feel you." he said. "When I was your age I use to feel the same way."

I stopped and thought for a second. Not the age issue again. "When you were my age?" I asked him. "Well how old are you now?"

"I turn 28 in December," he said. "Why, how old do I look?"

"You look about 25. Something like that." I answered.

"Oh okay. I'm feeling that. I still got it. Okay." He got quiet. "Is my age a problem?"

"No, I'm fine. You're fine." I said catching myself. "No, not you're fine, like you look good. You're fine like your age is fine."

"So, you don't think I'm fine like I look good?" he asked.

"Yeah, you look good. You look real good." I started to blush. "Just go to the next question!"

He laughed. "I don't want to make you feel uncomfortable. Okay, next topic. What's your sign? When's your birthday?"

"My birthday is July 6th. I'm a Cancer."

"Oh, Happy Birthday," he said. "What did you do to celebrate? Did you go out wit' cha girls? Ya fam?"

"Yeah," I answered. "Me, my parents and my sisters went out to dinner at this restaurant in Newburgh by the water, that I *absolutely* love."

"Let me guess—*Torches*," he said.

"Yeah, as a matter of fact, it is!" I said surprised. "How did you know that?"

"A good friend of my father owns that place. I go there myself, at least three or four times a year."

"Oh, cool," I said.

"I'll take you there for my birthday," he said.

"Aren't we a little presumptuous," I teased. "You don't even know me."

"Well then, tell me about yourself. What's your favorite song?"

"Ummm…I don't know. There are so many. If I had to pick one, I'd have to say—Can I pick a favorite slow song and a favorite fast song?"

He laughed. "No, you gotta pick one. Be it fast or slow. So go head."

"Umm—okay then. I guess I'd have to say, "The Lady in My Life" by Michael Jackson. I could listen to that song all day."

"Dope!" he said, "I love Michael Jackson! "Remember the Time" is my shit though," he said as he struggled to sing, *"In the park! On the beach! You and me! In Spain!"*

"Oh, see now, you need to quit that squealing!

He laughed. "Oh, you got jokes. Ma, my singing skills are sick! Girls stay creamin' over the notes that I'm singin'."

"Well not *this* girl," I laughed.

"You know that you are one of the most beautiful girls that I have ever seen in my whole life, Jaliyah," he said as he stopped laughing. "You literally took my breath away when I saw you. Just like in that song from *Top Gun*.

"*Come on now*," I said. "How many times you done run *that* line?"

"It's not a line," he said. "It's the truth." He paused for a moment. "I want to apologize too, for being such an asshole last night. I should have let you call me. I shouldn't have been such a hawk. I knew that you wouldn't call me though."

"You were right. I was not gonna call you. I was planning to delete your number as soon as I got to the crib. Maybe even in the car!"

"Damn, I was that bad?" he asked laughing.

"I was just not in the mood. It's so annoying being a girl sometimes. Every single dude has a confidence level that is through the fucking roof. No matter how he looks. How little or how much he can provide—every dude feels that he is God's gift, and he is gonna try to holla! It gets so frustrating at times!" I groaned.

"Yeah, well my confidence level is a little shaky," he said. "Not too many black women that I have tried to chat up are fond of this Scottish boy. *Well*, Scottish and German. They will say I'm cute or I have *swagger*, but it rarely goes any further. I don't know—maybe it's me and *my* insecurities."

"Scottish and German. Okay. Well, you definitely got a lil' swagger. You grew up in the hood, or are you just one of those rich white boys who ventured into the hood once you got old enough?"

"I grew up in Newburgh, not too far from where I live at now. No, my family was not rich. We were working class. One television for me and my brothers and sisters to watch. My parents are still together. I'm the baby of the family, the *troublemaker*. I've been locked up a couple of times for minor shit that happened back in the day. Like when I was in my late teens, early twenties. A few fights here and there.

I stayed in school the whole time though. I knew that I didn't really know what I wanted to do, but I just kept on going until I finished. I'm the only one who finished. Everyone else started getting married and having kids. I eventually ended up working for the family business just like the rest of my brothers, but I didn't start working for my father *right* after high school like they did. Both my sisters and my brother-in-law work for the company also.

He took a brief pause before continuing.

"As far as me venturing into the hood, I mean, Newburgh *is* the hood. It's where I lived. I have friends of all races and I have dated women of *all* races. I have always been accepted and embraced by people of all ethnicities. Of course I have had to deal with stupid people saying, *"Oh, Dominic thinks he's black.* Shit like that. But, this is me. This has always been me."

"Okay," I said, "I have never really *dated* a white dude. I mean, every one that I have gone out on date with has always ended up being insane."

"Oh no," he said chuckling.

"Most of the time when they'd bring me home to meet their parents or *whoever*, I'd get stared at like I had five heads. I just gave it up after a while. You know."

"Sweetheart, don't throw in the towel just yet. Let me at *least* take you out on a date or something. Nothing crazy." He got quiet and waited for my answer.

I gave in. *"Sure*, why not. Yeah, we can definitely go to dinner."

"Dinner?" he said, "Oh, no see, now that I got you to agree to let me feed you, we are gonna do breakfast, we are gonna do lunch *and* we are gonna do dinner all in one day. I'm gon' make a day of it wit chu'."

Surprised by his offer I said, "Okay, we can do that. Where do you wanna go?"

"We'll hang out in the city all day. Why not! The weather has been beautiful lately. I haven't been down there in a while. That's where we'll go. I'll come and pick you up, and then we can either drive down there or take Metro-North. I'll let you decide."

"Okay, just one thing," I told him.

"Anything Baby," he said sounding so fucking sexy.

"You gotta meet my parents first before I can go anywhere with you. They always want to meet any guy that I go anywhere with," I told him.

"No problem," he said. "Are you working Friday night?" he asked.

"Yeah, but only until 6:30."

"Okay, tell your parents that I will be there to meet them at about 8:00 o'clock on Friday. That way, I get to spend a little time getting to know them. Saturday, we are going to head out early, so I think that Friday would be a good thing."

I thought it over quickly. "Sure. I'll find out if they are going to be around and I will get back to you tomorrow."

"Good looks," he said.

I looked at the elapsed time on my cell phone. I had been on the phone with Dominic for over two hours. I suppose he noticed the time as well because he said, "Damn, I gotta be to work at 8:00AM sharp."

"Okay, so I'll call you tomorrow then," I said in my sweetest, sexiest voice. I wanted to leave him with something to remember me by until we spoke the next day.

"Cool. I'll be waiting. I can't promise you that I won't call you first though."

I laughed. "Do what you gotta do!"

"Alright then, shortie!" he laughed. "Sweet dreams."

"Same to you."

I plugged my phone into the charger and I went to sleep.

# part six
# wednesday

# chapter thirty-five

It felt good to have a DIVAS free day. I knew that I would be missing some crazy happenings, but they had enough drama to last them a lifetime. I decided to pay my Grandma Ruthie a visit. I called her to let her know that I would be there in about twenty minutes. To my surprise, my father answered the phone.

"What are you calling my mother for?" he said in his most convincing *serious* voice.

"Daddy," I said, "I'm coming over to see Grandma."

"Ma, Jaliyah's coming over," I heard him yell to my grandmother.

"Ooohhh, Boobie is coming over," I heard my grandmother yell in the background. "Did she eat anything yet? Tell her I have some chicken salad and deviled eggs here that I just made."

"No grandma!" I yelled into the phone.

"No ma, she didn't eat yet," my father told her.

"Your grandmother said that she made some chicken salad and—" his voice trailed off, "I'm sure you heard her. Look, I'm busy here J," my father said as he *hated* to be interrupted in the middle of playing Mr. Fix-it. "I'll see you in a little while."

"Okay," I said and then we hung up.

Exactly 30 minutes later, I pulled up to my grandmother's house. My father was outside on his knees planting some flowers for her in the front yard. My grandmother was right beside him holding a glass of ice water for him to drink.

*Baby Boy* is what she calls him. "*Baby Boy*, I got your water here for you."

"Thanks ma," he said as he drank the entire glass and handed it back to her.

My grandmother has this habit of never staying in the house or better yet, never staying put when someone asks her to. She always wants to be helping. She is such a strong, stubborn little lady.

"Do you want some more water Baby Boy?" she asked him.

"No ma, I'm good right now. Thanks."

I got out of my car and closed the door. "Grandma!"

"Boobie!" she yelled her voice sounding full of immense enthusiasm and joy. She ran over and hugged me.

"You came to see me!" She smiled. "You are so sweet!"

She ushered me into the house. "Come on in and let me fix you something to eat."

"Great. I'm starving grandma!"

"Oh, just go in the house and get some food already man!" I heard my father yell from behind a bush.

"Oh, hi Daddy. Didn't see you back there." I said as I chuckled with my grandmother and we went into the house.

She had a place all set for me at the table in the breakfast nook. All of the deviled eggs and the chicken salad were placed neatly in Tupperware with the lids off with serving utensils next to them. I went over to the sink and washed my hands.

"*Boobie*," she called over to me, "what do you want to drink? Aunt Sydney made some lemonade. There is some iced tea in here that I made yesterday. There's some—"

Before she could finish her sentence I said, "Iced tea!"

"Okay," she said as she brought the pitcher over to me.

Being at my grandmother's house is like *the* best thing ever. She always makes sure that you have everything you could ever want or need. Her food is the bomb too y'all. I can eat anything at her house, and it tastes amazing. I think that the fact that it's grandma's just makes it that much better.

Finally, I had my drink, my plate of food and I was ready to chow down.

"*Boobie*, I'll be right back." my grandmother said as she headed out the front door, "I have to see if Baby Boy needs anything."

"Okay Grandma," I said already polishing off my third deviled egg.

Once she came back in from checking up on my father, she asked me, "So Boobie, how is everything?"

"Fine," I told her through my chews. "I heard that Angie was over here yesterday showing you all of her wedding plans and stuff. I can't believe that anyone would *ever* want to marry her, but I guess some men are just that desperate." I smiled.

"You little jerk," my grandmother said as she laughed.

"I know, I know. Angie is a great girl. I mean she is *my* sister. Now, I cannot say the same thing for Nicole grandma. She is like in a whole 'notha league of her own. She has such a nasty disposition at times. I just want to….argh!" I said as I formed my hands in the air as if I were choking someone.

"Yeah well you the one made her like that," my grandmother said slyly.

"Nuh, uh," I said taking a sip of my iced tea. "Ooohhh grandma, you done put your foot and all your toes and toe-nails up in this tea here!"

"Is it good?" she asked.

"Yes. Everything is very good," I told her.

"Good. But back to Nicole. Your father told me that you and her were fighting at the house last week and he got knocked over to the side of the bed tryna break it up." She stared at me as if she were doing an interrogation.

*Dang, my pops got a big mouth,* I thought to myself.

"Grandma, I had just taken her all around here and there looking for stuff for her friend's birthday party and then I ask her to help me get the garbage together so I could put it down at the bottom of the driveway and she tells me that I gotta wait. So I said, wait my "a"-word, you gon' help me now. Then, she told me that if I can't wait, then she is not going to help me at all. So I said, "The hell!""

She told me to get out of her room and I said no.

Then she said, *"Fine, you can just stand there and look stupid all afternoon because I am not going to help you now."*

So I punched her. Then she punched me back and we started fighting. I guess my dad thought that we were playing, but once he realized that it was serious, he attempted to break us up. It was then when he rolled over the bed and hit the floor on the other side."

My grandmother just looked at me and shook her head. "Now why would you all fight like that over nothing?"

"Because I felt like she was disrespecting me. I'm older so she should listen to me."

"Do you always listen to your parents?" she asked rhetorically.

"No, but—"

She didn't let me finish. "You have always been a bossy little diva. Your whole life. You try to play the role like you're so sweet and innocent." She pinched me playfully, then said in a cute high-pitched voice, "But grandma knows. You can't fool me."

She looked at my plate that was now empty. "You want some more food?"

"No, I'm full." I told her.

"You know that you are grandma's girl, right?" she said smiling at me as she slid a twenty-dollar bill into my hand. "Buy yourself some lunch at work. By the way, how is your new job?"

"Grandma, the money is right, but my co-workers are lunatics," I laughed.

"Well, just go there and do your job. Don't mind what everyone else is doing."

Just then, my father entered the house. "Yo man, it's hot out there! Where's my water?"

My grandma looked at me and made an *oops I forgot* face before laughing.

"Coming Baby Boy!" and then she quickly disappeared, pitcher in hand, out the front door.

I stayed at my grandmother's house for a few more hours. I said my goodbyes and then I stopped by Pizza Hut and ordered a couple of pies and some sodas for dinner on the way home.

I wanted to wait until my father came in from my grandmother's house to find out if he was going to be around on Friday evening. My mother was home, so I began to tell her about Dominic.

"So, mommy, I met this really nice guy. His name is Dominic. He's 27-years-old. He has his Bachelor's degree and he is working toward his MBA. He has his own house, a car and he may even have pets. He works in construction and he does some freelance writing. He is extremely handsome and I believe him to be very sweet. He has a bunch of brothers and sisters.

He wants to take me out on a date. But get this, not just dinner. Breakfast, lunch and dinner. He wants our date to last the whole day! I told him how you and daddy feel about meeting anyone who I go out on dates with, and since he wants to take me out on Saturday, he wanted to know if he could come by on Friday evening to hang out and get to know everyone."

My mother just looked at me for a while quietly while eating her pizza. "Sounds good to me," she finally said after finishing a slice. "Your father should be around. You know Friday is usually our party night, you sure you want him to come on Friday?"

"Yeah," I answered. "Why not? It'll be fun."

"At least you're starting to come down in age. Quincy was fine, but too old for you. Oh, Kima was telling me how Uncle Ant was acting over the whole you and Quincy thing. You know he called right back after the two of you left and told us to nip that mess in the bud. Your father told *him* to handle it. That was the wrong thing to say. You know once he gets going, ain't no reasoning with crazy!" She started to laugh.

"Yeah, I told him that it wouldn't work out and he was cool. I think that he knew once he found out that I was Ant's niece."

"Now Lee-Lee, twenty-seven is still a little old, but it's more reasonable than thirty-five. *Come on now*." She picked up a cinnamon breadstick and took a huge bite out of it.

"Dang ma," Nicole said as she came into the kitchen to get some more pizza, "can your mouth open any wider?"

My mother threw her breadstick down on the plate. "About as wide as yours is gonna be once I put my fist in it! Mind your damn business! Take your ass back up into your nasty room that better be clean by the time I come up there!"

I laughed to myself.

"She gets on my nerves!" my mother said after Nicole was back upstairs and out of sight. "I'ma kill her. I'm telling you. Angie is on her way out. I'll be *too* glad once this whole wedding business is done with. Do you know that Nicole wanted her own, custom designed bridesmaid dress? I told her that she betta shut up before I snatched her bald-headed. Sometimes I just wanna wrap my hands around her scrawny neck and don't never let go!"

"Ma!" I laughed. "I know how you feel though. I apologize

for fighting wit' her like that last week. She just got on my nerves."

"I know. You ain't gotta tell me." She got up to get some more ice for her glass. "So, where did you meet this guy at?"

"At the mall," I answered.

"Always at the mall. Is he good-looking?" she asked.

"Ma, he is drop-dead adorable! He has the prettiest, brightest, grayest eyes that I have ever seen in my life! He has a dirty blonde, goatee, and…

"Blonde and gray! The hell you say!" my mother said loudly.

"Ma," I said, "why you yelling for?"

"Jaliyah, a white boy?" She got up and threw her plate away. "I done told you about them. I don't trust em'. No. Jaliyah, you marry a white man, he be done told the neighbors that you went on a trip, and he done really tied your black ass up and got you hanging in the damn basement!"

"Mommy, that's ridiculous!" I said laughing.

"I heard that happened to one of your cousins down in Flor-ida," she said as she straightened up the kitchen.

"Oh yeah?" I asked, "Which one?"

"Do it really matter? *She dead now*!" She put the soda back into the fridge. "Where is he from? What is he?" she asked.

"He is from Newburgh, but he is Scottish and German."

"A Nazi!" she yelled, "Oh hell naw!"

"Mommy! Please!" I laughed. "You are buggin out!"

"Brad Pitt is probably Scottish or Irish and German too, and you love him. Shoot, you'll watch him all day and all night!"

"That's Brad Pitt," she said. "He's a whole 'notha story." She regained her composure. "Okay, you know in this family we are not prejudiced. We accept everyone. But look at Angie, she's marrying a Japanese, Nicole only likes them Spanish boys and now you. When the revolution comes, I'm gon' be there by my damn self!"

"Mommy, it's just a date. No one said that me and him are getting married or anything like that. *Come on now!*" I shook my head in disbelief.

She caught herself. "You're right. There I go, putting the cart before the horse. I can't wait to meet him. I'm fine now."

"Okay," I gave her a kiss. "Cool. I'ma go upstairs and call Dominic and let him know that Friday is a go!"

I ran upstairs to my room and dialed Dominic's number.

"Hey you," he said sweetly.

"Hey Dominic. I just called to let you know that Friday is cool with everyone. I'll give you the directions and everything then."

"Great," he said sounding extremely excited. "Did you tell them about me?" he asked sounding a little worried.

"Yeah, well I told my mom. My pops isn't at home yet."

"What did you tell her?" he asked

"I told her your name and your age and what you do."

"Did you tell her that I was white?" he asked sounding a little worried.

"We *did* get to that," I told him.

"What did she say?" he asked.

"What is this, "Guess Who's Coming to Dinner?" My parents are the last ones who would care whether you were white, pink or purple. They just want me to be happy. I have so many extended family members who are Spanish, Japanese, Italian—whatever. My father was a cop in the city for twenty-plus years. It doesn't—"

He cut me off. "Word. Your father was a cop? You think that he's gonna run my information?"

"More than likely. He'll probably get one of my uncles to run your plates or whatever. No big deal." I was used to guys giving me that reaction. "Why you so worried for anyway? I thought everything you did was back in the day?"

"It was, but still—I want to make the best impression."

"Well, your best bet would be to put it on out there eventually. You don't have to worry about that right now though. We haven't even been out on a date yet. I might have the worst time of my life and tell you to lose my number!"

He laughed. "I doubt that baby. You might want the last stop of the day on Saturday before dinner to be the Diamond District so you can pick out your engagement ring, ya heard!"

"Oh, Dominic, *come on now*! You think that your company is that good? Oh, this I gotta see! I can't wait now! *Shit*!" I laughed.

"Well, we will see then. I can't wait to spend time wit chu' on Saturday. I feel like a little kid. I'm so excited. We gon do it all!"

"I can't wait!" I said smiling inside.

Just then, my call-waiting beeped through. I saw that it was Jacqueline.

"Dominic, this is one of my co-workers. Can you hold on a sec?" I asked him.

"For you I could hold on forever," he said sweetly.

"Bullshit," I said, then I clicked over.

"What's up Jacqueline?" I asked.

"Jaliyah," Jacqueline shouted, attempting to yell over all of the noise in the background.

"Yeah, Jacqueline, I have someone on the other line. What's up?" I said.

"Oh, I don't wanna keep you. I just wanted to know if you could come and pick me up from Carmen's crib. Everyone over here is on their bullshit and no one wants to fuckin' take me home," she yelled into the phone.

"Jacqueline can't you—," I remembered that Dominic was on hold. "Hold on Jacqueline."

I clicked back over.

"I thought you forgot about me girl," Dominic said jokingly.

"Nah, never that," I said. "Look, Jacqueline needs me to go out to Fishkill and pick her up from my bosses crib."

*"Word?"* he said sounding just as surprised as I was.

"Yeah, I know. I don't feel like it, but she has a kid at home and everything. I'll call you back on my way back home, okay."

"Okay, cool. My cell needs to charge, so let me give you my house number too. I don't always carry the cell around the crib, so just in case I miss ya call on one, you can get me on the other number," he said.

"Cool," I said as I took down his house number. "I'll call you back as soon as I'm on my way home."

"Okay sweetheart."

I clicked back over to Jacqueline and I told her to have her ass outside and ready to go because I wasn't coming inside.

# chapter thirty-six

I told my mother about Jacqueline's phone call and that I would be right back, so she didn't have to wait up. I got into my car and hit the highway. I arrived at Carmen's apartment complex in a matter of minutes. When I got there, I saw Jacqueline waiting outside just like I had asked her to do. She spotted my car and began to make her way over. I noticed that she wasn't wearing any shoes. I didn't even want to know the reasoning behind that.

She walked over to the car and was about to open the door and get in when Carmen came running out into the parking lot popping off at the mouth. Her hair was pulled back into a pony-tail. She had on a dingy, white, cut-off t-shirt, and some very short, cut-off, grey sweat-shorts. She wore black, flip-flops on her feet and had a half-empty Heineken bottle in her hand.

"Bitch, you betta bring your muthafuckin' ass back in this house before I fuck you up my damn self!" Carmen yelled out loudly, her voice echoing off the trees.

"Carmen, just go back in the house. Jah-dee is here to pick me up. Fuck it!" Jacqueline said as she started to sit down inside of the car.

I guess Jacqueline's nonchalant attitude pissed Carmen off because the next thing I know, she dropped that bottle to the ground, pulled Jacqueline out of the car by her hoodie, slammed her ass down on my hood and started choking the shit out of her. For some reason, the fact that she was choking Jacqueline didn't faze me and it didn't surprise me either. My whole thing was that, this was my new car, and they were fucking it up with their bullshit.

"Oh hell no!" I yelled as I jumped out of my car and attempted to pull Carmen off Jacqueline and both of them *off* my car.

Carmen jerked away from me on some bullshit, threw both her hands in the air and said, "Look, Jaliyah. This shit here doesn't concern you. So you need to keep your fucking hands to yourself and get back into your fucking whip!"

Now, I didn't know if she was drunk, or high or what. Nevertheless, I kept my composure and said, "Look! I do not give a fuck about the two of you fighting. Kill each other. Just get the fuck off of my car!"

"Bitch!" Carmen yelled at me, "Don't nobody give a *fuck* about this wack-ass fucking car. I been through two fucking Honda Civics in my lifetime already. Get over it!"

Now, I still wanted to give her the benefit of the doubt. I like to give people chances. Chances to right their wrongs. Chances to apologize. Therefore, I said, "Look, I don't know if you have been smoking or if you done drank a little too much back in the crib, but you need to check ya self chick!"

"Jaliyah, you *really* think that you're so *fucking* tough that the only way a bitch will step to you is if she's high or drunk. Bitch please! You *must* fucking be smoking if you think that dumb shit. Stuck up hoe! Playing that shy quiet role while you sitting back judging everyone in the fucking store! Bitch please!"

Now by this point, I was calling on the Father, the Son *and* the

Holy Spirit to keep me off her ass. I was thinking, *damn, I hadn't even been working at DIVAS a whole week! What the fuck did I do to her to make her so fucking pissed?!* Her whole fucking persona and everything had changed.

Chino and Janet came running outside.

"C, where you been at?" Janet asked Carmen before she noticed the looks on all of our faces. "What the fuck is going on?"

"Nothing, Jacqueline fucking called Jaliyah to bring her home and shit. She ain't want to pay her debt. She wanna walk around wearing the flyy sneakers and shit from Chino's connect, but then she don't wanna fucking pay up!"

Jacqueline yelled. "Carmen, I gave him the fucking money. I am not going to give his cousin head for some fucking sneakers. No, fuck that bullshit! I ain't dealing with this bullshit any more!"

Carmen charged at Jacqueline, but Chino held her back. "Baby, she paid the fucking money. Just, leave it alone!"

Chino looked over at me. "Jaliyah, what's the matter baby?"

"Nothing's the matter. I'm just about two seconds away from knocking this broad's teeth out. She's was all on the top of my car and what not like shit is fucking sweet!"

Carmen pulled away from Chino. "I am so fucking tired of hearing about that fucking car. It ain't even a mark on the shit. But here, you wanna be salty about something bitch!"

She picked up the Heineken bottle that she had dropped on the ground and threw it at my passenger side window causing it to shatter into what seemed like a billion pieces. "Be fucking salty now! Now you got a reason!"

"No bitch, now I got a reason to murder your ass!"

I ran towards Carmen with the strength of every MMA fighter that I had *ever* seen fight on television. I grabbed her fucking ponytail, wrapped it around my hand a good two or three times and repeatedly began to punch that bitch in her face. Lucky for her, I wasn't wearing any of my rings. Her face would have definitely gotten cut the fuck up by the way that I was punching her.

She finally got loose, and punched me in my chest dumb hard, damn near knocking the wind out of me. *Wow*, I thought to myself, *she really wants to beat my ass.* I cannot front. Her hand skills were decent, but they weren't stopping my ass. I was so fucking angry. I couldn't believe how she had tried to play me *and* Pearl! To my shock though, no one tried to break it up. I thought that the fight would never end. Eventually, someone in the complex called the Fishkill Police Department and my black ass along with her stupid ass were put in handcuffs, put into the back of the squad car and hauled off to jail.

"Jaliyah, I'm so sorry! I'm gonna call your parents and let them know what happened!" I heard Jacqueline call out to me as the cops put me in the squad car.

I thought that was the least that she could do seeing as how I had gotten into this bullshit because of her foolish ass. I used my one phone call to call my parents even though Jacqueline said that she would call them. I explained the whole story to them and they said that they were on their way over.

I was locked up for about an hour and a half and then released once my parents showed up to bring me home. I got charged with a misdemeanor and was told to show up for a court date. The arresting officer was an older man and he gave me a speech about taking the law into my own hands. He told my father that the police report was written clearly and precisely and I would not have any problems. He gave my father a reassuring nod. All I would have to do is appear in court and make sure that I had my receipts for the costs of the window repairs.

My father told me that Jacqueline had waited with my car while Nicole drove Angie over to pick it up and bring it back home. A friend of his told him that he had the window in stock and that he would have it fixed by the end of the day tomorrow.

All I would have to do is call up my insurance company and report it.

I heard it all on the way home. My parents weren't mad at me, they were just pissed that I didn't just walk away from the situation completely.

"What the hell happened tonight? You tell us that you're going to pick up some girl to give her a ride home and you end up arrested," my father exclaimed.

"Daddy, it wasn't my fault. That chick was fighting with Jacqueline all over my car, and then when I said something to her about it, she spazzed out, and freaking threw a bottle through my passenger side window. What was I supposed to do, just stand there and let her keep on with her foolishness?"

He took a deep breath. "Whatever. I want you to call up the District Manager first thing in the morning and let her know what went on tonight. Tell her that *I* said as of right now, you no longer work there! I am not gonna put your safety in danger in case this dumb broad decides that she wants to retaliate against you in some kind of way. No, it ain't happenin' captain!"

*"Lonnie,"* my mother said, "that woman don't even work in the store anymore. That girl Jacqueline said that she was fired earlier today for stealing money and clothes from the store. They banned her from coming within 200 feet of that store."

"For real mommy?" I asked. This was all news to me.

"Yeah, when your sisters went to pick up your car, they gave Jacqueline a ride home. Whoever else was out there when all of this happened was mad at *her*, and left her outside with your car. She rode home with Nicky while Angela drove your car home. Nicky said that she told her this whole long story about what happened earlier that day when you were off. She wants you to give her a call when you get in."

"Damn, they fired her?" *She did have a whole lotta clothes in her closet when I went to her crib that day.* I thought to myself.

"Everything will be fine Jaliyah," my father assured me. "Just call up the District Manager and let her know what happened. I have to think about if you should still quit or not. Just because she is banned from the store, doesn't mean anything. You still have to leave and walk in that parking lot when it's dark out and…." He stopped talking to think for a minute. "I just don't know."

"Lonnie, I forgot to tell you that Jaliyah has a date on Saturday and the young man wants to come over on Friday evening to meet us. Is that cool babe?" my mother asked, in an attempt to lighten the mood.

"Who's this guy?" my father asked.

"His name is Dominic Macculloch. He's twenty-sev—" I began to say before I was cut off.

*"Macculloch?* What is he, a white boy?" he asked me.

"Yes," I said not feeling like going through the same discussion all over again that I had just had with my mother.

"Oh, okay. Go ahead," he said

"He's 29-years-old. He does construction full-time and he is a part-time freelance writer. He is smart and he seems really nice from what I know so far. He wants to come by on Friday night at about 7:30 or 8:00." I finished.

"That's fine with me. You know that's our party night though and Uncle Ant and Aunt Kima are coming over with the girls. Aunt Tiffany and the boys are coming. I got a few of my boys coming thru. And I think your Aunt Pam and Aunt Sydney are coming by. Oh, and Sharisse is coming up from Brooklyn with her kids. Uncle Claude and Uncle Smitty may come by—so he'll get to meet the whole family."

My father smiled mischievously and looked at me through the rear view mirror then clapped his hands and turned up Ideal's "Whatever", on the radio. "Oh, we gon party hard!"

One thing my father loved to do was party. I guess after protecting and serving for twenty-plus years, you need to do something to take your mind off everything that you have witnessed during your career.

*"Whatever you wanna do uh uh,"* my mother sang along as she grooved along with my pops to the song on the way home.

I couldn't wait to get home so I could wash all the jail off me, then call Jacqueline, and find out what had happened yesterday when I was off. *What the fuck did Carmen getting her stupid ass fired have to do with me?*

First, I had to call Dominic and let him know about all of the drama that had happened between the time we last spoke until now.

I hoped that he was still up.

# chapter thirty-seven

I took a long, hot shower and then dialed up Dominic.

*"Dominic,"* I said once he picked up the phone.

"Hey Baby, what's up?" he asked me sounding half-awake but still happy to hear my voice. "What time is it?"

"About 12:30 in the morning. Look, I didn't mean to wake you. I just wanted to let you know that some crazy shit happened tonight and I will call you tomorrow or vice versa and tell you all about it."

"Bet," he said.

"Oh, and my father can't wait to meet you, I said.

"He can't?" he asked.

"Well, he said that it's fine for you to come by on Friday. You'll get to meet the family." I said laughing to myself.

"Good. I can't wait," he said.

"Okay, so I'll talk to you tomorrow then."

"Okay. Goodnight sweetheart."

"Goodnight."

I hung up with him and immediately dialed Jacqueline.

"Hello," she answered calmly.

"Jah-dee! What the fuck happened tonight? What the fuck did

you get me into? I got a fucking criminal record. I gotta get my damn window fixed. My pops is telling me that I may not be able to work up in there no more. I haven't even fucking gotten paid yet for the days that I *have* worked! What the fuck Jacqueline?" I yelled.

"Oh my God Jaliyah, you don't know how sorry I am! I will pay for the window, whatever you need me to do. Cab fare. Whatever!" she said extremely apologetically.

"No, that fucking skank is gonna pay for my goddamn window!" I interrupted. "What happened Jah-dee?"

"Oh, okay so today, well, *technically* now yesterday, was so fucking hectic. First off, there was no one there to open the store. Tina said that she had something to do, and that Carmen needed to be there to open. Carmen passed the buck to Janet. Janet passed the buck to me. And I said, *"Fuck it"* I ain't opening. I stood home until my scheduled time, which was two o'clock. So, eventually, I don't know, Carmen must have screamed on Janet or threatened to beat the shit out of her because Janet did eventually open the store at like twelve in the afternoon." Jacqueline said, her accent fading in and out.

*"Whuuuuuttttt?"* I said my voice low and deep. "Y'all opened late like that yesterday?"

"Yeah," she responded sucking her teeth. "Mind you, we supposed to be open at ten." She continued her story.

"So because we opened so late, the mall fined us $150.00. Tina would not have found out about it if she hadn't of been there when the fucking security guard came thru and served her with the paperwork or whatever it's called.

So Tina saw that we opened late and she started flipping or whatever. She threatened to call the District Manager and the corporate office. She was talking a whole lot of shit.

She kept on saying how Carmen was this and that. So, of course, she is saying all of this in front of Janet, and Janet is taking notes in her fucking *pea sized,* coked-out brain. So, Janet decides to call up Carmen and tells her that she needs to hurry up and come through because Tina is bugging out and she's gonna try and get her fired and what not. So, I'm staying out of it because, I am just *so* sick of the bullshit already.

About another hour goes by, and in walks Carmen with Robert and Chino by her side. Carmen looked me up and down and asked me why I was wearing sneakers with my outfit. I told her that my feet were killing me from the shoes that I wore yesterday so I wore my Jordans or whatever. She told me that she was going to write me up. I was like, *fuck it.* "Do what you gotta do." Then I walked away. Next, she walks over to Tina."

"Tina," Carmen asked as she removed her sunglasses to look her dead in her eyes, "what's this I hear about you trying to get me fired?"

"Carmen, you were supposed to be here at 9:30 this morning to open up this store. Where the hell were you?" Tina asked angrily.

"Um, look, I'm sorry, but unlike fucking losers with *ex-fiancés*, my life is more than this fucking store. Please believe. My fiancé is at home with me!" Carmen said rolling her eyes before flashing her engagement ring in Tina's face.

"Yeah," Tina said, "Well, which one is *your* man, because I see you walking around here flossin' Robert's engagement ring, but I also saw you on your knees, sucking Chino's lil' dick last night in the backroom behind some clothes while Robert ran to the CVS to get some batteries for your busted-ass camera!"

*"Now, Jaliyah,"* Jacqueline said as she took a moment from telling her story, "you should have seen the look on Rob's face when Tina said that shit. It's like— he didn't know that Carmen and Chino were fucking around. I mean, how could he be *so* fucking blind to that shit. Stevie Wonder could have seen that shit coming. But, back to the story."

"What the *fuck* is she talking about C!" Robert yelled, his voice thundering.

"I don't know what the fuck this lying bitch is talking about. I didn't even suck dick yesterday. *Anyone's.*" Carmen said jokingly.

"Don't fucking lie to me Carmen! What the fuck is going on with you and Chino? You fucking him?"

He got quiet as he waited for her to answer.

"HUH! YOU FUCKING HIM!" he yelled as his voice echoed throughout the entire store causing everyone to get quiet and a few customers to leave.

"Robert?" Carmen asked. "Do you really think that I would fuck *Chino* of all people? Short, scrawny, raggedy Chino. *He's my nephew for Christ sakes!"* she said as she shook her head surprised by his accusations.

She pulled him close to her. "Baby, I love you. You're my whole world." She kissed him.

"He's Melissa's son and Melissa is *not* your blood sister Carmen. And you still did not answer my fucking question! Are you or are you not fucking this nigga right here?" Robert said, tapping Chino twice in the chest forcefully.

"Look nigga, don't put your fucking hands on me!" Chino said in a deep, stern voice. "She's your girl, you handle her. Don't fucking touch me man!"

"Oh, look, the little bitch who dropped outta SUNY New Paltz cause he missed his moms, wants to speak up and act like a fucking man," Robert laughed with a crazy look in his eye. "You think that you're a fucking man because you're tapping a bitch, what, how old are you, um 23 right? Yeah, you think you're a man because you're tapping a bitch *seventeen* fucking years-older than you!?"

Janet spit out her water and laughed for a hot second before Carmen silenced her by turning to look at her.

Jacqueline stopped in the middle of her story again. "So here we are all like, "Holy Shit, this bitch is forty-years-old and out here acting a muthafucking fool every fucking day of her life. You should have seen how everyone reacted to that shit. We all gasped like we were in the end of the movie *Clue* or some shit. It was crazy! But, back to the story."

"I know how old she is nigga! She my mom's best friend. What the fuck you think. She's been in my life since I was born nigga. She's my godmother! So what! What the fuck is ya point?" Chino said getting heated.

"My point is, is you fucking her or is you ain't nigga?" Robert asked calmly using hand gestures for emphasis.

Chino stood there quiet for a second. Then he said, "Yeah— I'm fucking. I *been* fucking for a minute now. I ain't gonna lie."

Robert just stood there for a minute. Then he screamed in Carmen's face, "You hoe! I did everything for you. I woulda gave you anything. And you gonna go and fuck this little nigga?!"

"You was taking too fuckin' long to give it to me. I ain't got that kinda time." Unfazed, Carmen calmly said. "I'm sorry."

"Sorry, B," Chino said.

I interrupted this time. *"Whuuuuuuuttttttt?!"* I said extremely low and deep again. "So them niggas was *already* fucking. She just wanted Janet to fuck so she wouldn't feel as bad about *already* fucking?"

"Pretty much," Jacqueline answered. "Now, by the way that Robert was looking, I knew that he was about to do some crazy shit. He just stood there, with a deranged, psycho, Hannibal Lecter-ass look on his face, and then....yo...," her voice trailed off.

*"What Jah? What did he do? Girl, what did he do!?"* I begged for the rest of the story, hanging onto her every word.

I mean I was almost falling off my damn bed. It's just that the story was *that* good. My mouth was wide open.

*"What happened J?"* I asked again this time with a slight yell in my voice.

"He left." Jacqueline said just as calm.

"He left?" I asked.

"Yup, he snatched his car keys out of Carmen's hand and he bounced. No one knows where he went. His stuff wasn't in the apartment when we were all over at the crib so, he may have gone back to the city. No one knows right now. I don't know how Carmen is going to pay her rent because Robert was getting his disability checks or whatever from when he got hurt at his job. So, she's fucked right now."

"So, that was *his* car all along?" I asked.

"Yeah, that was his car. Carmen don't have shit! Chino really don't have shit, either. He gets his little hustles going on here and there or whatever, but never anything solid.

That's what the whole fight at the crib was about. But one thing at a time." Jacqueline said.

"So what happened next?" I asked.

"Oh, so" Jacqueline continued, "Robert left and then Carmen turned to Tina and said, "You happy bitch? Look at the shit that you fucking started up in here." Then she went dead in her face and said, "I'm gonna make your life a living hell. I'm gonna make you wish that you never came here to this store you fucking trailer park, bamma bitch!"

"Bitch, you won't have the time to," Tina said coolly as she walked over to the register to ring up a customer.

"Hi, did you find everything you needed, ma'am?" Tina asked the woman, who looked to be in her late thirties.

"Well, not for me," the woman replied. "It's for my daughter. She loves it here. I do too, because there's always some mess going down in this place! There's never been a time I've been in this store and no one's been fighting, cussing, or causing some kind of drama. I just love it!"

"Yes, while you ladies were having your usual *pow-wow* in the middle of the floor and not doing any work, we got hit—bad," Barbara the District Manager said holding up two handfuls of empty hangers. "Take a look over there," she said as she directed our attention to the front of the store.

"Yo Jaliyah, I kid you not mami, two whole rounders that were full with jeans when we had first came in, were empty. Nothing on that shit!" She started laughing.

"But Jameka *did* leave us a flyer on the ground next to the rounders for this party that he is hosting with a picture of him on it wearing a thong as his calling card.

*"Whuuuuuuuuuttttttt?"* I said again in my low, extremely deep voice. "Shit," I said laughing.

"Yeah, I know" she continued, "But we didn't even know that Barbara was coming through. She never visits the store! So, right away Barbara rips into Carmen. She fucking rips into Tina, into Janet and me. It was crazy. So she tells me to go and start straightening the store because it was fucking mess. *Then,* she tells Janet to get on register or whatever. Then she calls Carmen and Tina into the backroom with her.

So Chino is just walking around the store not doing shit as usual. Surprisingly, he ain't have nothing to say after everything went down.

Barbara has Carmen and Tina in the room for a good hour and then Carmen comes storming out of the room, tears streaming down her face. Makeup running. *The works ma-ma.* She walks over to Janet, and I make my way towards the register to see what's wrong or whatever.

So Carmen says, *"Janet, can you unlock the cabinet for me and give me my bags?"*

"What happened to your keys?" Janet asked her. "What's wrong?"

"Barbara fucking fired me for stealing company merchandises

and stealing money and some bullshit about using the phone here during non-business hours. Some stupid shit," she said sniffling.

Jacqueline continued. So then I asked Carmen what happened to Tina and she said, *"Tina got written up for the theft that just happened or whatever and she is now the manager here. Once I leave, I can't come back up in here. So y'all two, make sure you come by my crib tonight. I can't believe I'm finally out of this fucking hell-hole."*

Janet lowered her voice to a whisper. "Who do you think could have told her that you were stealing shit, C?"

Carmen sniffled again her voice cracking, "I don't know. You, Jacqueline, Michelle, Chino and Robert were the only ones who knew."

*"Didn't you bring Jaliyah to your crib before, C?"* Janet asked tryna stir up some shit in her brain.

Carmen stopped sniffling. "Yeah, but only for a hot minute. We went in, I smoked and we went up to the bedroom—," she stopped mid-sentence.

Janet raised a suspicious eyebrow. "You went up to the bedroom for what?" she asked full of attitude.

Carmen sucked her teeth. "That's where I rolled up at or whatever."

"And you probably had your closet door wide open that I *always* tell you to close and she probably saw all the fucking stolen shit hanging in ya closet, duh!" Janet said rolling her eyes.

So I said, "Y'all, I don't *really* think Jaliyah would tell. She hasn't even been here that long. Why the fuck would she want to tell on you Carmen?" I knew where the conversation was headed.

"So Carmen told me that she *guesses that I was right* and she told Janet that *she doesn't think that you would tell—blah, blah, blah. But,* she had already made up her mind that *you* were the one who had told on her," Jacqueline said.

Barbara came out of the backroom and said, "Carmen, you

have to leave the premises or I'm going to be forced to call the police and get them involved. We made a deal to handle this issue *in-house,* so please hold up your end of the bargain and leave like we agreed."

"I gotta go y'all. I'll see you later okay. Remember, come by the crib." Carmen hugged us both, and then she left with Chino.

"I don't know how they got home; I guess they took a cab or something. But they got there."

Jacqueline continued. "So, Janet was all upset and crying up until Carmen left, and then she said some slick shit like, "You play in the dark and the boogie man is gon' get you every time. Boo-yow!" Then she was fine. So, that made me think that maybe *she* was the one who dropped the dime on Carmen or whatever. I ain't really care. I was just happy that I didn't have to be harassed anymore at work.

Nadia came in. Who else, um, Taylor came in. Barbara ended up staying in the store with us until closing. She bought us all lunch. It was fun. Tina re-did the schedule according to the hours that everyone is available like it *should* have been done all along. Um, oh, and she did the typical *pep talk* saying how we were going to get through this and how we are a team and all of that bullshit. She told us to come in tomorrow morning ready to work."

"Is that it?" I asked her.

"No, not even close Baby Girl," she said laughingly.

"I still ain't even get up to the part of the story where you come in at. No, this is far from it."

# chapter thirty-eight

"Okay Jaliyah, what happened next, was like some shit straight out of a fucking movie. I swear this to you!" Jacqueline said sounding more wide-awake now than she had been all night. "We lock up the store. We are all walking out to the parking lot. We are talking about how crazy the day was. Yada, yada, yada. *Whatever.*

I head to Janet's car because we're supposed to go by Carmen's crib. Tina goes to her car. Barbara goes to her car.

Barbara gets into her car, starts it up, waves good-bye and drives off. Tina gets into her car, waves goodbye and drives off. Me and Janet wave back and drive off behind Tina. So, Janet and me are like, *that shit was crazy today!* You know, just talking about the day's events. All of a sudden, not one, but two of Tina's tires, pop off of her car and just bounce down the damn street almost causing like four or five cars to crash, and *then,* Tina starts swerving out of control until she hits the fucking guardrail over by the mall exit ramp!

Yo, Janet stopped the car and we both jumped out and ran over to Tina! Me and Janet are crying and screaming. We don't know what the fuck to expect once we get over to her car. So, her car is fucked up. But thank God, she ain't hurt.

Tina is like, *"Oh my God, I can't believe this. I just got my car inspected. I don't know how this could have happened?"* She's crying hysterically. She's shaken-up. It's obvious that me and Janet are thinking the same thing and we look at each other like, *Carmen? Naaaaahhhhh.* Why would she do some bugged-out shit like that?

We call the police and they come. The ambulance comes. They put Tina into the ambulance to take her to the hospital, and we decide that we are going to follow the ambulance over there to make sure that she's okay.

Before we get back into the car to go to the hospital, we go *back* over and take another look at Tina's car and it is *fucked*! So I'm like, *"Shit, she could've been killed."* So we're looking, and we're looking and then Janet whispers, *"Come here."* So I go over, and there are four little dusty, itty-bitty handprints on the side of Tina's black car. Now, nobody but Chino has little-ass hands like that, with his short, tiny boney ass!

So I said, *"Oh that shit is fucked up!* Them two muthafuckas are outta their muthafuckin' minds! Then we hopped into the whip, and went over to the hospital to see how Tina was doing. She was fine. Only a few scratches. They released her within an hour.

We dropped her to her aunt's house who is out of town right now. She is staying there until she gets settled in her place that DIVAS is renting for her. We made sure that she didn't need anything before we left since her car was totaled. She said that she was good, and that she would still be in tomorrow as planned.

On the drive over to Carmen's crib, Janet was like, we should tell Carmen about what happened to Tina, but we shouldn't say anything about the handprints on the car so *that* way if the police get involved and start asking them questions, they'll be caught off guard and won't have their alibis and shit together."

*"Whuuuuuuutttt?!"* I said again for what felt like the hundredth time. "I can't believe that they would do some extreme mess like that! The security cameras in the parking lot probably got their dumb asses all up on the video too. All up in the screen!"

"I know," Jacqueline said. "That's what I told Janet. So eventually, we pulled up to Carmen's crib and we agreed that we would just tell her that Tina was in a crazy car accident and her car flipped over crazy times and her tires flew off. This and that."

Jacqueline continued, "So we knock on the door and all we can hear inside is music blasting and madd niggas inside talking and laughing and what not. So Chino answers the door and he lets us in. We spot Carmen immediately drinking, smoking and bull-shitting over in the kitchen. She is laughing and having a good old time.

I turn to Janet and I give her the nod like come on, let's do it now, and *this* bitch shakes her head, *"No"*, madd fast. Yo, Janet straight up flipped the whole script and she ain't say *shit*! That's what the fuck *I* get for trusting a crackhead. I guess it was because, deep down she knew how Carmen got when she was drunk. Carmen offered her a drink and that dumb bitch immediately started drinking, rolled a blunt, and our plan went out the fucking window."

*"No she didn't Jacqueline,"* I said shocked because I thought that Janet was *really* gonna come through this time.

*"Yes she did,"* Jacqueline said. "I was like, *bitch, what the fuck are you doing?!* You supposed to have my back!"

She continued. "So, I just said *fuck it*, I'll do it by myself."

Carmen could look at my face and see that I wasn't feeling the whole vibe. So she got in my face and said, *"And what the fuck is your problem?"*

I told her how Tina had gotten into a crazy car accident on her way home tonight. I told her that she barely made it out of the mall parking lot and her tires flew off of her car and she swerved and hit a guardrail. Then I just stared at her with no expression whatsoever.

Then she goes to me, *"What the fuck are you staring at me for?* Bitch you betta step your ugly ass up outta my face and go get a clue before you get ya ass dragged through this house!" Then she laughed, and just kept on drinking her beer.

"Carmen, that's real foul if you had something to do with that shit. You could go to jail for attempted murder." I told her.

So Carmen said, "Well, I ain't have *shit* to do with *shit* so I guess I'll be staying right here," and she took her pointer finger and pushed me in my forehead twice or whatever like when she said, *right here,* she pushed me on my forehead—*hard.*

So I slapped her hand away and said, "Yeah, you'll be *right here* until the end of this month since Rob ain't around to pay the bills no more." Then I laughed.

She got pissed and she grabbed my wrist madd tight and said, *"Are you stupid? I'll fucking kill you Jacqueline!"*

Then Chino came over and told her to *let me go,* and that *I'm not worth it.* She let me go, and then she said, "Look Jacqueline, just give Chino his money for your kicks and get the fuck outta my crib!"

Janet said that she would drive me home, but Carmen said that if she drove me home she would make sure that corporate found out that *she* was stealing shit too. So, Janet just stood quiet.

Now Jaliyah, I had already paid Chino for my sneakers so I told her, "I already paid him for my sneakers last week. I ain't giving him shit!"

Then she got on some bullshit about me giving some nigga head. Some shit that I was joking about. I had said like a month ago that I love Jordans so much that *I'd suck a dick for em'.* Like that crackhead from *Menace II Society*. We all laughed, and that was it.

Now y'all, I had to interrupt her story right here and say, *"Well ma, you did suck dick to get inside of the club to see 50."*

She laughed. "Jaliyah, me and him used to mess with each other. Me and Tony had been dating exclusively for about a month or two. I could not believe that they were recording that shit. Then they had the *nerve* to put it up on the big screen in the club.

I didn't even know until I came back down to the dance floor. Me and him had done shit like that before plenty of times, but they never put it on camera or anything like that. I was just feeling nice and having a good time so it went down. That don't make it right, but that's all it was."

She got back to her story. "So, Carmen was on her bullshit tryna pimp *me* the way she be pimping Janet. Tryna get me to suck Chino's friend's dick or whatever. So I told her *no*, and I started to walk towards the door to leave. She ran after me, grabbed me and threw me down on the sofa, pulled my sneakers off my feet and was like, *"Where the fuck are you going with no shoes bitch! You gon' make good on what you said or else!"*

Now Jah-dee, seeing Carmen like this was not new to me, but I just ain't feel like going through it. So I said, "Or else what Carmen?" just as calm. Not flipping out or anything.

"Or else I'ma kick ya ass from here to your grandparents house, bitch!" she yelled.

Chino was still holding her back. Janet is fucking standing there not saying shit. All of these niggas are in the crib hyping shit up. I called a cab, but they said that they didn't pick people up from her address anymore because they never paid their fare. I didn't want to bother my grandparents, so I called you. You told me to wait outside, so I left and I thought that Carmen would've stayed her drunk ass inside, but I guess she wanted to come out and fight me or whatever."

She laughed. "Now I'm finished. The rest of the story is where you came in and you know that part."

*"Whuuuuuuuuttttt?!"* I asked, my voice deep and raspy.

"Girl, will you stop saying *what* like that like that. You sound nasty!" she laughed. "Your sisters are really nice. You all look alike."

"I know," I told her. "Everyone always tells us that."

"Your sister Angie told me that she's getting married," she said.

"Yeah, in a couple of weeks. I can't wait until she does it already. I'm so sick and tired of hearing about this freaking wedding!" I laughed. "No, I'm just kidding. I'm really happy for her. He's a nice dude. We all like him."

"She invited me," Jacqueline said.

"Shut up," I said jokingly. *"No she didn't.* Damn, by the time the wedding gets here, we gon' have to book another location. It's gonna be too many people!"

She laughed. "I wanna go. Shit, I never get to go nowhere nice!"

"Well, I don't know about how nice it's gonna be, but you should have a good time. You bringing a date?" I asked her.

"I got someone in mind," she said.

"Who?" I asked.

"I still haven't asked him yet. I don't even know if he'll be available. It's still up in the air right now," she said.

*"Whuuuuuuuuttt?!"* I said again teasing her.

"Ill, Jah-dee!" she said. "Stahpppp it!"

"Okay!" I said laughing. "I'm gonna take my ass to bed!"

"Me too," she said. "Don't quit Jah-dee. Barbara will be in tomorrow. Talk to her. She's good peoples."

"I gotta check with my pops and see what he says," I told her.

"Okay," she said. "Goodnight Jah-dee."

"Goodnight Jah-dee."

Then I drifted off to sleep.

# part seven
# thursday

# chapter thirty-nine

I woke up at about 9:30 that morning and immediately ran downstairs to tell my father about everything that Jacqueline had told me the night before. I explained to him why Carmen had been fired and how she wasn't allowed within 200 feet of the store. I told him that the District Manager would be in today and that I would talk to her and let her know what went on the night before.

"Talk to the District Manager and get specifics from her," my father said as he turned off the garden hose in the backyard. "As a matter of fact, get dressed. I'm gonna go in with you."

Now once my father said that he was going to go somewhere with me, that was the end of it. So I didn't argue with him. I just ran upstairs and got dressed. My father kept on his signature shorts, sneakers and t-shirt.

"I look bummy?" he asked me.

"I look good!" he said before I could even answer him.

I headed towards his black, Mercedes Benz and tugged on the handle for him to open it. He had just bought it.

"Yo man!" he exclaimed. "Just cause your little car is all

busted up don't be pulling on my doors! I'll kick ya ass!" he joked.

We arrived at the mall and saw two police cars parked out front. We walked inside and headed up the escalator to DIVAS.

"Jesus Christ!" my father said to me as we approached the store, "Do they have the music loud enough?" Janet Jackson's "All for You" blared from the stereo. As we walked in further we noticed that two police officers were standing by the backroom door talking to Tina.

"Baby Girl!" Janet, Jacqueline and Nadia shouted as they ran towards me and hugged me.

"What's up my peeps!?" I said playfully. "This is my father Lonnie," I said pointing to my father.

"Hi Dad," they all said laughing.

My father put his hand over his mouth and did a playful "girl-ish" giggle. "Hi!" Then he waved his hand like a true Queen. They all laughed. "Your dad is crazy Jaliyah."

"I know," I said. "It's nothing new to me. Trust."

"What's going on in here? Is Barbara here?" I asked. "Me and my dad want to talk to her."

"She'll be back soon." Janet said. "You know how Tina had that bad car accident last night, well someone tipped the police off about the little handprints on the car and about who they might belong to. The police went back to the security video and caught Chino on video loosening Tina's lug nuts. Carmen didn't help him, but she was standing there telling him what to do. They are both locked up right now." She winked at Jacqueline.

"I heard that they had just let Carmen out of her holding cell for fighting Jah-dee when they got the news about Tina's car accident; and they just turned her back around, and put her old, tired-ass right back in the cell!" Jacqueline said laughing hysterically, which made everyone laugh.

My father just shook his head. "Y'all girls are crazy." He

looked at me. "I guess it ain't no sense in you quitting now. They're locked up. You might as well stay. The money is good, right?" he asked me.

"Yeah," I said.

"Well, it's up to you?" he said to me.

All of the girls were staring at me waiting for my answer when Tina walked over. "What's going on here? You tryna get us robbed blind again Jaliyah?"

"No, she's thinking about leaving us," Jacqueline said as she made a sad face.

Tina grabbed me by the hand and said, "Girl you betta come on here!"

She looked at my father. "You must be her dad."

"Yup," my father said.

Tina continued. "Well, she is an absolute pleasure. She is so sweet."

"She better be!" my father said smiling. "Does she work today?" he asked her.

"Yes, she does. As a matter of fact, she's late." Tina said smiling.

My father turned and looked at me. "See ya!" he said loudly.

I reached up and gave him a kiss.

"Who's coming to pick me up?"

"What time do you get off?" he asked me.

"Six," I said.

"Someone will be here." My father said as he headed for the door.

"Bye ladies."

"Bye Dad!" they all screamed in unison as my father exited the store.

It had been decided. I was staying and I was happy that I was.

The hustle and bustle of the mall filled the store again. Tina grinned mischievously, then ran to the back and cranked up LL

Cool J's "Around the Way Girl". The beat boomed throughout the store, making everyone bounce along. Jacqueline nudged me with a smirk.

"That was one crazy night," she said, shaking her head in disbelief.

*"Definitely,"* I said, nodding in agreement. I stood in the entrance of DIVAS, the music pulsating, while the chaos of the night before began to fade.

That night *had* been wild, and nobody had any idea what was coming next. But if there was one thing we knew for sure, it was that we'd face whatever came our way—together.

# chapter forty

The day went by smoothly. It was so nice to be at work in a drama-free environment. I couldn't stop thinking about Dominic. I called him during my lunch break to fill him in on all of the details of my adventure-filled night.

"That twat better not have put a fucking scratch on you!" he yelled angrily.

"It's cool, it's cool," I told him. "I'm *so* excited for tomorrow night! I need it badly after everything DIVAS has put me through this last week! Jesus!"

"Me too," he agreed. "I'll call you tonight for the directions okay."

"Bet," I said using his classic line.

"See, I'm already rubbing off on you," he said laughing.

I finished my shift and I filled my sister, Angie in on everything that had occurred on the ride home. When we got home, we headed upstairs to her bedroom where my mother and my little sister Nicky were hanging out. With all of the week's occurrences, I had not even noticed that most of her stuff was already gone. She had been packing and moving boxes back and forth from my parents' house to her and Gil's new house since the middle of the month.

"Damn, you're all set, huh?" I asked her.

"Yeah," she said. "I can't believe that I'm moving out of here! I remember when I didn't want to move in, now I don't want to move out" she started to tear up. This of course made me and my mom start to tear up as well.

"This is my cue to leave!" Nicky huffed rudely before heading into her room, slamming her door and blasting "Certified Gangstas" by Jim Jones as loud as possible on her stereo.

This of course prompted my mother to follow right behind her and bang on her door. *"Nicky, open this goddamn door!"*

Nicky opened the door and my mother went inside and shut the door behind her. It was muffled, but I could hear my mother saying something about ringing her neck, then riding her neck, then throwing her ass down the stairs and breaking her neck.

*"You gon' miss this?,"* I asked referring to the beat down that my mother was preparing for my sister.

"Yeah J. I can't believe that in a few weeks I'm gon' be Mrs. Angela Tanaka," she said as she taped up and labeled another box.

"That's better than Macculloch," I said laughing.

"Macculloch?" she asked. "Oh, is he that white boy who's coming over here tomorrow night to meet Ma and Daddy, and then *hang you up in his basement?* I meant to tell you, Mommy and Daddy done invited the whole damn world over here tomorrow. We gon' have a cookout!" She snapped her fingers. *"Hey!"*

"Are you serious?" I asked her.

"As serious as Mommy is about beating down Nicole right now," she laughed. "That girl is crazy! She just gon' do what she wanna do! She's gonna learn the hard way!"

"Yup!" I said. "I tried to kill her last week. Her attitude is just *way* too much sometimes."

"I told you. Remember when me and her fought that time?"

Angela laughed. "She always knows just the right buttons to push!" I rolled my eyes.

"Dang, so we having a damn cookout?" I exhaled deeply. "This is gone be some shit here."

I built another box for her and we started to pack all of her stuffed animals.

Just then, my mother re-entered Angie's bedroom looking hot, sweaty and greasy. "I tried to ride her *neck*!" my mother said angrily and out of breath. "Oh, that girl makes me so mad! I can't wait til someone marries her ass and takes her up outta here! If not, I'ma take her out—permanently."

Me and Angie busted out laughing.

"It ain't funny." my mother said smiling.

She examined her figure in the mirror behind the door. *"Hey y'all, what do you think about me smokin' crack right up until the wedding?* Just for two weeks—I'll go down a whole dress size!

"Ma! Do not start that tonight!," Angie laughed as she threw a *Beanie Baby* at my mother.

"*Please* don't start!" I laughed, then grabbed a few more boxes from the hall. We spent the whole night giggling and joking as we finished helping Angie pack.

# part eight
# the weekend

# chapter forty-one

I didn't even see Dominic's car when he pulled up to the house. There were so many cars parked in front of the house that night that he had to park halfway down the block. All I know is that I heard the doorbell ring and there he was in all his glory holding a bottle of red wine for my parents and a bouquet of red roses for me.

"I brought this for your peoples, but I don't think that it's gonna be enough now," he said as he gave me a kiss on the cheek and I motioned for him to come in. I took the bottle from him. "And these are for you," he said as he handed me the flowers.

"You didn't have to bring me anything. That was so sweet of you."

He had on a pair of blue jeans that were loose fitting, but not baggy. He wore a yellow Polo golf shirt with blue lines across it and a fresh pair of low-top white Nike Uptowns. He smelled so good.

"I didn't know that y'all were having a cookout," he said as he sniffed the air, "but I'm glad y'all are cause I'm hungry than a mug!" He rubbed his hands together. "I was gonna take you out for dinner after meeting your parents, but cool. We could just chill here."

He took my hand. "Come on girl. Start introducing me so I can get to eating!"

I went and found my mother first. She was sitting outside in the backyard with my Aunt Pam and my Aunt Sharisse.

"Mommy, Aunties, this is Dominic," I said smiling from ear to ear.

"*Hi Dominic*," my mother got up and shook his hand.

He gave her a kiss on the cheek. "Oh my God, you and Jaliyah look just alike."

My mother smiled. "Everyone tells us that. You have to see her with her father though."

"You have a beautiful home Mrs. Whitfield." He admired the backyard. "I'm working hard so I can have a house like this one day. Right now, I live in a townhouse over in Chelsea. Nothing big but—"

"That's okay," my mother interrupted, "it's *yours* and that's all that matters."

"Hi D!" my Aunt Sharisse said loudly. "You like my niece!?" she asked. "She purrty right?!" she said taking a swig of her wine cooler.

"*Breathtaking* is more like it," he said smiling at me. He looked back over at my aunts who were obviously impressed. "Nice to meet you both ladies."

"You hungry D?" my Aunt Pam asked.

Dominic rubbed his stomach. "Yeah, I *could* eat a little something, something."

"Fix the man a plate!" my mother yelled. "We got burgers, hot dogs, chicken, ribs, steak, fried fish, potato salad. We got it all!"

"And it's all good!" my Aunt Pam added.

"*Dominic*," I called over to him from the table full of food, "what do you want?"

He walked over to me. "I'll take a little bit of everything sweetheart."

"Sweetheart," my Uncle Smitty said appearing out of what seemed like thin air. "How long you been knowing my niece that you can go around calling her Sweetheart?" he asked.

*"Uncle Smitty,"* I said as I gave him a murderous glare.

"Oh girl, I'm just teasing the man! Goddamn! You ain't gotta protect him!" he said laughing.

"Stop playing him so close!" He stopped laughing long enough to shake Dominic's hand. "How you doing man? I'm Jaliyah's Uncle Charles. "Everyone calls me Smitty though."

"How you doing man? I'm Dominic but everyone around here so far has been calling me *D*, so it's cool with me." He laughed.

"Nice to meet you man." Smitty put his hand on Dominic's shoulder and ushered him over to an empty seat. "Here man. Sit down and eat your food. I'll holla at you later." Smitty went to the cooler, pulled out a can of ginger ale to go along with his Jack Daniels, and he went back inside of the house.

*"D,"* I said, "I'm sorry I didn't tell you everyone was gonna be here like this. I just found out myself last night. I didn't tell you because I was afraid that you would change your mind."

He took a bite out of his hamburger. "You kidding me? I wouldn't have missed this for the world J." He piled some potato salad onto his fork and ate it. "I love a good cookout. That is one thing I love about my townhouse. I grill out damn near every night."

"Let me go grab you a soda," I said to him as I got up and headed towards the cooler. "What kind do you want?"

"Grape," he said.

"Grape it is," I said as I opened up the cooler and dug out a grape soda.

"Psssss….Jaliyah, come here!" I heard my Aunt Pam say.

I ran over to see what she wanted. "Mmm, y'all look really nice together. He's a cutie."

"I know!" my Aunt Sharisse said, "Make me wanna go out and get me one!"

"He is handsome," my mother said. "He almost got Brad Pitt beat!" She started laughing. "Go head back over there before he thinks we talking about him!"

"Okay," I said. I was to glad hear that my mother found him to be cute as well.

I walked back over to Dominic and handed him his soda.

"Thank you so much," he said looking me up and down. He took a bite of his chicken. "By the way, you are looking absolutely beautiful tonight J."

"You are looking quite flyy yourself," I commented back.

"Yeah," he said as he stared into my eyes.

*"Whoa ho...ho..!!!!!!"* my father exclaimed loudly as he approached Dominic and I in his signature outfit with his cap turned to the back and a rum and coke in his left hand. "Ain't that sweet. Y'all are sitting here staring into each other's eyes. How romantic!" My father looked me up and down. "Oh you got my daughter to put on a dress for you and everything. Look at that."

My father looked down at my feet. "Oh! You even got her to polish her toenails! Let me shake your hand, bro!"

"Daddy!" I yelled embarrassed.

Dominic turned beet red. He stood up to shake my father's hand and I held his plate. "How you doing sir? My name is Dominic."

"Dominic! Like Dominic the Italian Christmas donkey!" my father exclaimed as he broke out into the Dominic the Donkey song.

*"Hey, Jing-a-di-jing hee haw hee haw*
*It's Dominick the Donkey*
*Jing-a-di-jing hee haw hee haw*

*The Italian Christmas Donkey*
*Lalalalalalalalala. lalalalalaladidooda…"*

"Yup, just like the Italian Christmas donkey. My brothers and sisters use to tease me with that song growing up. I think my parents named me that for that sole purpose!" he laughed.

My father laughed too. "Well, go head man. Finish your food. Finish looking into each other's eyes. Because when that's done, we gone go down into the basement and party!"

"I can't wait," Dominic said laughing.

"Can you sing man?" my father asked.

"A little something," Dominic answered smilingly.

"Don't lie man," my father smiled. "I got microphones and everything set up downstairs. I'ma put you on the spot."

"I'm good. I can sing a little something." Dominic reassured him.

"Okay my man!" my father said as he gave him a pound. "Showtime is whenever you finish eating and looking into my daughter's eyes."

"Okay," Dominic laughed.

*"OOOOHHHHH LONNIE, YOU BOUT TO SING?!"* my Aunt Sharisse screamed from all the way on the other side of the backyard.

*"Yeah Reese,"* my father said as he rolled his eyes up in the air and walked away.

*"OOOOHHHHHH, I WANNA SING ATLANTIC STARR, 'FOR ALWAAAAAAAAYS,'* she yelled dramatically, blending scream and song."

"Come on Reese," my father, said unenthused.

Sharisse jumped up and ran into the house behind him, *"OWWWWW, TO THE BEAT Y'ALL! SO SWEET YA'LL! A FREAK-FREAK YA'LL!"*

She stuck her head back outside and looked over at me and Dominic. "Hurry up y'all, I'm about to tear it up!"

Most of the adults begin to file inside within the next hour while Dominic and I talked about anything and everything with my little cousins running around. I got to introduce him to Angie and Nicky, Angie's fiancé Gil, my uncle Ant and Aunt Kima and all of my cousins. My Uncle Claude was off jet-setting and couldn't make it.

"Does your father really have karaoke downstairs J?" Dominic asked me.

"My father has a whole damn nightclub downstairs!" I laughed. "He built it right after we moved in."

"No way," he said not believing me.

"I'm serious." I took him gently by the hand. *"Come on."*

I attempted to pull him towards the house, but instead, he pulled me close to him and gave me a quick, soft kiss on the lips.

"Oooooohhhhhhhh," I heard my little cousins say. "Ill, gross. They kissed."

"Mind yours, punk!" I yelled to my little cousin Adam.

"Baby," Dominic said laughing, "you don't gotta be so mean!"

"Whatever, they do need to mind they business!" I laughed. "Come on, let's go inside and see what's going on in the *club*!" I took his hand and we headed into the house and down the basement stairs.

Once we got down there, we were greeted with the "soulful" sounds of my Aunt Sharisse "singing" ABBA's "Dancing Queen".

*"YOU CAN DANCE...YOU CAN JIVE....HAVING THE TIME OF YOUR LIFE! OOOOHHHHH...SEE THAT GIRL....WATCH THAT SCENE...DIGGIN' THE DANCING QUEEEEEEEN!"* she attempted to belt out.

Once my father spotted me and Dominic downstairs he cut my aunt's song short. "Sorry Reese," he said as he shut her song off.

"Oh, hell no!" she yelled. "Fine, take your funky little mic. I was done anyway!"

My father threw on Gwen McCrae's "Funky Sensation" and everyone started to get down! He put on his fog machine and strobe lights as the disco ball in the middle of the room spun round and round.

"Wow, he really *does* have his own club down here." Dominic whispered in my ear. "Well, you know that you go to the club to dance so…," he pulled me to the middle of the dance floor. *"Let's do this….Girl!"* he said imitating Bilal in *House Party* when he asked Sidney to dance.

I cracked up. "You sure you gon' be able to keep up?" I asked him flirtingly.

"I was just about to ask you the same thing shortie," he said as he winked at me.

The music switched up and Jeff Redd's "You Called and Told Me" started pumping.

"Aw…see, you don't know nothing about this one here!" Dominic said as he clapped his hands and started grooving on beat to the music.

I was chilling, you know, doing my little cutesy dances or whatever because I felt like it was too early to give it all to him. I ain't wanna show out or nothing like that, you know.

"Yo," he said, as he put his fist to his mouth, "I thought for sure that you'd be able to dance a little better than that J!" he laughed. "Your swagger is too cool to just be posing to the beat!"

"Oh really," I said. "Okay, hold up."

I went over to my father and requested a song. I looked over at Dominic.

He laughed. "What you do, put in a request?"

"I got your request," I said looking at him with a sexy look in my eyes.

Beyonce's "Crazy in Love" started up. Everyone went bananas. Now, what y'all do *not* know about me is whenever a Beyonce song comes on, it's as if her spirit enters my body, and for that moment, I become her. I do that damn shit! I will fuck a Beyonce record up! Of course, I killed it! I twisted and turned. I went down to the floor and came back up. I swung my hair around. I did it all. By the time that song ended, I was sweating like crazy.

"Ma," Dominic said, "you killed it!" He gave me a pound. "Damn, see I knew you had that in you. I could tell by your attitude. Tryna play that shy, cute role. I like a girl that will get down and do her thing. Have all the bitches in the club jealous and shit!"

"One In A Million" by Sanchez began. Dominic took my hands into his and pulled me close to him. We danced to the music. He kept the beat the whole time. He could *really* dance. Like the white boys in *You Got Served*! He didn't lose it after a few minutes either. He *really* had rhythm.

"I'm having so much fun with you Jaliyah. Damn, we doing it all! Dinner, dancing….your Aunt Reesee's live performances. I love it!" he laughed.

Just then, the song faded out and my father took the mic to sing. "This song is dedicated to my oldest daughter, Angela. As you all know, she is getting married in a couple of weeks. I hope to see you all there."

The crowd erupted with, *"You know I'm gon' be there! You'll definitely see me. I ain't gon' miss that shit!"*

My father continued. "If you have not RSVPd as of yet, don't just show up. I will not be working the door. I'm gonna be inside sitting down somewhere. Therefore, if you have *not* gotten on the list, see Angela or Gil before you leave, or else you are *not* getting in. Don't be calling me up on my cell neither. Not me, not Deena, not Jah-dee or Nicky. None of us. And y'all know Nicky will *answer* her phone and just tell you that she ain't tryna hear it."

Everyone laughed.

"Big facts!" Nicky chimed in.

He finished his song intro with, "And to Dominic, if this night and tomorrow's date with Jaliyah goes well, we may see you there too my man!"

"I hope so!" Dominic yelled out to my father from the table that we were now sitting down at. He looked at me, *"Will I be there J?"*

I smirked. "So far, so good."

The music started up and my father began to sing "Lullabye (Goodnight, My Angel)" by Billy Joel.

Of course, Angie began to cry along with all of the other women in the room except Nicky. She just rolled her eyes at the whole thing. When my father finished singing, everyone cheered and clapped. Angela went over and gave my father a huge hug and kiss.

*"Dominic, my man!"* my father shouted into the microphone. "I didn't forget. Come up here and sing a little "shumptin', shumptin" as you said earlier.

Dominic hid his face with a napkin on the table. He looked at me and smiled.

"You don't have to go up there if you don't want to. He's just kidding," I said to him.

"No," he said, "I'll do it." He winked at me as he went up to the mic and flipped through the collection of songs. He whispered his selection into my father's ear. I saw my father mouth the words, "Are you sure man?" to him. "Cause we'll talk about you."

Dominic laughed and shook his head yes.

My mother looked at me. "Can he sing?" she mouthed.

I shrugged my shoulders and mouthed the words, "I don't know. I don't think so." back to her.

The music started up. Michael Jackson's "The Lady in My Life" erupted from the speakers.

*He remembered,* I thought to myself.

He began to sing. His voice was so smooth and rich.

> *"There'll be no darkness tonight*
> *Lady, our love will shine*
> *Just put your trust in my heart*
> *And meet me in paradise..."*

My whole family began to scream, cheer and clap for him. My mother and the rest of my family who were downstairs looked over at me and smiled. You could tell that they were impressed.

"Damn, that boy is good! Justin Timberlake ain't got shit on him!"

Dominic continued to sing,

> *"...So let me keep you warm*
> *Through the shadows of the night*
> *Let me touch you with my love*
> *I can make you feel so right..."*

When he finished singing. We stood up for him. He was *so* good. I coulda beat his ass, pretending that he couldn't sing on the phone the other night! I felt so special. The fact that he remembered that " The Lady In My Life" was my favorite song *AND* he sang it to me. I was elated. I gave him a huge hug and I kissed him on the cheek when he came back to the table.

"Boy, you can blow, you can blow, you can flow, toe to toe!" my Aunt Sharisse said as she hugged him. Then she leaned in close and whispered. *"Tell my brother, that you want to sing a duet with me so he'll let me get back on the mic and sing one more time, okay."*

Dominic laughed. "A-ight, what you wanna sing?" he asked her.

Her eyes opened wide and a huge smile crossed her face, "Tell Me if You Still Care" by the SOS Band. You know how it goes?" she asked him, her eyes full of excitement.

"Yeah, I know it. Definitely," he said.

What Auntie Reesee *didn't* know was that my father had already peeped her whole stee-lo. As soon as Dominic got up to approach my father, my dad got on the mic and said, "Reesee, your time on the mic is up! It ain't happening!" he said. "But, Dominic here can sing another song by himself and you can just sing along quietly in your seat."

Reesee gave him the finger as she polished off wine cooler number ten.

My father laughed. "Nah man, your voice is amazing. I thought that you were gonna get up here and play around man. Wow."

"I love to sing. Not as a career, but just in my free time. In the car or the shower. Places like that. I appreciate it though sir. Thanks for the compliments."

I looked at my watch. It was already after midnight.

"D!" I called over to him.

"Look, my daughter's calling you man. You better go. I've seen her cut dude's off for much less," my father said to him.

Dominic chuckled, and then came over to me.

"It's already past twelve," I told him.

"Shit, it's that late. I'm having such a great time." He tapped me on my chin. "Tomorrow will be great too though." He clapped his hands together and said, "Okay, come around with me to say my goodbyes to everyone. Then, I'll say good-night to you and I'll see you tomorrow. How's that work?" he said.

"Fine with me," I said.

I didn't realize how many people were up in the crib until Dominic decided that he wanted to say goodbye to each and every one of them. My Aunt Kima took a picture of the two of us before he left.

"Let me get a jacket," I said. "I wanna walk you to your car so we can have a proper goodbye. I know my little cousins are running around here hiding somewhere tryna be nosy. Little bastards."

I opened up the downstairs coat closet, took out one of my father's jackets and put it on. "You ready?" I asked him.

"Yup."

"Okay, let's go."

I walked him out of the driveway and about four cars down the block. I couldn't really see what type of car he had. I could only see that it was black and big.

"What kind of truck is this?" I asked him tryna make it out in the darkness.

"It's an Escalade," he said.

"Oh, okay. Go ahead D!" I said laughing.

"Is your car fixed yet?" he asked me.

"You know what," I said, "I ain't even check. Hold on a minute."

I ran back up the block and saw that my car was one of the cars parked on the street. I went around to the passenger side window.

I ran back over to his car. "Yup, it's fixed!"

"Good," he said. "Your pops came through, huh?"

"He always does," I said.

"Oh so you and your sisters are like Paris Hilton and Nicole Richie—huh?"

I smiled at him. "On a much smaller scale—but yes.

"I see, I see," he said smiling. "Well it is really chilly out here, so go inside and try to get some sleep even though they seem like they ain't gone stop rocking til the break of dawn in that bitch!"

"Tell me about it," I said.

He leaned in, pulled me close and kissed me softly on my lips like before, but this time, he slipped me a little tongue. His lips were *so* smooth and so soft. He caressed my lower back and slid his hand down to my butt before patting it softly.

"Sweet dreams," he said.

I gave him a hug. "Call me when you get home, okay."

He got into his car, started it up and said in his best Tony Montana impression, "Ju got it main!

He followed me in his car and watched me walk back into the house. I waved, he waved back and then he drove off.

I went inside and told everyone that I was off to bed because I had to get up early the next morning. Our first date was about to go down and I couldn't have been more excited.

# chapter forty-two

Saturday had *finally* arrived and Dominic called me at about seven-thirty that morning to say that he would be at my house by nine. We had decided that we would drive down into the city and worry about parking once we got there. *What was I going to wear?* I walked out onto the front porch in my bathrobe. There was not a single cloud in the sky. The weather was perfect. The weather report said that it would go up to the mid-70s that day.

I chose to wear a simple white tank top, with a long, brown and pink bohemian-type flowing skirt and a pair of really cute brown, sandals. I layered on few anklets and bracelets to accessorize. On my neck, I wore a simple cross that I had gotten from my grandmother years ago. I pulled my hair back neatly into a bun and secured it with several bobby pins. I carried my large, pink crocheted shoulder bag and made sure that I had my lipgloss, mirror, clear mascara, hand sanitizer, brush, mints, gum, a little thing of hair gel for fly-aways, my wallet, some cash…you know. *The norm.*

My parents and my sisters were all awake and downstairs. My mother was in the middle of making breakfast. My father was already in the backyard trimming the hedges. Angie and Nicky were planning their days.

"Angie," I said. "Jacqueline told me that you invited her to the wedding."

"Yeah," she said cheerfully, "is she cool?"

I thought about it. "Yeah she's cool. We'll have fun."

"I'm so glad that you and Gil are paying for everything, as many damn people as y'all are inviting!" my father yelled from the backyard. "Me and your mother got off easy paying for your honeymoon! All my goddamn money!"

Angela began to cry—yet again. "I'm gonna miss these mornings. Waking up and just talking around the breakfast table."

This time though, me and my mother couldn't go there. I wasn't even tryna chance messing up my freshly washed faced or make my clear mascara run. And my mother was busy putting the food on the plates.

*"I can't go there wit' chu' right now boo,"* my mother said as she piled some eggs, toast and bacon onto a plate for my father, "but I got chu' later."

Nicky just looked at Angela like she was crazy, rolled her eyes up in the air and said, *"Whatever"* to herself quietly.

It was 8:45AM when the doorbell rang. He was early.

I ran downstairs and opened the door to see Dominic standing there with another bouquet of roses. This time they were pink and they matched my outfit.

"Thank you!" I said. "You did not have to get me more flowers boy! Dominic's here!" I yelled as I let him in.

"Good morning everybody," he said as he waved and smiled.

My father came in from the backyard and washed his hands. He then went over and shook Dominic's hand, "Sup man!"

"Good Morning Mr. Whitfield. I just wanted to stop in and say hello before me and Jaliyah headed out on our date."

"Don't like to waste the day!" my father said loudly. He

looked over at Dominic and smiled before saying, "My man!" loudly. He gave him another pound. "Well, have fun and I will see you later." My father leaned over and gave me a kiss before he sat down to the breakfast table to eat.

"Call me to let me know where you are every now and again," my mother said as she placed Angie and Nicky's plates on the table." I gave her kiss.

I leaned over and kissed both my sisters. "See y'all later."

Dominic said his goodbyes to the family and we were off.

We left my house and walked over to his shiny, black Cadillac Escalade that gleamed in the sunlight.

"See now, this is nice! I couldn't really get the whole effect of it last night. You got the rims going on and everything! I like this here! Pop the locks so I can get on up in here!" I said laughing.

"Oh, you feeling my ride? Okay!" he smiled as he unlocked the doors.

We got in, he backed out of the driveway and we hit the highway. It was an almost two-hour ride into Manhattan from where we were. We rode down to a lot of old school hip-hop. Pete Rock and CL Smooth, Grand Puba and Nice and Smooth were just a few of the artists we listened to on the way down. Dominic knew every lyric, every ad-lib.

"Damn, you should be on the record," I joked to him.

"I used to listen to these songs all the time when I was a youngster." He smiled at me. "I love hip-hop music."

He held my hand the whole way while he was driving. Well at least until he got into the city, then he had to use both hands to zig and zag in and out of traffic.

"What do you want to eat for breakfast?" he asked me. "Do you want a whole big spread for breakfast and then a light lunch? Or, do you want something light for breakfast and then a heavy lunch? Or, he asked me do you want both heavy or both light?"

"Decisions, decisions," I said teasingly. "Um, I'm not really a breakfast person, so I'll take a small bottle of apple juice and a warm croissant or a muffin for breakfast, and then we can do it up real big for lunch."

He smiled. "I was thinking the same thing."

We stopped at a café on the corner of Prince and Broadway and surprisingly found parking not too far from the restaurant. We went inside, sat down and enjoyed our light breakfast.

"I'm really happy that you decided to give me a chance J," he looked into my eyes for a minute and stared at me, his face full of joy.

I laughed.

"What's wrong?" he asked me.

"You got, some cream cheese, right here," I said as I reached over and wiped it off with my napkin.

"Oh shit," he said embarrassed. "What an asshole. I'm here thinking that you're laughing and smiling because I'm so irresistible and I have goddamn cream cheese on my face!"

"You're not an asshole," I said. "You don't have to be embarrassed around me. Wait til you get to know me a little better. You know that show, *Newlyweds* with Nick Lachey and Jessica Simpson? My family and all my friends tease me and say that I'm the black Jessica Simpson."

I pointed my fork at him after I took a bite of my fresh fruit. "*You* better never call me that though, or else it's gon' be me and you!"

"You ain't said nothing but a word!" he said laughing. "You finished?" he asked me.

"No," I said with a playful attitude.

"Well," he said imitating me, "Can you finish so we can get out of here and hit our first of many stops today?"

"*Fine,*" I said as I finished my fruit.

Dominic paid the bill and we got ready to get into the car when he said, "You know what, I'ma just leave my ride here, and me and you can cop a couple of Fun Passes and hop the trains all day. That'll be a lot easier." He looked at me. "I mean unless you too prissy to get on the subway!"

"What, are you crazy? I'm the gulliest chick you will ever meet in ya life son!" I said with crazy bass in my voice imitating a dude, before flashing my nastiest *Beanie Sigel* stink face. "Don't sleep!"

He laughed. "Okay, I see you! Let's get it then!"

"Let's go!" I said excited for what the day would bring.

We went *everywhere*. FAO Schwartz, Times Square, Nike Town. We had lunch at this Cuban Restaurant in the village. We went to South Street Seaport. We went on the Intrepid where I had *never* been. We even took the Circle Line.

I had been to Manhattan so many times. I had even *worked* in Manhattan. But I had never had this much fun in Manhattan. It was all so Paul Varjak and Holly Golightly in "Breakfast at Tiffany's"! We concluded our day of fun with dinner at this restaurant called, Tropica in Grand Central Station. I didn't even know that it was in there.

Our dinner conversation went something like this.

"I am so daggone tired I can't even see straight," I said to Dominic while taking a sip of my raspberry iced tea.

"Me too," he said rubbing his forehead, "I'm pooped!" He raised his eyebrows for emphasis. "I had a great time today though. This is one of the best times I have had in a long time. Last year was pretty shitty. I was feeling down. It's like, once you have the car, the crib, the job, you want that extra. You know. You want the wife, the kids and the drama that comes with it. It's a good kind of drama though. I want that."

"Yeah, well Angie is well on her way to that drama that you want so much," I said as I started in on my salad. "Speaking of Angie," I paused, "yo, you rolling with me to her wedding or what?"

"What?" he said, "I was about to ask you if you was rolling out with *me* to the wedding!"

We both laughed.

"I'm in the wedding party and everything so, I'll just tell Angie to put you at a table with Smitty or Reesee or someone and once the dancing and everything starts; I'm yours for the night. Cool?"

"Cool," he agreed.

We laughed and talked for about another hour and then we hopped back on the subway to Prince Street, hopped in the whip and rode home to the sounds of Smokie Robinson and The Miracles. We reached my house at about 1:30 that morning. We kissed, said goodnight, and I went inside. I actually stood there, smiling in a daze just like the girls do in the movies.

Butterflies were just a fluttering every witcha way inside my stomach. I was smitten with him. I reached into my bag and took out the photo strip that we had taken in a photo booth at the Broadway Arcade. All I could think about was the next time that me and him would be together. I walked into the family room to see my mother and father cuddled up together under a blanket watching "Coming to America". My mother was asleep.

"I'm back," I said quietly. "It was amazing. I had so much fun today!"

I gave my father a hug and a kiss.

"Yeah, he seems like a nice kid," my father said as he took a sip from his glass of red wine. "He knows his wine too." He raised his glass to me and winked his right eye. *"Salud."*

"Silly!" I responded. "I'm going to bed."

I took my shower, and my phone rang about five minutes after I was snug in my bed. It was Dominic.

"J, I had a great time tonight. You're real cool. But, I knew that already," he said.

"I've been home for a minute. I just wanted to shower and get into bed before I called you up. You know. Give you a chance to get settled."

"I had a good time wit' chu' too. You showed me one of *the* best times of my life," I laughed. "But you *already* knew that I'm sure."

"Maybe I'll come by your job tomorrow and say hello," he said.

"Maybe I'd like that," I responded.

"Okay, so as always, sweet dreams and I'll call you tomorrow."

"Same to you," I said, and then I hung up the phone.

# chapter forty-three

The next day at DIVAS, it was business as usual. The music was playing and the cash registers were racking up the sales. Dominic stopped by during my lunch break and we went and ate at the TGI Fridays downstairs in the food court. Once we finished eating, we kissed and hugged each other goodbye and I told him that we would speak later on that night.

All of the tension in the store had been released and there seemed to be no ill feelings amongst any of the girls. Barbara informed us that Michelle would be returning to the store the Monday of the following week.

*Welp, there goes my big raise,* I thought to myself.

Michelle would take Janet's position as assistant manager and Janet would be bumped up to co-manager, Tina's old position. To my surprise, Barbara *hadn't* decided to demote me even though I had not been working there long, and Carmen had promoted me to spite Michelle. None of the drama that the girls had been angry about really seemed to matter without Carmen there. Everyone had a clean slate. The store was going to be run the way that it was *supposed* to be run, and that was fine with all of us.

The day seemed to fly by and before we knew it, closing time had rolled around. There were hardly any returns to put away. There weren't any rounders or displays to straighten either. Tina ran that store like a drill sergeant. She wasn't mean or anything like that, she just kept reminding us that the more we did during our shifts, the less we would have to do once it was time to head home.

Jacqueline and I began to count down the registers while Tina, Nadia and Janet continued to straighten up the store. All of a sudden, the strangest feeling came over me. I felt as though someone was staring at me. I looked up towards the front gate that had been pulled down and locked and I saw a woman wearing sunglasses, with very long, bright red curly hair and a tan trench coat like Carmen San Diego wears, briskly walk past the gate and our window displays out in the hall.

"Maybe it's just someone passing through waiting for one of their friends to get off of work," I said to myself.

I continued to count the register down. After about a minute, I looked up and saw the person again. I could not make out who it was because they always moved as soon as they saw me looking in their direction.

I whispered to Jacqueline, "Jah-dee, I think that may be Carmen out there looking in here. I keep seeing someone staring at us and when I look up, they run out of sight. Look, just keep counting the register and I'll make a yawn sound or something, and then you look over at the gate."

"Okay," she said nervously.

I began to count the pennies. "Argh…," I yawned.

"Oh, shit!" Jacqueline whispered back. "Yeah that's her. She always wears that outfit when she's up to some shit. The last time I saw her wear it, we were all at Applebee's and she said that she was going to the bathroom and she straight up dipped on us and skipped out on the fucking bill."

She laughed. "She thinks that it's a great disguise, that's why she *never* switches it up. That's a wig that she has on by the way. It's called the, "Jessica Rabbit!"

We both began laughing hysterically.

"What are y'all giggling about over there? Finish counting so we can get up outta here!" Tina screamed over the sound of the vacuum cleaner as she vacuumed the insides of the fitting-rooms.

I motioned her to come over to the register. She turned off the industrial sized vacuum cleaner and headed over in our direction.

Once she got to the counter I said, "Tina, Carmen is here. She has been hanging around the outside of the store. Do you think that we should call the police and let them know that she is in violation of her court order?"

Tina looked over to the gate.

By this time, Carmen knew that we had all seen her so she snatched the glasses off and screamed, *"Y'all bitches got to come out sometime and when you do, Tina, I want your ass bitch! You wanna talk shit about whose dick I'm sucking and get me fired you bitch! I got something for you bitch! I'll be outside! That way I won't be in violation of a muthafucking thing while I'm fucking your ass up!"*

"Fuck you, you old out of work crazy bitch!" Tina yelled back as Carmen ran off past the windows and out of sight.

"I'm calling security," Janet said as she ran over to the phone. "How did she even get out of jail?"

"Don't call security," Tina said as she began to put away the vacuum cleaner.

"Why not?" I asked her. "That bitch tried to make you crash your damn car. She likely to do any damn thing! I wouldn't be surprised if that bitch is packin' heat!"

We all looked in Jacqueline's direction.

She looked surprised. "*What?* I don't know if Carmen has a gun. If she does she ain't never show it to me."

Then we all turned to look at Janet.

She looked just as stunned as Jacqueline did. *"I have never seen her with a gun either!* She does know a lot of crazy people and I wouldn't be surprised if she has Chino's mother *and* God knows who else out there waiting to kick all of our asses."

She went to snort from her ring and found it empty. "Shit, I forgot that I quit now that I'm gonna be getting piss tested! I'm having a panic attack! *I don't want to go out there, I'm scared of her!"*

Tina threw her arms up in the air and then went over and unlocked the cabinet under the register so that we could get our things and get ready to go. "Chile please. I walk with God! He's my security. I ain't gon' have this bitch having me afraid to live my life. Shit, she knows where I live. Let her come on! She wanna fight outside, shit we could do that too!"

She regained her cool. "Are you two finished counting down them registers?"

"Yeah, we just finished," Jacqueline, answered her.

"Okay then. Let's get ready to get outta here," she said her voice full of enthusiasm.

Tina gathered all of the money and receipts from that day's sales and she put them in a pouch. She put the pouch in the safe, locked it up and then went into the backroom to shut off the lights. "Let's go!"

Now I can't lie, if my father had known that Carmen had come around the store making threats and we didn't call anybody because Tina had decided that Jesus was our security that night, he would have called me a damn fool! I'm not saying that my father doesn't believe that God has your back, he just believes that God don't give you a mind to be stupid. However, there is also the old saying, *"God takes care of fools and babies."*

We walked out of the backroom exit into the side parking lot where we had decided that we would all park our cars so we could always leave in a group. We looked around to see if we saw Carmen. Janet and Jacqueline had told us all on our way out that Carmen usually drove Chino's mom's car whenever she couldn't get a hold of Robert's. She told us that her car was an old, beat up ice-blue Ford Taurus. We continued to scout the parking lot. No Carmen. But to the left of us all the way at the end of the side lot was the rusty and beat up Taurus.

*"That's the car,"* Jacqueline said.

"Great, it's all the way down there and we can't seem to find Carmen so why don't we stop looking for her and let's just go home! Call it a night!" Janet exclaimed as she jumped in her car, started it and drove off so fast her tires squealed. "I'll see you all tomorrow!"

"I swear yo, Janet is such a flake!" Jacqueline yelled.

"Well, Carmen's here somewhere. Maybe she realized that her stupid ass would go back to jail and this time they'd keep her ass if she started any shit." She looked over at me. "Jaliyah, can you take me home?"

"Not a problem. Hop in." I said to her smiling. I turned to Tina and Nadia. We're gonna go. Nadia, we'll see you tomorrow. Tina, be careful. Just keep a look out and you should call the cops to let them know something just to be on the safe side."

"Will do," Tina said.

I clicked my car alarm to unlock the doors. I had just opened up my driver's side door and was about to get in when I heard a familiar voice holler out, "What's that shit you was spoutin' the other day Miss Mouth! Huh?! See a bitch, slap a bitch! Hmm, well I see one, two, three, *four* bitches out here, and I'm gon' slap each and every single damn one of em', so which one of y'all bitches wanna get her face slapped damn first! Cuz Jameka is here to put the *P* in pain for *every last one* of you hoes!"

Jameka charged towards me wearing some tight, blue-jean, cut off shorts, a wife-beater with an ironed-on picture of New

Edition on it and some neon yellow flip-flops. He had the nerve to have his hair wrapped up in a bootleg, Louis Vuitton durag and Vaseline all over his face.

I threw my bags into my car and slammed the door. "You and who, might I ask is gon' slap *me* bitch?! You better take your broke-down, Skeletor-looking, boney ass on somewhere and get on up outta my damn face before I slap the high holy hell outta your foolish ass!"

My remarks enraged him. "What?! Skeletor? Bitch are you outta your mind? Me and who?! Me and who?! I got your me and who bitch!"

Jameka turned around and began to scream out like a banshee, "JUICY! REE-REE! MUFFIN! ROYALTY!"

He turned back to look at me. "Mmm hmm! Who's talking shit now!? Me and who?! Me and who?! Me and these bitches! That's who!" Then he began to gesture with his hands as if he were Vanna White on *Wheel of Fortune*. "Bitches, meet my *Circle of Sisters*.

Four larger than life girls came from out of nowhere and surrounded me.

Jameka laughed. *"And this is the Black Expo honey!"*

I looked at the four girls and began to size each one of them up in my mind. Shit, it wasn't no use. They were some big-ass broads B! *What the fuck!* I thought to myself. *What am I gonna do now?*

Suddenly Tina yelled out, *"Dana!"*

The big girl that Jameka had referred to as "Juicy" looked over in Tina's direction. "Cousin Tee-Tee? Cousin Tee-Tee, what you doin' up here? I thought that looked like you but I just knew it wasn't cause you live all the way down in Greensboro girl!"

They ran over to each other and started to hug.

Jameka began to smile. *"Oooooh Juicy, this your cousin girl?"* He asked immediately changing his mood entirely.

"Yeah!" Juicy said proudly. "This my cousin twice removed on my mama's daddy's side!"

"Oh, well den—*Hey cousin!*" Jameka yelled as he ran over to hug Tina. He glanced in the direction of me, Jacqueline and Nadia and rolled his eyes playfully. *"So...I guess we can be cool since y'all are cool with my girl Juicy's cousin and erry-thang."*

He opened his arms to embrace us all. *"Come on, give me some loving."*

We hesitated at first, and then we figured, *"What the hell."*

As we stood there hugging and introducing ourselves Jameka, noticed Carmen tip-toeing from out of the bushes in an attempt to quietly make it back to her car which like I said before, was parked *all* the way at the end of the parking lot.

"Excuse me, I have a question!" Jameka asked quietly, confusion in his voice, "What is y'all *fish* of a manager doing with a wig on creepin' and crawlin' over there outta them bushes?"

I grinned and evil grin and said, "Oh, she's waiting to beat the ever loving shit out of Cousin Tee-Tee here! You ain't know?!" I laughed.

Juicy's smile turned into a scrunched up, crunched up snarl. *"Don't nobody fuck with Cousin Tee-Tee!!"*

"Oh hell naw! Ain't gon' be none of that now!" Jameka shouted. *Circle of Sisters*, let's roll!" Jameka and his crew took off towards the bushes!

Carmen, realizing that her cover was blown, sprinted out of the bushes and bolted towards her car in an attempt to reach it before Jameka and his crew reached her ass. The girls and I didn't even bother hanging around to see what happened next. All I know is that when we drove out of the parking lot, Carmen was running around in circles, red wig blowing in the breeze and all, with Jameka's *"Circle of Sisters"* hot on her trail.

Later on, Juicy told Tina that Carmen had a bunch of razors, a screw-driver and a tiny handgun on her.

There was no doubt about it, that evening we were definitely *all* fools and Jesus; well He *was*, *is* and will *forever* be our homeboy.

After all of the chaos that day, things at DIVAS ran smoothly. We still had our fair share of drama every now and then; but nothing like when *Carmen* was in charge. Although Jameka was cool with us, he would still sneak in every now and again and hit us, leaving us with rounders full of empty hangers. Life at DIVAS settled into a new rhythm, one that, while not perfect, was a vast improvement from the madness of the past.

# part nine
# the wedding

# chapter forty-four

## The Wedding

Two weeks passed, and before I knew it, Angie's big day had arrived. She had become *Mrs. Angela Tanaka,* and it seemed like all of Dutchess County had been invited.

*"Look over here please. Okay, now say money!"* the photographer shouted happily as he took our pictures on the steps of the elegant mansion that Angie and Gil had rented out for their nuptials and reception.

I was so sick of taking damn pictures. Angie had the photographer just a snapping away from the time we got dressed, to the limo ride over, up until now. Angie looked beautiful. She wore an off the shoulder, Disney princess-style dress that poofed on the bottom. Her train was as long as a damn subway car!

Surprisingly though, with all of the crying that Angie had done up until the ceremony, she really held it together during her vows. She didn't shed a single tear. But, you will *never* guess who did cry! Nicky with her mean, surly ass! She was a mess. Boo-hooing throughout the whole damn ceremony. She would not shut up! I don't know what came over her mean ass.

She had been throwing back mimosas like they were going out of style that morning, so maybe that had a little something to do with it.

We were all standing around outside waiting while the photographer took pictures of my sister with Gil's family. I spotted Dominic checking me out from the corner of my eye. We had been on several dates during the two weeks leading up to my sister's big day. Everything was great. I could not have asked for more.

*"There you are,"* I said. "I was looking all over for you. Well as much as I could considering that I've been stuck here taking pictures since before they said, "I do".

"You're a fucking knock-out! Just like the first time that I saw you that night in the store," he said as he kissed me on my cheek. All of a sudden, his expression changed as he looked past me.

"What's wrong?" I asked him.

*"Your sister invited the weed connect?"* Dominic asked confused.

*"What?"* I asked confused as well.

I turned around to see Jacqueline walking up to me, arm in arm with *Robert*. "Wow!" I said shocked as hell, "You made it, and with a date!"

Jacqueline leaned in and kissed me on the cheek. Robert did the same. "How you doing Jah-dee?" he said. "Long time no see." He looked at Dominic and gave him a pound. "What's up man? How you doin?"

"Really good since I met this girl right here!" Dominic said giving me a squeeze of comfort on my shoulders.

I glanced over at Robert. "Where you been at boy? I haven't seen you in a minute.

He shook his head and smiled. "I had to bounce and clear my head. Jacqueline was there for me through all of the bullshit. Her son plays ball with my little nephew. I was dropping him off one day and I saw Jacqueline. We talked out our differences and we've been kicking it ever since."

I pushed Jacqueline playfully. "Slut, you ain't tell me!"

She playfully pushed me back. "I wanted to, but you know how it is. I didn't want to jinx it. *I really like him!"*

"Jaliyah, come back over here. We got a few more frames to take before the reception starts," I heard my mother yell.

I rolled my eyes. "I gotta go y'all. But I'll see you inside." I ran over and finished taking pictures with the rest of the wedding party until it was time for the reception to begin. Once we were finished, it was time to par-tay!

"Ladies and gentleman for the first time ever as man and wife, give it up for Mr. and Mrs. Gil Tanaka!" As Alicia Keys's "If I Ain't Got You" played in the background, Angie and Gil danced their first dance as man and wife. The MC invited everyone to join in and dance with them. I locked eyes with Dominic from my seat and we joined each other on the dance floor.

He sang to me as we danced. I looked around the room to see who was there. Angie had invited *everyone* and their mama. Jameka was there sporting his newly acquired, *Jessica Rabbit* wig, a silk, baby pink, strapless evening gown with a huge split up the leg and some strappy sandals. Juicy, Ree-Ree, Muffin and Royalty were there also.

Tina and the rest of the DIVAS crew had gotten an invite because Angie went in there one day to pick up some last minute bikinis for her honeymoon and they gave her a discount. The next thing you know, Janet and Nadia are picking out their dresses from the DIVAS *Elegance* collection in the back of the store, which by the way, ain't that elegant! Let me just make that clear! I think I even saw the damn Korean lady who used to do our nails back when we lived in Mount Vernon.

"Nah, that couldn't have been her," I thought.

Just then, Angie and Gil came over and began dancing next to me and Dominic. "Is that Cathy from Everlasting Nails?" I asked her mid-twirl.

"Yeah, they're all here!" Angie said as she directed my attention to their table.

The whole freaking nail crew from Everlasting Nails was up in the damn wedding. They took up a whole damn table. She had truly gone and tripped. The song ended and they cleared the dance floor for the father daughter dance. I noticed that Trey and Alicia, Cheyenne and Christina, Mos and Lena and Jacqueline and Robert were all sitting at one table. I knew that Trey and Mos would behave because they had their girls by their sides.

The song finished, and I brought Dominic over to their table so I could introduce him. "Hey y'all!" I said holding his hand.

"What up J," they all said happy to see me.

"This is my friend Dominic. Dominic these are all of my friends. "That's Trey, Mos, Cheyenne, Christina, Alicia, Lena, and you already know Jacqueline and Robert."

"Nice to meet y'all," Dominic said as he waved to everyone at the table.

Cheyenne ran over to me and said between clenched teeth, "What the fuck was your sister thinking sitting me at the table with that bitch, Lena! She got one more time to look at me funny and I'ma shank her ass with my shrimp fork!"

I hugged her and whispered back, "*Please* don't do that. This is Angie's wedding. Look at all these damn people she has here. It's a damn circus already!"

I exhaled and rubbed her upper arm. "When I get married, I don't give a good goddamn who you shank, but please try to behave tonight."

I poked out my bottom lip. "For me. *Pretty please.*"

"A-ight Jah-dee," she said sucking her teeth.

I guess Ms. Christina's insecure ass thought we were getting a little too close because she got up from her seat and approached us with a snide, *"Is there a problem?"*

I folded my arms hard and looked her up and down, "Yeah bih—"

"Jah-dee," Shy said happily, "it's Angie's wedding. *Remember, marriage. Happy. Fun!"*

I rolled my eyes. "Yeah, I remember. Have a good time y'all." I smiled at the table.

Dominic put his arm around my waist. "What was that all about?"

"Nothing. But just make sure that you keep all sharp objects far, far away from Shy—and me!" I smiled at him and gave him a quick peck on the cheek.

The music started up for the father-daughter dance, and Dominic and I sat down at my friends' table. My father and Angie danced to Beyonce's "Daddy". I couldn't hold back my tears, *and* I didn't have to because I was the only one smart enough to wear clear mascara. *Just kidding.* I was so happy for Angela. She had been through so many ups and downs with so many different assholes. I had seen her cry herself to sleep more times than I can remember.

Then one day, she met Gil Tanaka at an office Christmas party. He worked in the mid-town office, while she worked downtown. When they met, he was just an associate broker in training, now he was one of the *top* brokers at his firm. He had brokered some huge deal by himself a few months before the wedding that earned him a commission of about $975,000 *after taxes*! Crazy right. I guess that's why he and Angela decided that it would only be right to invite 975,000 guests to their wedding!

After Angela and my father finished dancing, they did the mother-son dance. And then *this* dance. Then *that* dance. Finally, the party started! Johnny Kemp's "Just Got Paid" rang out from the speakers. Balloons and confetti dropped from the ceiling, the lights went dim and the strobe lights came on.

Everyone started to jam! Angela took off the bottom part of her gown which turned it into a cocktail dress. Once she did that, everyone knew that it was about to be on!

*"Owwwwww to the beat y'all!"* my Aunt Sharisse screamed as she ran onto the dance floor and began to get her groove on.

*"Come on Deena!"* I heard my father yell to my mother as he pulled her over to the dance floor. "Let's do it baby!"

Everyone from our table got up, ran over and went to work. My little sister Nicky was tearing up the dance floor like she was Ciara on speed. She danced to every single song with everybody. She danced with my father. She danced with both Gil and Dominic. I even saw her and my mother laughing and hugging at one point. Uncle Smitty and Uncle Claude were there hammin' it up for the videographer.

We did "The Bump". The "Electric Slide". The "Cha-Cha Slide". We even took it back to 1977 and "Got on the Good Foot"! By the time Luke's "I Wanna Rock" came on, I felt like I was gonna die. Gil's family was keeping up too. His mother put her hands on the floor and her ass in the air as Luke chanted, *"Face down ass up that's the way we like to fuck!"*

The funniest part of the night was when my mother and my Aunt Tiffany battled my Aunt Sharisse and my Aunt Sydney to "Break Dance-Electric Boogie" by West Street Mob. They had their *B-Girl* stances down. The only thing that was missing were their shell-toe Adidas, a few gold rope chains and a piece of cardboard. I didn't even know that they *all* knew how to break-dance! None of them could get outta bed the next morning though. I just thought I'd share that little bit of info.

Jacqueline and Robert were dancing while kissing and hugging the entire time, while Trey and Alicia were arguing about every half hour. Alicia would storm off the dance floor mad, then they would both get back on it smiling. I knew that Trey was in love because he didn't look at another female the *entire* night. Oh no, wait, he *did* sneak a few peeks at Jameka until I told him that *she* was indeed *he*.

Mos and his date were having a great time, except for the few times we had to keep her and Cheyenne from trying to kill each other. And speaking of Cheyenne. Mmm, mmm, mmm. I don't know what Angie was thinking telling her that she could bring *Christina*. Their asses needed to be censored. You would have thought they were the entertainment from Gil's bachelor party the night before. They were outta control! Just plain trashy. Running their hands up and down each other's bodies. Kissing. Snaking and winding every witcha way! Thank God for strobe lights and the fog machine! It was bananas! Of course, none of the men in attendance seemed to mind. They couldn't keep their eyes off them. I even saw Gil and my pops getting their peeks on with their mouths open a few times that night!

And what can I say about James "Jameka" Charles y'all. That's his full name. He took the floor and brought down the house honey! He even got the DJ to play "Greatest Love of All" so he could do his nightly routine from Club Cavalier. Him and his *Circle of Sisters* had a ball. So did all of the girls from DIVAS. Janet didn't sit down the whole night, and constantly waved her left hand in the air to make it a point to show everyone that she was *ring free*.

The reception wound down around two in the morning. The final song of the night was Jagged Edge's "Let's Get Married" remix—something smooth you could dance to, but didn't have to go all out for.

# chapter forty-five

As Dominic and I danced the last dance of the night, I realized that regardless of what happened from that moment on, I would always remember that night.

Back then, who would have thought that Trey and Alicia would wind up getting married a year later and having a beautiful baby girl the following spring. Or, that Mos would chat it up with Gil at Angie's wedding and eventually become a successful real estate broker down in Miami Beach. Cheyenne eventually completed her CPA degree and does everyone's taxes each April like clockwork.

Who would have thought that Janet would make it all the way up to the DIVAS corporate headquarters and end up being Barbara, the District Manager's boss? Or that Jacqueline, Robert and her son would up and move to San Diego and be expecting their third baby in a couple of weeks. Tina eventually left the Poughkeepsie store and moved back to Greensboro. She and her fiancé got back together and are set to marry this year. All of the other DIVAS girls eventually ended up going their separate ways. Chino eventually got out for good behavior and word on the street is that him, his mother and Carmen are living down in the Sound-view area of the Bronx.

Miss Jameka Charles officially left James behind, and *her Circle of Sisters* (which me and my sisters are now honorary members of) are still running around, wreaking all kinds of havoc throughout the Hudson Valley.

As far as my family goes, they are just fine! Everyone is still partying hard and acting a damn fool! My parents just celebrated their 30th wedding anniversary. We threw them a huge anniversary party. All the players came! Reesee, Uncle Ant, Uncle Smitty, Aunt Tiff—everybody! We had a great time.

Angie and Gil are still together and have since added two baby girls named Jada and Chelsea to their family. Nicky is still a bitch, but we love her. She graduated from college, got a good-paying job and made the decision to move out of my parents house as soon as she could after my mother's many failed attempts to *literally* snatch her bald-headed.

I only worked for DIVAS for about six more months, before I landed a job as an executive assistant to the Director of a beverage factory. I moved out of my parents' house about a year later, and I have been on my own ever since. Like I said in the beginning, I still have not finished school and I don't have *a clue* of what I want to do with my life. But, I'll figure it out.

Though there were times when DIVAS caused many a girl perpetual shame and an abundance of regret, that store will *always* hold a significant place in my heart. Aside from four of the most amazing girlfriends that anyone could ever ask for, DIVAS gave me a story to tell that will *never* go out of style.

Oh, and as far as me and Dominic go; now *there's* a story that would blow your fucking minds!

The End.

# acknowledgments

With a heart full of gratitude, I want to thank my incredible family and friends for their unwavering support and love. To my beautiful daughter Jada—you are my light and my greatest inspiration. To my sweet cat Willow, whose gentle presence and playful spirit has brought so much joy to our lives. And to my dear friend Raymond—thank you for reminding me of my gift when I needed it most. I love you all so much.

# about the author

Erica-Faye Nicole Williams is a native of Mount Vernon, New York, and the proud mother of one daughter. She's also a devoted fur mama to her beloved cat, Willow. When she's not writing, Erica-Faye enjoys painting and spending time with her daughter. *Divas of Dutchess* is her debut novel, marking the beginning of her journey as an independent author under her Starlight & Belle Publishing imprint.

# spotify playlist

**Loved the drama, laughs, and chaos inside *DIVAS*?**

Keep the energy alive and step even deeper into Jaliyah's world with the official *Divas of Dutchess* soundtrack—carefully curated to match every twist, turn, and fierce moment of the story.

♪♪ **Scan the code to listen on Spotify and explore more bonus content!**

www.ingramcontent.com/pod-product-compliance
Lightning Source LLC
Chambersburg PA
CBHW020247010826
48973CB00006B/1687